Now or Never

Brand of Justice
Book 14

Lisa Phillips

TWO DOGS PUBLISHING, LLC.

eBook ISBN: 979-8-88552-291-5

Paperback ISBN: 979-8-88552-292-2

Published by: Two Dogs Publishing, LLC. Idaho, USA

Cover Design by: Sasha Almazan and Gene Mollica, GS Cover Design Studio, LLC

Edited by: Christy Callahan, Professional Publishing Services

Now or Never

Chapter One

Kenna Banbury had long considered clothing to be a form of armor. These days she could use real armor —the kind of bulletproof vest designed with a pregnant mother in mind. Horrible as it sounded, there were places in the world where that was necessary. She wouldn't have imagined it in her own life, but then so much of what had happened over the past few months was previously unimaginable.

Mostly she was just trying to forget her time as a captive of their enemy so she could feel normal. If that was possible. It seemed more like the essence of who she was had been left shattered on the floor of that deep-sea platform.

"Ready?" Jax stopped at the entrance of the restaurant, the backdrop of the downtown Boston skyline behind him. Lights everywhere. Traffic, even after nine on a Friday evening.

"I miss Wyoming."

"No more hiding." He smiled, reminding her of her own words—the ones she'd said to him just a few weeks ago. "Time to get back to work."

He hauled open the door, and she stepped into this little alcove of humanity where surfaces were covered with white tablecloths and the lights and conversation were set to "low." A maître d', slender and in her fifties at least, with a sharp bob and aggressively straight bangs, looked down her nose.

"We're meeting someone." Kenna scanned the dining room. "I see them. Thanks." She passed the gatekeeper and headed for the expanse of tables. No idea where they'd find the Chief Medical Examiner. She kept scanning, aware of Jax behind her.

No matter what she did, where she went, or what they faced, her husband would be here with her. Behind her, watching her back. In front of her, protecting her and their baby from whatever threat came at them. Hopefully, nothing life threatening happened in this restaurant.

But then, that was why they were taking these cold cases.

Finding the lost and forgotten had become a way for her to try and put herself back together. Their child would be born into the kind of world where she would need her mother and father there to protect her every minute of every day.

Jax gently squeezed her hip, and she let him take the lead, threading through tables to the far corner. He reached his hand back, and she clasped it with hers, needing that bit of connection as much as he did. Neither of them had said as much out loud, but it was far better to work on cases anyway. Saving other people and solving crimes that no one else had been able to solve had become a life's work for Kenna over the years—from an FBI career to private investigator and now as a husband-and-wife team, and the friends who had become family along for the ride.

Away from the traffic of the kitchen door, the Chief Medical Examiner sipped a glass of wine, as though unwinding at the end of a long week. She spotted their approach and watched them close the distance to her table. At forty-seven, she was young for the position she held, though the wear and tear of the job was evident in her eyes.

Jax dropped Kenna's hand and shifted to the seat on the right, so she could sit across from the Chief ME.

"I'm here to meet with someone." The woman's voice sounded like a rough northern sea. She still had her blazer on over a white blouse. No jewelry. Makeup that had worn off, but her bright lipstick outlined her displeasure.

She probably thought she was here for a date. Not that they were going to accuse her of professional misconduct.

"We're the *someones*." Kenna slid onto the chair, thirsty but not willing to drink something that could be tainted when the director of the CIA and the president had been killed that way just a few months ago. "Kenna Banbury and Oliver Jaxton. We're private investigators—unofficially, at least in the state of Massachusetts." She watched for a reaction to their names, but there wasn't anything overt in the steady gaze of the other woman. "We're investigating a case you worked six years ago."

"So you know who I am? And somehow you think—what?—that I can help you?" She took a sip, and the crimson wine stained her lips. "More likely you're reporters here to ask me about something entirely different so you can dig up dirt and discredit me. All for a salacious story."

Kenna had worn slacks and a nice shirt with no sleeves,

but which hung blousy around her middle—not really disguising her pregnancy, also not drawing attention to it. She was six months along but didn't really look it. Over the blousy tank top, she had pulled a heavy jacket to ward off the winter chill in Boston and boots with tread, because no way was she going to risk slipping.

She reached in the inside pocket of her jacket and pulled out the wallet she used as a cred pack. Back in her FBI days, she'd carried her badge and ID card in this leather fold. Now she pulled out a few of the private investigator licenses she held.

"Arizona, Utah, *and* Washington?" The Chief ME pushed those aside on the tablecloth and discovered Colorado and California under them. Her drawn-on brows rose.

"I get around. Which means I know what I'm doing, and I'm *not* a reporter." She glanced at Jax, who laid the file he'd brought with him onto the table. "We know you're Doctor Eleanor Walsh, and you've been the Chief ME for the City of Boston for over five years." She pulled the file over but didn't open it yet. "You aren't married. You live alone. By all appearances you have chosen to dedicate your life to your career, which is an admirable thing. You give a voice to those who can't speak for themselves, and because of that, justice is served."

Dr. Walsh held Kenna's attention with a steady gaze. She had blond hair, threaded with evidence of her years, and her reading glasses were probably tucked in her brief-case on the floor. She never left her work in the car where it could be stolen. She brought it with her always.

In the time they had spent following her and researching Eleanor Walsh, Kenna and Jax had learned she was meticulous. Which was what made this particular case so intriguing.

Kenna continued, meeting Walsh's steady gaze right back. "Six years ago, you performed an autopsy on Samantha Ambrose. Fifteen years old. She'd been missing for over a year when she was discovered deceased in an alley on the other side of this city. That case has long since gone cold, though not for lack of trying on the part of Detective Withers."

"And you're here to solve it?" Walsh sipped her wine. "When no one else can? There simply isn't enough evidence to find the killer. That's what cold cases are. And despite the local news and media, there's no grand conspiracy going on when a young woman is murdered. It's simply a tragedy."

"That's where we come in." Jax took the top sheet of paper. "This is a copy of the autopsy report you completed at the time. I'll let you see for yourself, but you reported the cause of death as 'Hemorrhagic shock due to penetrating injuries.'"

"If I listed that as the cause of death, it's because it was the cause of death." Walsh shifted in her seat. "I didn't come here for...whatever this is."

Kenna had more questions and didn't want to do this on the street outside. "It's been a long day for you, I'm sure. We won't take up too much of your time."

Dr. Walsh stared at the sweating water glass.

"Please look at the autopsy." Kenna paused. "We'd like to ask you about a theory we have."

Walsh reluctantly took the papers and the photos they had printed off, images they deemed relevant. "It's not my business to deal in theories. I report the truth of what is evident at the time of the autopsy. Anything else isn't in my purview."

"I take that report, extrapolate theories, and investigate," Kenna said, "hoping I'll discover what really happened and who is responsible for the death of a...child." Her throat tried to close on that last word.

A lot of people might not consider a fifteen-year-old a child, but it depended on perspective. Samantha Ambrose might have considered herself to be practically an adult. She might've lived life independent of her parents, and whether that was what started her on the path that led to the end of her life wasn't something Kenna could draw conclusions on—at least, not yet.

Bottom line, an adult should have protected her, but no one did. Her vulnerability made her the target of a predator, and she wound up dead.

"We know she didn't bleed out in that alley," Kenna pressed. She swallowed against the dry feeling in her throat. "The police never found the place where she died. All we have is this." She tapped her index finger on the stack of photos. "One of those stab wounds killed her. No hesitation, just a quick stab and twist."

"She fought back," Dr. Walsh said, her tone guarded.

"The other stab wounds were more random. The one that killed her was precise."

Walsh looked like she was trying not to squirm. "What are you saying?"

"You reported what you saw in front of you on the body. And noted what you didn't see."

Kenna couldn't fault her solely. Not when each of the parties involved had failed Samantha Ambrose. The officers who arrived on scene first, Dr. Walsh, and the investigating detectives. Every superior officer or boss. Every person who handled evidence testing. All of them, combined, had a part to play.

Kenna continued, "She had defensive wounds on her arms, but no abrasions on her knuckles. Given the evidence in front of you, would it be reasonable to conclude she might've been killed with that first stab wound, and then each of the other wounds could have been *applied* after the fact?"

Walsh frowned.

"The defensive wounds are simply slices to the underside of her forearms. Those random stab wounds on her torso were far shallower than the one that killed her, a quick in-out motion." Kenna leaned forward in her chair. "Is it possible Samantha Ambrose was murdered by someone meticulous who then used the knife to cover up the lethality of that first strike by making it look like she was killed by someone out of control? That she could have fought back, or that the murder might've been committed in rage and anger instead of cold calculation?"

Walsh flipped through the pages, her wine forgotten. "However it can be interpreted doesn't change my recounting of the facts of the evidence."

"She'd been fed only bread and water for days. Her weight at the time of her death was nearly twenty pounds lighter than what her parents told the police."

Walsh looked up from the papers. "You think she was held captive."

Kenna had read the detective's report after interviewing a couple of school friends. Samantha Ambrose had pulled away from them and started to hang more with people she worked with at the coffee shop—a place open until two in the morning on weekends.

Walsh eyed her, flustered—her face pink. "You just came here to run a theory by me?"

"No." Kenna shook her head. "I came here to ask why you concluded she was the victim of an attack that the detectives took as random violence. The result of a teen pushing boundaries and getting herself into trouble. Why you disguised the truth that she might've been killed by someone with military training."

A server in a crisp black shirt and black pants stopped beside their table, a white apron tied around his waist. What would be chin length hair was tied back behind his head, the bottom half shaved. "Are these people bothering you, ma'am?"

Chapter Two

"Are you bothering this guest?" The server turned to Kenna and Jax. "You shouldn't be bothering our guests. Especially if you aren't going to order food."

Kenna glanced over at him. "We're about to leave."

"It's fine, Philippe." Dr. Walsh waited till he left, then said, "I reported the evidence. What conclusions are drawn from it aren't my jurisdiction. I do autopsies, and I testify in court."

"Now you run the entire medical examiner's office for the City of Boston." Kenna laced her fingers together on her knees.

"You were promoted just a few months after this case," Jax said. "Seems like interesting timing to me."

"What are you insinuating?" Walsh lifted her chin. "I earned the position I have through hard work and—"

"Dedication to your job," Kenna said. "We caught the speech on YouTube. There's no need to repeat it for us."

"And yet you think I bribed my way, or slept my way, to the corner office?"

Kenna kept her expression impassive. "I think someone...encouraged you to report this as a random act of violence perpetrated in the heat of the moment."

"I never said that's what happened." The Chief ME stared at Kenna, her jaw set.

Jax folded his arms. "Your conclusions, and the way you interpret evidence, sway the detectives. They draw conclusions from what *you* tell them."

"And you told them this girl fought for her life but wasn't strong enough to prevent her death. Which I suppose, in a way, was true," Kenna said. "It's simply that it happened over a period of weeks between her capture and her inevitable death."

Walsh's expression hit on a frown, just for a split second.

Yes, Kenna knew what she was talking about. She knew what it meant to be held against her will, convinced there was no way out. Waking up every day wondering if it would be the day she died. Being pregnant...

Not something she needed to think about right now. She and the baby were safe. Or at least as safe as they could be given their enemy was a dangerous group of people whose entire goal was to manipulate worldwide events. The reflex to comfort herself and her baby had her hand moving toward her abdomen, but she caught herself before drawing attention to the fact she was pregnant.

Jax took her hand and laced his fingers through hers. No matter who was paying attention, or if no one saw, they were a united front either way.

Kenna held tight to his hand and looked at Dr. Walsh. "I *am* going to find the person who did this to Samantha Ambrose. Not because her parents are offering a reward, or because I might be able to spin it and have the district attorney file corruption charges against you. But because Samantha Ambrose can't speak for herself."

"So the question is," Jax said, "did you record the evidence in this way because you were pressured to do so, or because on this particular day you simply decided to rush through and cut corners?"

Walsh shifted, clearly uncomfortable. "If you believe me incompetent just come out and say it."

"Who encouraged you to do this?" Kenna asked. "Seems like no one really cares about the victim. She wasn't anyone important. Why brush it aside?"

"This is off the record," Walsh said, her voice hushed.

Kenna didn't bother explaining again that they weren't reporters. She simply nodded.

"I don't know who it was."

"How did they contact you?"

"A note in my mailbox." Walsh sighed. "I never learned who they were. I never met them."

"What did you do with the note?"

"I destroyed it."

Kenna tried not to be disappointed hearing that. "What did the note say?"

"Those who don't fall in line—"

"—are cut down in their prime." Kenna's stomach flipped over. Or the baby was moving. Maybe both. Either way, the topic of conversation and the smell of hot roast beef was getting to her.

Walsh frowned. "How do you know that?"

"I've heard it before." She squeezed Jax's hand without intending to. "How did you know what to do, based on just that?"

"There were...pictures. Of Samantha Ambrose. Instructions to interpret the evidence in a way that would lead the detectives to believe it was random and vicious. The result of the victim's choices." Walsh swallowed. "Then my boss used that same saying about falling in line. I knew they got to him as well, and we were both being manipulated. Three weeks later, he died in a car accident."

Kenna said, "Calling it an accident implies no one is at fault."

Walsh nodded.

Jax squeezed her hand, and she took that as the signal to wrap this up.

Kenna glanced over at the server and saw him talking with a suited man who had slicked-back black hair threaded with gray. The owner, or manager. She dug a business card from her leather wallet and put it on the table. "If you think of anything that might help us find whoever did this to Samantha Ambrose, please call us."

Kenna held tight to Jax's hand all the way to the door. Outside wasn't a place she could relax. That only happened in their valley in Wyoming. The five-acre piece of property he had bought when he sold the townhouse in Phoenix.

A black-and-white police car passed them on the street, lights and sirens going. In a hurry to get...somewhere else.

Before they got within fifteen feet of the car he clicked the locks and turned on the engine using the button on his key fob. Just in case someone had set an explosive device in their car.

Meanwhile, Kenna was walking a fine line trying to balance the truth she knew with what her husband needed to do to make himself feel secure. To do what he felt he needed to do to protect her and their baby.

Jax didn't open the door, but turned and leaned against it instead. He pulled her into his arms, and she stood between his feet. Kenna hugged him because she could, and she wanted to. In his embrace she could *almost* forget all the crap that swirled around them on a constant basis.

"That was a lot." His voice rumbled under her cheek. "Do you want to talk about it?"

"Not really." She sighed.

He chuckled, and she enjoyed the feel of it, smiling to herself. Soon enough it would be time to reconvene. But not on the street with people and traffic. In a spot where he felt the need to pay half of his attention to her and the other half watching her back for any potential threats.

He tipped her chin so he could see her face. "We need to call Maizie back. My phone rang a couple of times while we were in there."

Each time he mentioned the young woman they had officially adopted, Kenna always watched for the nuances of what he wasn't saying. Maizie lived in Colorado in an Airstream under the watchful eye of trusted friends. The teen had escaped a horrifying situation and become a friend and the kind of family they watched out for.

He'd told Kenna everything that happened while she had been a captive of their enemy, *Dominatus*. How Maizie had been manipulated into withholding information from him that had been used to coerce her. She wasn't the only one who didn't show him the footage and images of Kenna being held. He and Maizie had worked through what they needed to work through and were getting back on the right footing, but she still wanted to know where he was at with the young woman they'd adopted.

Kenna had turned down both the offer to look at the images and footage and the invitation he'd given her to talk about the experience beyond some of the basics. Jax had been there, on the same deep-sea platform, when he'd come to rescue her and been captured himself. He knew a lot, or thought he knew enough, and she was grateful he wasn't going to push her if she didn't want to talk about it.

As far as Kenna was concerned, the rest didn't matter.

Kenna was determined to live this life on her terms. To focus on her husband, on keeping their baby safe as much as was within her power, and on solving the cases that made her feel most like the person she was supposed to be.

"Maybe she has information about this case." Kenna kissed her husband because she was free, and she could. And even if she woke up back in captivity, she was going to enjoy the dream.

He held the car door for her, and she slid in.

Kenna grabbed the bottle of water in the cup holder and twisted the cap open. Not something she ever took for granted, considering how many times in her life she'd been unable to do even that much with her hands.

"Good?"

She glanced at Jax and nodded. "I'm good."

It was getting easier to pretend.

Whether he noticed or not, she didn't know. Either way, he pulled into the flow of traffic and told his phone to call Maizie.

It rang a couple of times, then she picked up. "Hey, guys. How did it go with the ME?"

Kenna could picture Maizie's face, all that thick blond hair in whatever style she was trying this week—the latest was diffused curls. Huge blue eyes and pale skin. The girl was gorgeous, but on the list of things Kenna had to worry about, it was a distant cousin to future problems.

Jax turned a corner with one hand and reached over to hold hers with the other. "Someone left her a note, and the boss corroborated what she was supposed to do."

"The guy who died in that car crash? I can't believe no one thought that was suspicious."

Kenna turned her hand over and laced her fingers with Jax's. She'd already finished the entire water bottle. "People see what they want to see. Could've been a busy week for the state police, or whoever responded treated it as an accident and didn't ever consider anything else."

"I could send everything I have to...someone. Get them to reopen the case," Maizie suggested. "Should we do that?"

Kenna paused. "It might come out in the course of the investigation. But right now, I'd rather focus on finding the person who killed Samantha Ambrose."

"I've been working on that. When you guys didn't pick up, I called Ramon, and we tossed around some ideas. I'm not saying I hacked the military, or that it's even possible to do it, but I happened upon a list of soldiers who lived in the area around the time of the murder. Based on your parameters of height and weight, and age, I narrowed it down. But it's still a long list."

"How are we going to narrow it down even further?" Kenna asked. "I'd rather not have to knock on all those doors and see if a murderer greets us."

Jax navigated the icy city roads, concentration on his face. He needed to be extra careful, as the salt mix laid down had been driven over and refrozen by fresh snow. All of it made a slushy mess.

"I think we should take a look at the scene again," he finally said. "Unless we come up with a better idea."

Kenna squeezed his hand. "Wanna get some sushi on the way?"

He grinned.

Maizie exhaled loudly. "You're not supposed to eat raw fish while you're pregnant!"

"I know that." Kenna smiled. "I only eat the kind that's cooked. It's better anyway." Giving up coffee was bad enough, though she just drank decaf instead so it wasn't totally like she'd given it up.

"Yes, we can get sushi." He squeezed her hand back.

"Maizie, send us the list you narrowed down," Kenna said.

"I'm also looking at Samantha's social media, back before her parents co-opted her accounts for their fundraising." Her voice had a tone.

"What did they need money for?"

"Ostensibly, the funeral. Though, it seems like they cremated Samantha, so they probably didn't need all the money that was raised. At first, they were posting regular videos asking for information. Gradually, that petered out and now it's quiet. But their personal accounts have a whole lot of vacation pictures." Her voice still had that tone. "I guess they kept some of the money as a reward for any information leading to the arrest of her killer. But within a few weeks, they were taking regular trips to Hawaii, or France, or England. Cashing in on people's goodwill donations after Samantha went missing."

Kenna frowned. "They acted the part when we met with them. Offered us five grand to find her killer."

"I don't wanna be cynical."

"Be cynical," Kenna said. "It'll keep you alive longer."

Chapter Three

Kenna didn't like the silence that greeted her statement. "So...how are we going to narrow down the list of soldiers?"

Neither of them responded to her question.

She looked at Jax. "What?"

"Being cynical keeps you alive?" Jax pulled up to a stop light and looked at her.

"I always think everything is a trap."

Maizie's voice came through the car speakers. "Are you really quoting *The Princess Bride* to us?"

"It's a great movie," Kenna said.

She'd watched a lot of them with Jax the first few weeks after he rescued her. They'd gone through so many classics, nostalgic favorites that weren't as good as they remembered, and timeless cult hits. New movies, old movies, and none of them depressing or scary. It hadn't entirely worked to pull either of them out of their funk. But it had helped her at least not think about the ever-present threat for a while. Or how impossible it was going to be to take down *Dominatus*.

Kenna had no intention of getting into a conversation

about what was going on in her head. They thought they wanted to know, but they'd regret asking in the end. It was better to just...

She blew out a breath. "Can we focus?"

"I'm trying to narrow the list down," Maizie said. "But I don't even know whether to rule out people who are dead or keep them on the list."

"Hmm. Good point." She took a moment to admire Jax pulling away from the stop light. Why did that stir up attraction in her? Aside from pregnancy hormones, that was.

They'd spent every moment of the day together for a few months now, soaking up the togetherness that had been denied them for the weeks she'd been captive. Probably it would wear off eventually, but she almost didn't want it to.

Jax said, "If the killer is dead, there won't be a way to prove beyond a shadow of a doubt that they're responsible. There was no DNA on the body from her assailant."

"I've been thinking about that." Kenna paused. "What if she was killed, then undressed, and they washed the body completely clean? Which was why there was no evidence and the only blood was transferred from her clothes. They re-dressed her and dumped her in the alley."

"They?" Jax looked over at her.

She shrugged one shoulder. "Figuratively speaking. One person—the killer. It could have been more than one, though. Or someone else helped him cover it up."

"Assuming it was even a male who committed the crime," Maizie pointed out. "Though from the angle of the stab wound that killed her and the depth, it was definitely a bigger and stronger person, most likely a male."

"A male with military training," Kenna added. She could see Samantha being strangled if it was the heat of the moment. Or beaten, or a messy stabbing. But that wasn't what had happened. There was far too much about this that seemed cold and calculated in a way that crimes of passion never were. "Possibly more than one person."

"I'll start looking into the people I have on this list, alive and dead," Maizie said. "Zeyla has a contact at the Department of Defense, apparently. She said she can dig up their actual personnel files and find out if any of them had a violent streak they couldn't control in a way it was being put to good use as part of their normal duties."

That sounded like the result of a conversation between Maizie, Ramon, and Zeyla about violence and military personnel. Kenna was of the opinion that anyone could commit violence if they were pushed to the edge and felt they had no other choice. Some people were more comfortable with it, for whatever nature-or-nurture reason life handed them, or could be trained to the point they were.

All Kenna cared about was what kind their killer was. And, if he was alive, where to find him so they could turn him and the evidence over to the police.

"Sounds good," Jax said. "Anything else?"

"I was looking into those other missing persons Kenna sent me, trying to find a connection between any of them and Samantha Ambrose."

This sounded interesting. "Anything?"

"Not without the military angle," Maizie said. "Other than that, there's no connection between her and Samantha." She went quiet for a second. "Her name is Megan Tiller. Seventeen, so two years older than our victim. She had a boyfriend six years older who was in the army. Around the time of Samantha's death, Megan went missing as well. Her mom is the only parent in the picture, and she doesn't seem to care much. There's nothing on her socials about her daughter being missing all these years. The police report is closed, and it's noted that she dropped out of school a few weeks before and told her mom she was going to California with the boyfriend."

Kenna straightened in her seat. "The boyfriend? That's the military connection between this Megan and Samantha?"

Before Maizie could answer, Jax said, "Sounds like it's only a thread of a connection between the manner of Samantha's death and the boyfriend. The fact that another young woman went missing shortly after she did..."

"Could be an overlap." Kenna had seen it in another case, a serial killer who disposed of one victim and all too soon claimed another, sometimes before the previous victim was even killed. "Samantha was dead, so he took Megan."

But if the boyfriend was responsible, why would he do that? It could be that Megan found out what happened to the other young woman. Or they might not be connected at all.

"Megan has never shown up," Maizie said. "Not so far as we can figure. Although, it is possible she's a Jane Doe who was never identified."

"What about the boyfriend? Is he on the list you came up with?"

"Yes," Maizie said. "But he's dead. There's no one to question. Mitch Caudelle was deployed to Afghanistan a month after Samantha's death and died a few weeks before he was supposed to come home."

"Keep digging. This is the best lead we've had so far."

"Got it."

Jax reached for the dash screen. "Catch you later, kiddo." He ended the call with a stab of his finger and didn't waste any time saying, "Those who don't fall in line..."

"I'm not finishing it."

"You know what it means."

Kenna laced her hands on her lap, biting her lip.

"If this case connects to *Dominatus*, that is significant."

"Sometimes it seems like everything in my life does," Kenna muttered.

She squeezed her fingers together hard enough that her forearms twinged with something that wasn't quite pain. Just the mild discomfort of a pulling sensation. For years, the tendons in her forearms that had been severed and repaired by surgeons were a source of intense pain. Then along came their enemy, trying to do her a favor. Now she invited the familiar pull that used to be pain where they'd repaired her forearms because it meant she was still who she'd been before they came into her life.

"I'm not ignoring it," she added. "Or burying my head in the sand."

Jax pulled over into the parking lot of a high-end grocery store she knew had a sushi counter. "You're pretending..." He shook his head. "I wanna say you're pretending they aren't a threat, but I know that isn't true."

"I'm not in denial, and I'm not refusing to see the truth."

"You wanted to get back to work, but you don't want to take any cases that have anything to do with them."

"Exactly."

Jax glanced at her. "How is that not denial?"

"They don't get to define everything about me. They've taken enough from us—and from our lives."

"We have to stop them."

She shook her head. "That's not a fight I want this child born into." She laid her hands on her baby. *Their* baby. "They don't get to control any more of my life. It's time I decide for myself what I want to do every day, and it's not going to be reacting to the last horrible thing we learned they're doing. I'm done getting knocked back and trying to strike at them in response."

He didn't reach for her.

Hot tears filled her eyes. "I'm sorry, but I just can't right now."

"You don't have anything to be sorry for."

"Neither do you, so don't start with that either." Everyone knew angry tears were better than sad ones. "None of this happened because of a failure on your part." She shook her head because it was as ridiculous now as it had been the first time he'd voiced the idea aloud. She'd have laughed at his suggestion of culpability, but there wasn't anything funny about any of this. "Let's just work this case, then go home to Wyoming."

"Knowing they're still out there?"

"I've taken down so many of their players. You've taken out a handful yourself. Doing that almost cost us everyone we love."

"It's always a risk."

"I'm supposed to accept it, and the cost, and just to do the right thing?" She shook her head, one of those hot tears rolling down her cheek. Regaining her sense of who she was helped her feel more like herself than she had in a long time, and taking a stand felt more *Kenna* than anything. Even if the stand she took was to do nothing that had anything to do with them. "I'm not willing to lose anyone. Not now, and not ever."

"That's what keeps me up at night, praying in the wee hours of the morning." He cleared his throat. "Trying to figure out how we can get on with our lives knowing they're out there."

"It's easy. We're already doing it."

"I thought we were being called to take them down," he said, carefully. "Before you were captured, that was our ultimate goal. Then I got a taste of exactly what you're talking about, wondering every minute of every day if you'd been killed or if I would ever find you."

"You did." She shifted in the seat and put her knee up, so she could face him. "It wasn't anyone else who showed up on a speedboat to rescue me from that buoy. It was you." She reached for him, and he met her halfway.

His forehead settled on her shoulder and he wrapped one arm around her back. He needed to cling to her, and she knew exactly what it felt like to be in that place where there was such a powerful need to hang on. Because she lived there.

Kenna held tight to her husband while he did the same with her.

So much between them went without saying, but it was possible she should have said more the past few weeks than she had.

Keeping her own counsel was necessary for her sanity, and for the sake of all of them, but she could give him something. "I need to feel like me." Her voice sounded like gravel in the dark interior of the car. "Not like a pawn in their game."

"I know." He didn't move, and she felt his breath brush against her neck. He pressed a kiss to her pulse. "Nothing about my life right now is what I thought it was supposed to be. It's all a new kind of normal. But I'm not necessarily saying I want to change anything."

He lifted his head then, and she nodded because she knew. He'd have told her if he wanted to do something different.

"But Kenna...I'm not dealing with what you're dealing with. I don't know what you know."

"We're on the same team. We both want our child born in safety."

"It seems like that might be wishful thinking." Again with the gentle tone. "We know what they do. Eventually they'll come after us. They'll come after *her*."

She stared at his hard-to-read expression and tried to find the words to explain what was wrong about that statement.

But the words wouldn't come.

Chapter Four

Rain hammered incessantly against the wall of windows all lined with crisscrossed wire. The din outside, heavy gray sky, and miles and miles of ocean surrounding them cast the room in low light. Personally, Kenna would flip all the lights on and make things in here as bright as she could.

Maybe *Dominatus* didn't want to have to pay a huge light bill on their deep-sea platform in the middle of... She had no idea where they were. It wasn't the Caribbean, that was for sure. Not with this constantly gray weather.

Kenna stared at the bowl of stew in front of her, the rain swelling in her ears until it was all she could hear. She pushed a couple of carrot chunks that were still hard around the bowl with the plastic spork they'd given her. As if she didn't know how to use it as a weapon.

Mystery meat popped to the surface.

Kenna held her breath and stood. One foot over the other off the bench seat. Down to the end of the row. She just about made it, narrowly missing the edge of the trash bag stretched to its limits over the rim of the plastic can.

Bye-bye, bread roll.

That was the best part of the meal, usually. It was hard to mess with a basic roll, even if it was bland. Butter made everything better.

Her stomach heaved again, but nothing came out, even though she gagged.

A cup of water appeared in front of her.

She looked over at Dr. Marcus Buzard—one of them anyway. Kill one, and another pops up. She tried not to think about *Dominatus* and their science experiments. Especially since she *was* one of their science experiments currently.

"Drink it." He shoved the cup at her.

Kenna took a sip. The water tasted like salt—like the rain hammering against the windows. When it was empty she chucked it in the trash can while trying to swallow the taste out of her mouth.

Buzard stared at her, his eyebrows heavy under the smooth skin on the top of his head. No lab coat today, which only made her wonder if it was covered in blood from a horrifying experiment on someone else captive in this place whom she hadn't met yet, and now someone had been tasked with bleaching out the stains.

Two pens and a pair of reading glasses in his shirt pocket. She could use both to injure him. She could use his tie to strangle him. But what was the point in all that effort? The room was rimmed with guards, all of them armed with stun guns and batons—and syringes.

Kill one, and another pops up.

"Since you're finished eating..." He snapped his fingers, and two guards pushed off the wall, striding toward them. "You have an appointment."

She held still, and they stopped a few feet away.

Noise erupted from the loudspeaker on the wall beside the double doors that led to the hallway. "Doctor Buzard, the retrieval team has returned."

Kenna shuddered. The voice. It was the same woman from the videos.

Her mind flashed with images of war. Uprisings. Genocide. Mass graves. Things that happened unless *Dominatus* controlled the world. Unless they created humans to their specifications, trained them, and set them in positions of power across the world.

Those who don't fall in line are cut down in their prime.

She knew they were brainwashing her. They'd started the first day, pushing her to exhaustion and keeping her hungry and thirsty. Forcing her to "earn" food and water so the baby stayed safe within her.

She'd tried to resist. To comply outwardly and yet, within her mind, retain her sense of self.

She'd tried.

Failed.

Tried.

Failed.

Who cared what they wanted to tell her, or what she had to say she believed. She had to protect this baby growing in her womb until she could either escape or was rescued. There were no other options.

Lord...

What was the point in praying? He hadn't answered any of her pleas yet. She hadn't felt the peace she was supposed to possess, or a sense He was with her. It felt more as if *Dominatus* had claimed this place for their purposes and He was not welcome. Like they had shut God out of their domain, and no matter how much she prayed, the requests didn't even get through the shadow of darkness that hung over everything here.

Seconds later, the doors at the far end flung open. Two familiar faces whose eyes she wanted to scratch out. The retrieval team were two men she had met months ago. Researched. Hunted. Now they were here.

"We got it, Doc." One of the men from that retirement home came over, lifting a tackle box to show them. Four— she had since learned his name was Linus.

The other was Five, but she didn't know his real name. He had pale clammy skin and hung back behind his friend.

"Good," Buzard said. "Take it to the lab. I want to get started with the tests this afternoon."

She moved without thinking, aiming for the tackle box.

Linus swung it back out of reach, laughing. "Got your boyfriend's juice right here. Shame we had to hurt him." He cackled. "Actually, it was fun."

Buzard pushed her back. "Give it to me. Take your friend to the infirmary and get him patched up before he keels over and makes a mess."

Linus spun, shoving Five in front of him.

Buzard turned to the guards and motioned with his chin. "Section four."

She inhaled a sharp breath through her nose. *I don't want to go there.*

She could still taste the bile in her mouth as one of the men grabbed her arm and dragged her between two tables and their bench seats. She focused on keeping her feet, staying upright and not thinking about what she would be forced to watch for hours. Until her eyes stung and she could barely keep them open. They would inject her with something to keep her awake, push her past her limits, and then test the baby's vital signs.

If you kill my baby...

She had no recourse. No power here. She couldn't fight them off or defend herself.

There was no way out.

Buzard pushed out the double doors into the hallway. She'd tried to plead with the men who worked security. There weren't many, and none had been sympathetic. Far as she'd been able to tell, there weren't more than a couple of dozen people who lived and worked on this platform. Some kind of deep-sea research station, or it used to be an oil well. She had no idea, and all the signs on the walls were in Russian. At least it gave her an idea of the neighborhood they were in.

Focus on that.

At least until a scream echoed down the hall. A high sound that cut across her threadbare nerves and left her senses raw.

The tight grip of the guard's hand on her arm got her attention. She stumbled along the hall, trying not to let go of what little control she had over her emotions, her thoughts, and her actions. It wouldn't last. She knew that.

She also knew she had to fight until she couldn't fight anymore.

A door swung open at the end of the hall, and a woman stumbled out of the room there, blood on the scrubs top over her torso. Blood on her hands. Her face. Stringy hair hung down either side of her head. She spotted them and froze.

"Brandon!"

Kenna jumped at the shout so close to her ear.

The man holding on to her yelled again. "Get her out of here."

Another man appeared at the door, holding a knife with a three-inch blade.

"Take your toy somewhere else."

The woman started to turn. Brandon grabbed her from behind, one hand over her mouth, and dragged her back into the room.

The door slammed shut.

Bile rose in Kenna's throat, even though there was nothing in her stomach. The woman didn't scream again, but as they passed, a puddle of blood seeped out from under the door.

"Guess that's one case you don't need to solve."

The two guards laughed like that was actually funny.

Kenna's ears rang. One of the men hit the button for the elevator and then rolled the door up like a garage. Not the first time she'd thought of jumping down into the shaft. Taking her chances with the drop and the stationary horizontal surface at the bottom.

But ending two lives in one shot wasn't how she wanted to escape this. It seemed far too much like a gamble that she could end it fast and as painlessly as possible. She had no idea if it was far enough down that the chance she'd die would pay off with a swift end.

She also didn't want to spend her last moments regretting what her death would do to Jax when he found out they were both gone. She wanted to see the joy in his eyes when he found out about their baby.

That meant figuring a way out of this hell.

And never giving up the fight until she did.

Chapter Five

PRESENT DAY

"This is a longshot at best." Jax sat in the driver's seat, sipping from a paper cup. Outside, the snow that had fallen overnight blanketed the residential street in a layer of white that made it look nicer than it really was.

Kenna, in the passenger seat of the parked car, bit into her warm double chocolate muffin and tried not to groan aloud. After she'd savored it for a second and swallowed some of the mouthful, she said, "You have somewhere else to be?"

"Yeah, our land in Wyoming."

She glanced at him, the muffin held aloft in front of her face. The street around them was as empty as it had been for most of the morning except for the odd delivery driver and the mail van. Two rows of houses, plenty of cars in drives and on the street—not the nicer ones that spoke of huge payments but the used models that were more common to people who couldn't fork out hundreds every month for something flashy.

"Eat your snack." He lifted his chin to her neglected muffin.

But they needed to talk about this. "You wanna leave Boston and go back home?"

"Well, yeah. You're happier there, and so am I."

"What happened to 'time to get to work?' That was yesterday."

He snorted, shrugged. "I can change my mind. Wait ten minutes, and I'll change it back. Or I'll decide we should go to Hawaii."

"Too hot any time of year."

"Maine."

She smiled. "A moody coastline that's just mist twenty-four seven. Now you're talking."

"Hard to solve a murder when you can't see your hand in front of your face."

"Who says we'll be solving a murder there?"

He smiled just enough that she could see the change on his face and leaned over to kiss her. "Mmm. Chocolate."

She pushed his chest gently. "Get your own."

"Bet they have those muffins in Maine."

"If they don't, we could rent somewhere with an oven, and you could make an über-healthy, high-protein version that's 'good for the baby,' and I'll pretend to enjoy it."

His eyes closed for a second and his chest shook, but no laughter escaped.

"I love you."

He kept his attention on the street. "I know."

"Did you have a nightmare last night?" She had been shaking off the effect of hers all morning, trying to forget the images that had been burned into her mind. The ones that hovered like ghosts in her dreams.

He said nothing at first.

"Jax."

"It's enough to know you did as well."

And yet she hadn't shared with him any more than he had with her.

He said, "Don't worry about me, okay? You're safe. We're together." He pulled in a full breath and blew it out slowly. "I need a way to combat the fear, and getting in the Word this morning helped a lot. I've got a call later with a couple of my Bible study guys." He reached over and squeezed her knee. "I'm okay."

"Still, you want a way to take them down so it's finally over." She ignored the sick feeling in her stomach and tried not to think about her faith and the way it had slipped from her heart in the middle of all that fear and the pain.

The fear seemed to have taken up residence in her life instead, in a permanent way. She couldn't seem to shake it. And how could she, when this was far from over?

"You want this to be done, and I want another muffin."

She didn't really but wanted to move this conversation back to something safer. And if she couldn't eat a double chocolate muffin in the second trimester of pregnancy, then when on earth was she supposed to be able to eat one? This was exactly the time to enjoy herself and not care about calories. Plus, Jax had fed her potatoes, egg, and cheese for breakfast, so this was a totally valid pre-lunch snack.

"I want a way to guarantee your safety," he said. "That probably means we have to take them all down in one go."

"There's no way to do that."

"As far as you know. Which means we haven't found the solution yet."

Kenna wanted to share his optimism, but she couldn't see how they'd be able to take down the entire *Dominatus* organization and keep their baby safe in the process. She wasn't about to watch him go off to battle with a dangerous enemy and stay behind. Even if their friends went with him as backup, she could still either lose him to the fight or she would become a pawn in the middle of it all.

Kenna swallowed a mouthful of water. She'd thought about hot chocolate, but with the muffin, that was too much of a good thing. "Promise me something."

"As far as it's within my power to do it."

She figured that was a decent way to approach the whole balance of marriage. But wasn't sure he'd want to make the promise once she said what it was.

Down the street, a school bus turned onto the road and immediately stopped.

"Morning class but not afternoon?" she wondered aloud.

The first child got off the bus, and Jax said, "Looks like preschool or Kindergarten."

"They're so cute."

"So cute you forgot what you were going to say?"

"Fine." She sighed. "Maizie offered to turn a photo of you and me into a composite of what our child might look like."

"Sounds terrifying."

She managed to find a smile.

"What am I promising?"

Kenna reached over and found his hand, lacing her fingers with his the way she had in the early hours of the morning when she needed that connection as well as the feeling of him surrounding her. The man who slept between her and the door, so that any threats would reach him first. "That if you do figure out a solution, you won't leave to go finish it."

"I won't put you in harm's way."

They didn't need to rehash that conversation. The one where she pointed out that danger was everywhere, and at least out here solving cases, they were aware of the potential threat enough to manage situations.

The idea was to not go stir-crazy in the RV, on their admittedly gorgeous land, spending the rest of their lives wasting away from inactivity. There would be seasons in their lives when they could do that, like after the baby was born. But until then, she had to stay active.

"And because I won't put you in harms' way," he continued, "the only solution is to allow *Dominatus* to continue and for us to do nothing about them. Live and let live. Always wondering when they'll show up to steal our child from us. Or tear us apart some other way. Knowing they're destroying lives, and we knew and didn't stop them."

"We can't fight them. They're too big and too dangerous." She shook her head.

Right then, a boy no more than five years old with tan pants, rubber boots, and a heavy coat trudged along the salted sidewalk. His ears were red, but he held a wool hat in one hand. He stopped in front of the house.

"Isn't that the residence?" Kenna asked.

Jax let go of her hand. "Yes, it is. You think that's his house?"

She shook her head. "If he lives there, he doesn't want to go inside."

"The man who owns it has been dead longer than that kid has been alive." Jax shifted in his seat. "But someone lives there. A light is on inside, behind the blinds in the living room."

"He's just standing there." Her heart broke at the sight of this lonely little boy on the sidewalk outside a house that might not be his. Was trepidation holding him there, not wanting to go home? That, or he should move on. Get to his house. If he lived here, what about that house made it so he didn't want to go to the door and step inside?

A million scenarios all roiled in her mind. One of a thousand ways this little boy could be suffering inside the walls of that house.

"We need to keep talking about how to get out of this stalemate," Jax said. "So we have a plan for what to do about *Dominatus*."

The front door of the house opened. A slender woman stood there in slim jeans and a thin sweater with long sleeves pulled over her hands.

The little boy saw her and darted toward her, his backpack bouncing side to side as he ran. All the way into her arms. She crouched and held him to her, hugging each other tightly in the doorway.

Kenna sniffed.

"That's why we have to fight them," Jax said. "So we can live in suburb with a white picket fence and kids who ride the bus to school and play sports and take music lessons. So we can go to sleep at night and rest and not lay awake wondering when the threat will come. We have to eliminate them so they're no longer a threat."

"You sound like Bear."

"It's a good plan."

Kenna shook her head, watching the door to the house close. "A missile isn't a plan. It's just a missile. They don't know where to fire it, or when. What they need is intel."

Another point of contention.

"So let's get it for them," he said. "Isn't there a way we

can find out when the next *Dominatus* meeting is? We could pass Miami Security International, or what's left of them, the coordinates, as well as the date and time of the meeting. Let them take care of the rest."

Kenna's eyes burned. "I want that dream of yours, though not so much the suburbs."

"I thought it was *our* dream."

"If it was, there would be a dog in the mix. Something goofy and lovable." She turned to him, taking his face in her hands to bring him close to her. "I want that. I do. It just feels like too much of an impossible dream. I have to worry about *now* every minute of every day, and I have to worry about the next minute. I can't even contemplate the day this child is born right now."

"It's coming in a few months. We need to find a midwife, and a safe place for you to have the baby."

Kenna squeezed her eyes shut and shook her head. "I can't..." She tried to breathe. To think.

"I know." He held her arms. "I think you should talk to Elizabeth, or someone else. Work through the panic you feel."

"I need the fear." She held his gaze with hers. "I need to remember to be afraid every moment. It's what will keep this baby safe."

"But you won't let it stop you from living your life? You're going to have to fight for that as well."

She didn't worry about the flat tone he used to say that. "I'm not hiding. But I'm also not dangling myself out as bait. I'm done playing their game. I do this my way."

"Do what? Solve cases?"

"No, live my life."

He drew her to him and kissed her passionately, and all that fear and anxiety and desperation arced between them light lightening. The give and take between them was both solidarity and a battle of wills. She wanted to feel his frustration and powerlessness, because it meant he felt the same as she did contemplating what the future held.

Kenna gave back as good as she got, pouring all the desire she felt into that steamy car kiss. Leaving them both breathless. They were in this with the same commitment, a hundred percent on board.

For each other and for their child.

"I have an idea," she said.

Jax lifted one brow.

"Hold that thought for later. This is about our case." She ignored the amusing disappointed look on his face.

He kissed her again. "This case is connected to *Dominatus*. So by working it with you, I'm working on my goal of figuring out how to take them down and your goal of ignoring their existence."

"I've been trying not to think about what that medical examiner said." Kenna winced. "They wanted the murder covered up."

"Means we need to solve it."

"I would've done that anyway, regardless of whether they're involved."

"I know." He squeezed her knee. "What's your idea?"

Chapter Six

"We're looking for a house in the area and we want to know what the neighborhood is like," Kenna told Jax, keeping her voice low as they approached the front door.

He knocked, and she shifted beside him—noting he did the same—probably also trying not to stand on the doorstep like a cop. Like two cops, one of them pregnant.

She unzipped her jacket and tucked her shirt tighter around her abdomen. Where a moment ago it would've draped and hidden her six-months-pregnant rounded belly that wasn't all that big anyway, now it was on display.

"Good idea," he whispered.

She tucked her hands in her maternity jeans pockets, also emphasizing the bump under her shirt. Over in the front window, the blinds shifted. Someone looked out to see who was on the doorstep. She knocked again, a jaunty rhythm she tried to make sound light.

When the door opened, Kenna was smiling at Jax. It was the first thing whoever answered saw, and she trusted Jax to protect her if it came to that. She would take the lead from his hold on her hand, because he would alert her if she needed to move. If his fingers tightened suddenly, or he spun her around, there was danger.

She looked over her shoulder, already smiling. A pang of recognition hit her, as in that instant she knew what kind of situation this young woman lived in. But she had learned a long time ago not to let how she was feeling on the inside show in her expression.

"Hi, sorry." Kenna turned from her husband to the slender woman in the doorway. "Sorry to disturb you."

Megan Tiller. Seventeen when Samantha Ambrose was killed six years ago, missing that length of time despite her parents' meager attempts to find her. Or the police, who had deemed her as a runaway who'd taken off with her boyfriend. Escaping home, looking for something else.

Jax eased an arm around her waist. "We're thinking about moving into the area."

"Gotta get out of our apartment before the baby comes." Kenna put both hands over the baby. "You know how it is. Maybe you don't—I don't know you. But we did a viewing over at a house down the street."

The young woman looked a little shellshocked. Exhausted, which wasn't unprecedented with a young child. Behind her, the hall remained dark.

"What's this neighborhood like—if you don't mind us asking?"

Megan hesitated. Her hair could use product and styling, but it was clean. Could be she simply didn't have the money for those things. She wore clothes that were probably purchased from a secondhand store or which she'd kept for a long time. Indications a person was on a strict budget were often simply that. Nothing more.

And sometimes they were a sign of the kind of situation Kenna believed this was.

Megan Tiller had dropped off the map. She lived in a house that was still owned by the boyfriend she'd had years ago, the one who died months later in Afghanistan. Someone kept up the payments, and no one had ever told the mortgage company that he'd died. Kenna couldn't figure how that'd been allowed to continue. Unless you were *Dominatus* and you wanted this woman to remain here, no questions asked.

Megan held the door with one hand and sucked in a choppy breath. "It's a nice enough neighborhood. Quiet." She shrugged one shoulder, and the sweater slipped a bit. Kenna caught the edge of a purple mark on her neck.

Jax rubbed a hand over Kenna's hip. "What about local schools?" He motioned to a hook just inside the door, where the kid had hung his backpack.

Megan looked at it and practically flinched. "Fine, I guess. It's school."

"That helps!" Kenna said, excited but not so loud she would startle this woman. "We won't need one right away, with this one being little. But eventually, we'll want to know she's going somewhere that's safe, where she can learn and make friends." She grinned so wide it felt stiff, and she hoped it didn't look totally fake. "This is probably an imposition, but we've been out a while and I really have to pee." She exhaled a flustered breath. "Is it okay if I use your bathroom?"

Kenna started to step inside before she was even finished with the question. As if Megan would never have any intention of saying no. Anyone with a good-willed heart would let a pregnant woman in a door rather than force her to walk into it, and she banked on the fact Megan wasn't a bad person. Kenna had seen the way she cared for the child who'd come home.

The way she hadn't left the house.

How she'd waited for him to come in and they'd embraced the way they did.

This was a woman who cared for her child no matter what was swirling around her. She was a protector. A survivor.

"You can't come in." Megan froze, her voice nothing more than a whisper.

Kenna looked around the dark interior of the house, dimly lit by lights overhead with missing bulbs. The hallway was stark but clean, nothing on the walls. Thin old carpet covered the hallway floor.

"Megan, we know who you are," Jax said in a soft voice. "Are you safe here? Do you need help?"

Kenna turned to the living room, where the little boy sat on the floor with his back to the wall. Knees curled up. An old metal train with faded paint was on the floor beside him. He held a small plastic bowl, two Cheerios in his fingers. He stared at her.

She stepped up to the threshold and saw there was only one recliner, over which someone had draped a US Army blanket. No couch. A coffee table beside the recliner had an ashtray on it, which accounted for the cigar smell in here. Big TV on the wall, wires hanging down connecting to the box on the bookcase under it.

Nothing on the walls.

Plenty of people didn't have much material wealth, and abuse happened in every stratus of society. Kenna bit her lip. *Don't assume.* Poverty didn't mean Megan wasn't happy with her life, or finding contentment in her choices. So what if she and the kid had nowhere to sit.

Kenna wanted to look through the whole house and get a complete assessment of the situation. Instead of doing that, she turned back to Megan. "My name is Kenna Banbury and I'm a private investigator. This is my husband, Oliver Jaxton. He works with me. We're a team."

"Are you even pregnant?" Megan stared at her with a hard expression.

"Yes, I am." Kenna gave her a moment with that. "We do want to help you. But we'd also like to ask you about Samantha Ambrose."

Megan flinched, but it was barely visible. Kenna might not have seen what she thought she did.

"I'd ask if we can talk, but it doesn't look like there's anywhere to sit in here." Kenna waved to the living room. "Do you have a kitchen table?"

"You can't be in here." Megan bit her lip.

Jax held out his hand, and Kenna clasped it, though they were further from each other than she'd have liked. "If you or your son are in danger, or scared about anything, or if you feel trapped...we can help you."

Megan shook her head vigorously.

Kenna took a wild guess. "There are places you can go he won't find you."

"No, there aren't," Megan whispered. "I don't know you guys. You need to leave *now*."

"Are you expecting him to come home?" Jax's hand tightened around Kenna's. "If you get your things and bring your son, we can leave. He *won't* find you."

"I can't leave the house."

"Megan, I can't leave you here," Kenna said. "Not knowing you're in danger. The police—"

"You don't understand. I *can't leave the house*." She gasped but didn't say more.

Kenna wanted to ask what *Dominatus* wanted with the two of them, or if it was because their captor held enough sway to get what he wanted. The homeowner was the one who was supposed to have been Megan's boyfriend at the time of Samantha's death. If he was dead, and not the one who forced them to be here, then who was the person keeping her living in this fear?

Jax said, "We know you didn't even leave to meet your son at the bus." He paused. "I'm guessing you don't even check the mailbox."

Megan stared at him, no unshed tears in her eyes. Just a slender woman with straight shoulders who had withstood who-knew-what in the past six years.

"Does he hurt your son?" Jax was fighting his frustration.

This woman didn't need to see him lose his cool, but Kenna knew for a fact he was close to it. All because this family was in danger and her husband felt the way she did when it came to rescuing those who needed it.

Megan's jaw flexed.

Kenna wanted to tell her that her son was beautiful, but that might not be a good thing in Megan's world. "What's his name?" There was so much more to say, but starting there could help Megan begin to trust them.

"Joseph." Megan didn't look at the boy. He hadn't moved from his spot on the floor, or eaten any more of the after-school snack since they came in.

Kenna needed a plan. "If you tell us everything about him, we can make sure the police take him down. He'll be arrested, and it will never fall on you. We'll go after him like it's a personal vendetta, and he'll have no clue why until we explain he double-crossed us in business. Something like that. You'll be safe, and he won't come after you."

"One of them will."

"Because they're connected to *Dominatus?*"

Megan's eyes flared. Her body curled in on itself, a defensive reflex that had become instinctive. A way to protect herself against the threat.

"We know who they are," Kenna said. "We've gone up against them before and survived. We can do it again. If it keeps Joseph safe, it will be worth it."

Jax's hand flexed around hers. She wasn't going to trade their baby's life for Joseph's, but neither of them was prepared to walk away when another child was in danger.

Kenna continued, "We have friends who can keep you both safe from them. Friends who know exactly who *Dominatus* is and how to hide from them."

Jax nodded, relaxing slightly but not much. "It's true. We *can* do this for you both. But you have to trust us enough to go with us. Take the chance and be free."

"He'll kill me."

"We're going to make sure that doesn't happen to you or Joseph." Kenna had to get through to her. "And we don't want to leave you here, but we will if you think it's best. Don't think we'll forget about you. It's going to become our mission to make sure you're set free of this. Whatever it is. You deserve to feel free. Safe. To find some happiness. Everyone does."

Megan stared at her, and Kenna got the feeling she might as well be speaking a different language. Safety and happiness weren't words Megan understood. The life she lived had no room for those things, or wishing for them to be true.

"We know what it's like to be scared. To not know what *Dominatus* is going to do next." Kenna paused. "We know what it's like to be trapped. And we can help you."

A tiny whimper came from the living room.

Kenna glanced over at Joseph and saw his attention on the front window. Before she could say something, the front door moved.

A man's presence filled the space at the end of the hallway. But it was more than where he stood. It was the air in the home. "Why is—"

His eyes narrowed on Jax, this heavyset man with a barrel chest and shaved head. A tattoo up the side of his neck.

Kenna moved, propelled by Jax tugging on her hand or her direction first—she didn't know which it was. Jax let go of her. Kenna swept Megan into the living room and out of the hall where Jax faced down the man who had entered.

Megan sucked in a breath, her gaze on Kenna's gun, which she'd drawn.

Right. But there were safer ways for a pregnant woman to keep two charges protected. She palmed her cell phone with her off hand and speed-dialed the number she'd programmed.

Ramon answered before the first ring. "Almost there. Two minutes."

"Hurry." She hung up.

A gunshot exploded in the hall.

Chapter Seven

Megan sucked in a sharp breath. A thud in the hall sounded a second before the threat stumbled into the room and fell to the floor, his face flush with anger. Kenna shifted enough to untuck the material she'd tucked around her pregnancy belly.

"Jax?" Kenna didn't want to ask, but she had to know.

"I'm good." Jax appeared at the doorway, holding his gun. "Tried to fight me for it. Found out what happens when he goes up against someone his size." His jaw was set, indicating to her that her husband wasn't happy. For several reasons would be her guess.

Kenna's focus was Megan—and Joseph. "Go to him." She indicated the boy in the corner, and Megan rushed across the room, gathering the child against her. The boy tucked his head against her hip, his arms around her legs, holding on tight. As close to safety as he could get.

The guy got up off the floor of the hallway, tension and anger in every line of his body. "The two of you get out of my house!" The assailant's voice thundered in the room, the lack of furniture making the sound echo off bare walls and floor.

Megan and Joseph both flinched at the sound and moved closer to the corner of the wall as far from him as they could get. But the guy didn't even look at them.

Kenna moved her gun into view, matching Jax's stance, but with her hips back into her coat, making the sides hang where they might disguise her front. Or at least not make it obvious she was pregnant.

Far as she could see, this guy didn't have a gun.

"That's the thing," Jax said. "It isn't your house."

Kenna picked up the line of questioning. "The name on the mortgage is Mitch Caudell, but he died overseas six years ago. So who are you?"

"The person who lives here!"

"Call the police. Tell them we're here and you want us to leave." Kenna shrugged. "We're happy to be escorted from the premises."

A tendon in his jaw ticked. He had no intention of calling the police. But she did.

Before she could reach for her phone again, the front door slammed open and footsteps in the hall preceded Ramon and Zeyla rushing in a second later with their guns drawn.

"Everyone good?" Ramon moved into a defensive position in front of Kenna so she got a good view of his jacket and jeans, and the back of his head, but not much else.

"We're good," Kenna replied.

But Megan and Joseph still looked scared for their lives.

Zeyla scanned the room, clocking each person. Taking in more than the average citizen. Cataloguing threats and assessing the situation. "Take the woman and the kid out. I'll make it look like self-defense."

Jax said, "We don't murder people in cold blood."

Kenna agreed with her husband's statement but wasn't going to immediately discount Zeyla's idea. She found she was more willing to find gray areas these days than she'd ever been before in her life. Just not right now in front of two innocents.

"Megan, you and Joseph come over here." She held out a hand, around Ramon.

Megan looked at Kenna's Hispanic friend.

"He's here to protect us," Kenna said. "And we're all here to protect the two of you."

She started to move, Joseph still clinging to her leg. The guy grabbed her, pulled them both in front of him, and swung his arm around her neck. Megan swallowed a scream, her eyes pleading with them to help her.

Kenna ducked back behind Ramon, fully confident her husband and two friends would take care of the situation. While they called out orders to him to let her go and put his hands on his head.

"911, what's your emergency?"

"We need the police," Kenna said. "This guy is hurting his girlfriend and child."

She told the dispatcher the street address and described the house. When he asked more questions, she gave as much information as she could, explaining she was a private investigator here to ask about a cold case murder.

They talked long enough for him to say, "There's a patrol car pulling onto the street now."

"Thank you." Kenna hung up, whether the conversation was over or not.

She ducked into the hall and heard Megan yelp, then opened the front door and waited for the uniformed officers to park. She waved the two of them over, both guys in their thirties or forties. "Thank you so much for coming."

When the two men entered the hall and went into the living area, Zeyla and Ramon were both gone. Jax alone stood guard over the three—the captor and his two victims. "He won't let her go. He just rushed in and grabbed them."

The two cops moved through the space with confidence. Both had heavy gear on their belts and overcoats over their uniforms. Beanies were tucked into pockets, and neither drew their weapon.

One moved to Jax's space to face off with the captor. "I'd like you to step outside with me, sir."

The other said, "I'll stay with these folks."

Kenna was supposed to go with Jax, though. "I don't want to leave my friend. Megan was really scared when he rushed in and grabbed them. Can I stay with her?"

That solved part of the problem. The guy who lived here with them would spin a tale about protecting his house as if they were the assailants who had come in uninvited. Until Kenna managed to reveal the reason he didn't want to call the cops in the first place.

"Maybe Megan and Joseph can come outside with me?" she suggested.

Kenna was as worried as she likely appeared. Sure, she could play the pregnant card and use her condition to convince the cops she was about keeping people safe. Which was true, and not something that only applied universally to anyone having a baby. But she'd used the pregnancy in her favor enough today. Eventually, it would feel like using the kid as a set piece to do her job. Which was exactly what *they* did. Not something she wanted to define her.

"Sir, you wanna let them go outside?" The officer's

question didn't sound much like a request, more a test of the boyfriend's intentions.

The guy huffed. "These do-gooders. They think they can take her from me. They're probably from some weird religion."

His hold on Megan shifted enough it looked less like he was trying to detain her. Which was better than blatantly strangling her, but the cops hadn't seen that. This guy was good. He kept it tight when he had to, which meant no one had figured out what was going on with Megan.

Not until Kenna and Jax knocked on the door.

She wanted to thank God, say a prayer and be grateful for Him leading them here. But was that what had happened? She wondered how far His control of their lives extended when Jax considered his life yielded to the Lord... but Kenna wasn't so sure about hers.

Megan whimpered.

"Ma'am, come with us." The police officer waved her and Joseph over.

The abuser didn't want to let her go but couldn't argue.

"Sir, put your weapon away."

Jax complied with the other cop's order. "He's a dangerous man. Don't turn your back or underestimate him. We believe him to be the person who killed Samantha Ambrose six years ago."

Kenna would have said the same thing, just so that the police officer took extra caution. It might even save his life in the next few minutes. They couldn't control what the assailant did next, but the cop knew now to be extra wary.

She backed up into the hall, and Megan came with her. Joseph, too. "Megan, when was the last time you went outside?"

The girl stopped in the hall, the cop listening to their exchange.

"You and Joseph are going to need coats, okay? It's really cold out."

Megan said, "Joe, get your jacket."

The little boy let go long enough to grab it off the hook by his backpack. His shoes were lined up neatly in a way no child would do. So had Megan straightened them? Making sure things were precisely in their place before "Dad" got home.

"Megan, do you have a coat?"

The young woman shook her head.

Kenna tugged off her own and held it out, making sure the shirt she wore covered the gun at the small of her back. "Pregnancy is making me much warmer than usual. I'll be good for a few minutes." Meanwhile, without it, the young woman would be far too cold. She motioned it closer to Megan. "Please, wear this."

Megan took the coat and slipped it on while Kenna went to the front door, trying to come across as nonchalant. Remaining calm and levelheaded, and showing kindness. All things that she didn't need to pretend, but which a police officer would notice.

She opened the door and stepped out, watching Joseph slip his shoes on. "Do you need help with your zipper, buddy?"

He nodded and stepped over the threshold.

Kenna knelt on the front walk and waved him over. She got his zipper lined up. "This is a nice coat. Does it keep you warm?"

He didn't answer.

She got the zipper to the top. "There you go." She smiled, and he returned to Mom's side.

Megan had the coat overlapped in front, so she was surrounded tightly by the warm material.

Kenna's skin chilled, but she would be fine for a moment. "Megan, there isn't a perfect solution here. We can all only do our best. But if you need help, if you're scared for your safety and Joseph's and you want to get out of this house, there are places you can go."

She wasn't going to promise he would never find her, but she wanted to.

The cop glanced between Kenna, Megan, and Jax on the far side by the door. There was barely room on the front step for him to be outside, but he stayed tucked against the open door.

Jax winced. "I hate to say it, but if you have information about the death of Samantha Ambrose, it's going to give the police more reason to keep you safe. It might even be something they can talk to the feds about."

The cop said, "You're dangling witness protection?"

"I was FBI for years. I'm not promising anything, but we don't know what Megan knows. She could be exactly the person the US marshals are in their business to protect." Jax shrugged. "Someone wanted Samantha Ambrose's death covered up and Megan might be able to tell us who and why."

Witness protection might not be enough to hide someone from *Dominatus*. She'd considered it, but even that might not be secure enough to keep them from finding her, and Jax, and their child.

There might be nowhere on earth they could hide...

If *Dominatus* was looking for them.

"We're here because Megan went missing around the same time." Jax's tone gentled. "Megan, were you held here against your will the last six years?"

Megan Tilley clutched her son's shoulder. She nodded.

Kenna said, "Is the man inside that house the father of your son?"

There were limited options as to what could have happened between two men and two teenage girls who had gone missing from their lives. One person was responsible for Samantha's death, and one person was inside that house facing a serious jail sentence.

Megan just stared at her.

"What is his name?" the officer asked, pulling out his phone.

"Carl Allerton."

"He keeps you here against your will?"

Megan managed to nod.

"Does he hurt you or your son?"

"That's not..." Megan's voice sounded hollow. She covered Joseph's ears, then said louder, "He isn't my son. But I'm the only one who takes care of him. I'm the only one who protects him. You can't take him away from me. I'm all he has."

Kenna glanced at Jax, whose eyes widened. "Megan, who is his mother?"

"Samantha was." The woman swallowed. "But they killed her."

Chapter Eight

"Carl Allerton is nobody." Zeyla dropped the file folder on the small round table in the hospital café, tucked into the corner of the lobby.

Kenna pulled out a chair and sat, aware of Ramon and Jax getting drinks for the four of them. "No one is nobody."

Around them, a smattering of people had gathered. An old man reading from a newspaper, drinking out of a china teacup on a saucer. A couple of doctors, or residents, in light-blue scrubs. A guy who gave "dad" vibes having a tense conversation with a teen boy.

Zeyla gripped the back of the chair. "Fine, he was a soldier along with Mitch Caudell. Basic training together, in a unit together. Carl pulled out early. Mitch got redeployed."

"After they kidnapped Mitch's girlfriend, Megan, and a younger girl who they killed."

"According to Megan," Zeyla said.

"What's *that* supposed to mean? She's upstairs having every abuse she's ever suffered catalogued and photographed so the police can use it for evidence. Like it's a piece of paper left behind, or a fingerprint on a knife. They're going to take apart her life and leave her to figure out how to put it back together on her own."

Not only that, but with the connection to their enemy, she might be in danger and that would pose a serious risk if she was left to fend for herself. Only if this turned into a federal case—like a corruption charge against those in power who had covered up the murder—did Megan have any shot at a witness protection deal in exchange for her testimony.

"Seems to me however this shakes out, she's in danger." Kenna glanced at Jax, who frowned as he approached the table.

Ramon didn't look any more pleased about this situation than her husband did.

Kenna would have said Ramon was her best friend, if they even needed to categorize it. They had each other's backs, and that was what counted.

"Thanks for coming in, both of you." She glanced between him and Zeyla. "I didn't know you were nearby when I called, but I'm glad you were."

Given the size of this country, and the fact they'd supposedly been working a case elsewhere, that was an interesting development. Two minutes away sounded more like they'd been on call, ready to assist at any moment. Not just because she'd called on a reflex, and they'd been nearby. She'd contacted Ramon not even knowing if they'd be able to help. Something she wasn't going to unpack. It simply turned out they were, and she was choosing to be grateful for it.

Jax shifted his weight from foot to foot, not because he was nervous. More likely he wanted to get moving to burn off some pent up frustration.

She wasn't surprised he'd ensured she was protected.

He pressed his palm to the table and leaned down to kiss her, light and quick. "Yesterday, when it became clear there might be the slightest *Dominatus* connection with this case, I called them. They came."

Ramon sipped his coffee.

Zeyla folded her arms across her chest. "You're welcome."

Kenna smiled at her cousin, knowing the other woman was just as on board with protecting the people in this chosen family as the rest of them were. She didn't exactly know what, if anything, was going on between Ramon and Zeyla and if they were more than just friends, but she was glad for the support.

Jax pulled out a chair, and Ramon dragged one over after confirming the older man with the newspaper didn't need it. He rotated it and sat leaning against the back. "So what do we know about this guy? Other than the fact that he kept her after his friend died."

Kenna had spoken to Megan in the ambulance on the way over here, Joseph tucked to her side. The EMT hadn't been able to do much, considering she had no pressing injuries and didn't respond to any of his requests. She had answered Kenna's questions, though. Probably because that made it easier to ignore the EMT.

"Megan told me that she'd already moved in with Mitch before she was reported missing. Neither mom nor her dad paid much attention, and no one really cared where she went. The police did come to the house to ask about her, but Carl is the one who answered the door back then. They were roommates at that point, so Carl told the cops that Mitch and Megan had left town. Headed for Florida, or California, he didn't know which. They bought the whole story, and no one ever came back to ask about her. No one knew she was being held there, abused and tormented into not even stepping outside the front door."

"So sad." Zeyla shook her head. "They didn't follow up and never checked anything else."

Kenna hadn't read the missing person file but figured that was likely accurate. "I'm more interested in going back and talking with Doctor Elenor Walsh about how she not only misconstrued the cause of death, but how she also neglected to include the fact that the deceased had recently given birth before she died."

Jax reached over and put a hand on her knee.

"Where's the connection to you-know-who?" Ramon looked around, like saying the D-word aloud and mentioning the name of their enemy was taboo. Or risky.

She'd done it a moment ago. "I'd love an answer to that. It could be a number of things."

Zeyla sat back in her chair. "Mitch. Carl. Some other parentage of the kid. It could be Samantha's parents, and they wanted her death covered up. For whatever reason scumbags do that sort of thing." She drifted into a slight British accent. "Megan. The cops investigating. Some witness, or bystander. Who knows."

"Hopefully, we can narrow it down more than that," Jax said. "I'm praying Maizie comes up with something."

Ramon glanced at Kenna, but she wasn't sure why. She held his gaze until he shrugged.

"Wanna tell the rest of the class?" A slight smile tugged at Jax's lips.

Kenna pushed out a long breath. "It's nothing."

Ramon shook his head. "Zip. Zilch. Nada."

"Yeah, yeah," Jax said. "But I want to thank the two of you as well. We appreciate the backup."

Zeyla shrugged. "You should've shot him before we got there. Or let me do it. This whole thing would be a lot easier to contain."

"But we'd lose the chance to question him," Kenna pointed out.

Jax glanced at her, a guarded expression on his face.

Before he could speak, she said, "Fine. I'm not the one who's going to question him. You know what I mean."

"Maybe you guys should head back to the RV. Let Zeyla and I take care of the next steps." Ramon kept his tone all innocent, like he wasn't suggesting the pregnant lady go take a nap.

At least he hadn't told her to calm down.

Ramon lifted his hands. "It's just a suggestion. You're the one who said Megan might be in danger."

Zeyla narrowed her eyes. "I'm feeling the need to make sure the local social services department lets Joseph and Megan stay together."

Kenna shrugged. "Even if that was a good idea it's not our fight. It might be the worst possible thing for Joseph to continue to live with her, and foster care would be a blessing. We have no idea. Given the police are involved, it's not even necessarily up to us to make sure Megan is safe."

Zeyla looked impressed. "So you're turning over a new leaf, not determined to save everyone in the world anymore?"

"Or you just don't want to be anywhere *Dominatus* is involved?" Jax paused. "You'd rather be a million miles from any of them." Like his statement was a confession of her darkest secret. When he was actually outing her to her friends.

Ramon straightened back from the chair, his brows rising.

Zeyla chuckled. "That'd be nice." She let out a long sigh. "I tried that once. Told Mum I was done. I was out of the game. Lasted a good few days until one of them approached me at the grocery store. Best of luck to you, trying to ignore them." She lifted her paper cup and toasted Kenna.

"I'm not doomed to fail. I'm living my life." She folded her arms across her chest, resting them on the baby, who suddenly kicked at the spot where her right arm lay. Kenna jumped.

"What is it?" Jax uncrossed his arms and leaned toward her.

"The baby kicked me." She took his hand and touched it to the same spot. Little Miss kicked at his hand, pushing a few times in a row against his palm.

He smiled at her, so much wonder in his eyes.

"Did you guys pick a name yet?" Ramon asked. "Because Ramona is pretty good."

Zeyla snorted into her cup and started choking on coffee. "There's no way." She coughed and barked out a laugh. "No way."

"What?" Ramon said. "It's a good idea!"

Kenna smiled at her husband, only partially paying attention to the other two and their antics. He smiled back, but the kicking seemed to have died down.

"We're making a list." Kenna chuckled. "Sorry, but neither of your names are on it."

"Zeyla is a great name, but it's not for everyone." The other woman shrugged. "I'll see if I can get in to talk to Megan, find out what she knows about"—she glanced at Ramon—"*you know who.*"

"I'm not that bad," he said. "But to be fair, the last one

of those people I met nearly killed me." He rolled his shoulders. "Who just blows themselves up?"

"I'm just impressed they covered up use of a military armament on US soil." Zeyla pushed her chair in, and the two of them headed across the lobby of the hospital.

He eyed Kenna. "I'm guessing you want to go see Doctor Walsh again?"

"What's there to learn?" She shrugged. "Walsh covered up the pregnancy, and the family cremated her. If there's any evidence, it's gone now. The family needs to know so they can get a DNA test run. If Joseph was my grandson, I'd want to adopt him."

"You're a good person, though." Jax smiled for a second, then said, "We could make a packet, get Maizie to anonymously send it to someone in the DA's office so they can start an investigation. But if *Dominatus* wants this all hush-hush, that might put another life in danger."

"Exactly." She nodded. "I keep turning down paths and realizing I have no idea what to do with the road ahead. I just know I want to be where you are and have this baby safely."

"That's a lot just by itself. All the rest of it on top of that is enough to drive a person into a psychologist's office—or to a counselor."

She nodded but didn't want to talk about doing that. Not right now when the list of people she could trust was so short.

Jax's phone beeped on the table. He flipped it over to see the screen. "It's a breaking news alert."

"What's going on?" She took a sip of the smoothie he'd bought her.

"A bomb just went off in Washington, DC, on a city street. Several cars were blown up."

"Seriously?" Kenna said. "Any fatalities?"

"The number of casualties is unknown yet, but there are deaths and injuries on the scene. And a limo belonging to a Croatian delegation looks like it was the target." With his head dipped to his phone, he didn't see her reaction. "Apparently, they're in town for a meeting with the president about a peace treaty between our two countries."

She stared at him, not allowing her mind to show her memories she wanted to keep locked up tight. *None of our business.* "That's scary. How horrible."

Jax nodded. "There's going to be a taskforce busy for weeks working this. Hope they find the bomber soon."

She took another sip of the smoothie, which tasted sour in her mouth. "Me, too."

Movement across the room caught her attention. When she looked she couldn't believe who she saw. The smoothie got stuck in her throat, and she coughed, swallowed it, and managed not to choke.

"Everything okay?" Jax glanced from her to the spot across the room. "Did you see something?"

She looked again, but he was gone.

Kenna shook her head. "Just a ghost."

Chapter Nine

Sitting outside was preferable at any time, but in the winter on the outskirts of Boston? Not so much. Kenna had the heater in the RV running, a mug of steaming decaf coffee in front of her, and the laptop open on the small dining table. On the screen she dragged facial features onto a blank canvas she was using to build a composite sketch of the man she'd seen in the hospital waiting area.

"Who is he?" Maizie's voice came through her laptop speakers. Kenna had the volume turned low because she was up early but Jax was still asleep. In the corner window of the video meeting, Maizie peered closely at the image.

"Someone I thought was dead. Or hoped was dead." Kenna deleted the eyes because they were too far apart and scrolled down the list. "Maybe I didn't see him, I just thought I did."

"That happened to me a lot." Maizie's gaze shifted to something else on her screen as she typed on her laptop keyboard. The view around her was the Airstream trailer Kenna had grown up in, the one her father had owned, currently parked on a hillside in Colorado on property owned by Kenna's former boss from the FBI—now retired—where he lived with his wife.

"Elizabeth helped you work through it?" Kenna found eyes that were close enough and dragged them onto the face.

"You could talk to her. Let her help you."

"I'd rather forget the whole thing."

"Is that a good idea?" Maizie asked. "We're not supposed to stuff it down. We're supposed to deal with it so it doesn't come back up and bite us when we least expect it. Because trust me, *trauma*—I hate that word—always resurfaces at the worst possible moment."

"Want to talk about it?"

"You're the one that's supposed to be talking about it!"

Kenna glanced at the slider separating the bedroom from the living area of the RV, then to the window over the kitchen sink.

There weren't more than a handful of occupied spaces in this campsite. Either they lived here year-round, or they were in town to visit relatives and didn't mind braving the cold. Jax had mentioned Florida, and she had to admit that didn't sound too bad right now. Except that it would feel like trying to run as far from *Dominatus* as she could get and that's what being in Boston was supposed to be.

"I'm not running."

"Well, yeah," Maizie said. "But you're avoiding all of it, even if you think you aren't running away. But I think you are."

"The case connected to them, but I didn't drop it. I stuck with it, and now Megan and Joseph are safe." Kenna took a sip of her coffee and scrolled through the images of lips.

"Hmm."

Kenna ignored that. "Zeyla and Ramon are going to go and see Samantha Ambrose's parents today so they can relay what Megan said about her death. They'll probably want to do a DNA test and find out if Joseph really is her child."

"We should all do that. Find out if any of us are related."

"Might be better not to know." Kenna tried to keep the conversation light. "I'm not sure I can handle any more surprises."

Maizie laughed gently. "It's probably just wishful thinking. I mean, you and Jax are basically my parents now, but that doesn't have anything to do with genetics. Could be cool though, with you and Zeyla. Her mom, and Bruce and Ramon, and all of us."

"You think Ramon and Bruce will turn out to be brothers?"

Maizie laughed louder. "Maybe not."

"We're family. We don't need to be blood relatives," Kenna said. "But I get what you're saying. It would be nice to know we're connected like that as well."

Maizie let out a sigh. Her phone pinged, and she looked at the screen. A smile pulled at her lips, and she actually blushed a little.

"That looks interesting." Kenna tried not to sound like she was prying. "What's his name?"

Maizie blushed a darker shade of pink. She brushed a hunk of thick blond hair behind her ear and cleared her throat. "Uh, no one."

"Right. Just a school thing? You're in a group project together."

Maizie rolled her eyes. "Fine, his name is Travis."

"Have you done a deep dive background check yet?"

"No, *Mom*."

Kenna smiled. "I can do one. What's his last name, date of birth, and social security number?"

"If I knew those things, I wouldn't tell you."

"I'll find out from Zeyla."

"No, you will not."

Kenna chuckled. "Fine, I'll back off."

"You just want me to think you've backed off when you have no intention of doing that."

"Who me?"

"Pregnancy is giving you this real mama-bear thing."

"And as a result, you're safe. We're all safe."

But Dominatus is still out there.

She knew what everyone in their family unit of friends was thinking. They expected her to be gung-ho on board with taking the big evil organization down when they had no idea how to do that.

"Hey." Jax put his hand on her shoulder.

Kenna flinched so hard coffee spilled on her lap. She winced, set the mug down, and rubbed the thigh of her leggings.

"Sorry." Jax handed her paper towels, then wiped the table and under the mug.

She pressed the bundle to the wet fabric on her leg.

"Did I burn you?" he asked.

She shook her head. "I should've heard you coming."

Instead, she'd been deep in her thoughts and distracted by the cold terror of facing *Dominatus*. Everything she'd buried in her mind and was currently actively trying to avoid thinking about—let alone facing. Let *alone* actually going up against. All of it swelled up like a wave that threatened to drown her every time she even thought about any of it.

"Hi, Maze." Jax gave her a wave, then turned his head and kissed Kenna. "Hi."

"Good morning." She smiled. "Don't worry, I'm good."

He nodded, and the assessing gaze dissipated from his expression. "What are you working on?"

"Proof I'm not ignoring this. I'm just not sure if I really saw this guy or not." She shifted on the seat, moving toward the window so Jax could sit by her after he'd poured his first cup of coffee.

It wasn't six thirty yet, but these days it seemed like she didn't sleep nearly as much as she used to, and then a day or two later she made up for it. As if the baby had decided on her own rhythm already and Kenna was along for the ride. When it happened, she enjoyed the quiet morning by herself, and when she slept, Kenna enjoyed the peace of being curled up in blankets alongside her husband. Either way, she didn't have to face life outside the door of the RV.

"Who is he?" Jax put one arm along the back of the seat, his fingers on her shoulder in a reassuring touch.

"A bad guy. If this guy is loose in the world, we have mega problems. There will be a trail of ugly murder scenes behind him."

"Then we need to find out so he can be shut down before he comes after you."

Jax was probably right about that, but still she said, "We don't know if I would be the target."

"Not something I'm willing to wait and see on." He said it so matter-of-factly.

Kenna found it hard to argue with him. "Not going up against a serial killer would be great." Especially not one who hurt people because he got a kick out of suffering. "I'd rather not to do that anytime, let alone pregnant."

The fact she was even saying that was a testament to

how much in her life had changed. Things had shifted, and life became more complicated. The stakes of the work they did were higher—much higher—when they went up against the shadowy organization that her family wanted to take down personally.

She wasn't exactly dragging her feet. More like flat out refusing to engage, past the work she'd always done. Work like saving Megan and Joseph from the situation they'd been in.

"So how do we find out who this is?" Maizie peered at the sketch now. "I can't search every DMV database in the country and the military, and every other facial recognition program. It could take weeks, and he might've killed a hundred people by then."

"I'll touch base with Amara," Kenna said. "See if she knows him."

Jax made a *hmm* sound in his throat, shifting on the seat. He took a sip of coffee but said nothing.

"Anything else, Maze?"

"Isn't there always?"

The young woman was right, but Kenna didn't know how else to change the subject. "Hit me with it."

Maizie's gaze shifted in a way Kenna could tell she was looking at other screens.

Kenna focused on the sketch for a second, long enough to decide she'd put it together as close to the real thing as she could.

"Bear messaged me again. He wants to talk to you. They're working on a plan, and he needs your input."

Kenna wasn't sure she could avoid it much longer. "Put something on the calendar. How are things going at the platform?"

Jax shook his head. "I'm still surprised *Dominatus* hasn't just blown the thing away."

"Or they don't consider it a breach of security to leave it there." Kenna shrugged. "Could be they have a different plan for the security team who took it over and we just haven't seen what it is yet. Or whoever was in charge is gone in a way they can't report in. Which means the head honchos don't know the platform was taken back and everything going on there was shut down."

"Makes sense, in a way. But only if they really do run things so separately with different factions and groups like splinter cells and no cohesive leadership. If everyone is doing their own thing and no one reports to anyone else, I guess this could happen and they wouldn't retaliate. Or come looking for revenge." Jax shrugged. "Just seems inefficient."

"Or it's the path of least resistance."

Maizie said, "What do you mean?"

"They don't have to have checks and balances, someone giving orders and everyone reporting in." Kenna paused. "Seems more like they have a general goal, and everyone goes about it in their own way, however they want to do it. So you've got a whole lot of rogue operations, and over the long term, they get where they're going. But it doesn't make change very quickly."

"Like I said, inefficient." Jax squeezed her knee under the table.

"They didn't explain to me exactly how it works," Kenna said. "It was more like one-world government propaganda trying to get me to buy in to the overarching plan."

"That doesn't sound like fun." Maizie winced.

Kenna hadn't shared even this much about her experience as a captive on that platform, but now that she'd started, she found she could say, "It did feel a lot like they were trying to brainwash me. Makes me wonder if they could trigger me and I'm suddenly mindless doing their bidding."

They'd seen it before, but with the use of chemicals. Hypnosis or suggestion? Those were the things that kept her awake at night. Wondering if she was free, but still very much their pawn.

She just didn't know how to be certain she wasn't. Aside from staying as far as she could from any of their operatives. Living her life—her way. Relying on her husband to protect her, possibly even from herself.

Jax tugged her close with his arm and kissed her forehead. "That's why, whatever we do, we do it together."

She nodded. "Agreed."

On the screen, Maizie started typing. "I'll ask Bear to have his people go through the records they found when they took over the facility. Maybe there's something in the files about that kind of experimentation."

"Thanks, Maze." Kenna smiled. "Don't worry about me. Jax has it covered. Zeyla and Ramon are nearby if needed. We're good."

The girl didn't look any less worried, but said, "Okay." She looked at her phone again, but without the flushed cheeks. "I should go. I have some English homework to finish."

"Have a good day."

Maizie said bye, and the call ended.

Jax nudged her shoulder with his. "That's what you're worried about? Being brainwashed?"

"Among other things. I'm not writing you a list. We don't have enough paper."

"I can't fix it."

Kenna reached for his hand. "Fixing it might be what you feel like you should be doing, but it's not what I need."

He lifted his gaze, and she saw all the fear and turmoil in her reflected in her eyes. "What do you need?"

"Not to be corny, but you." She smiled.

"That would've been corny."

Kenna leaned into him. "I need you. Here, like this. I need us to be together, doing what we can. Trying to enjoy what our lives are and not getting too caught up in someone else's war. There's a whole world out there. Why do we have to be the ones to sacrifice everything to fight this big bad evil? It's too much. We can't possibly survive that fight, and it's not giving up to say that. It's realizing we have too much to lose to go after them."

"It sure feels like giving up. But you're right. We can't risk this to take them down. Not when we don't have a good plan, or a way to take them out."

"I wouldn't mind a plan to severely undermine them." Kenna worked her mouth back and forth. "But I can't figure out how to do that either. I don't want to be near any of them for long enough to figure out how to get them to destroy each other."

"Sounds like we need to pray." He bowed his head and spoke aloud, giving all their fear to the Lord. Asking for wisdom on how to fight this evil, and protection for every member of their family.

To her ears, it sounded like clanging cymbals. Like the words hit the ceiling and bounced back down, going nowhere.

Kenna squeezed her eyes shut and just listened to the sound of his voice. She'd given up straining and groping in the dark for a peace she wasn't going to find.

It had left her months ago.

Chapter Ten

Later that same afternoon, Kenna entered the hospital room right after Jax. "Hey, Megan." She smiled at the young woman tucked into the bed sheets and blankets. Dressed in a gown that revealed the angry bruises on her forearms, and places where she had been grabbed by someone with a punishing grip. "You asked to see us."

The girl nodded, wringing her fingers together. "Thanks for coming."

"How are you feeling?"

Jax hung back by the door, leaning against the wall. Probably trying to look unobtrusive. Or at least, nonthreatening.

Kenna went and stood by Megan's bedside, tugging off her coat and laying it on the chair because the hospital had the heat cranked.

Megan shrugged one shoulder. "They want me here for observation. Whatever that means." She shook her head.

"Are you worried about Joseph?"

"The social worker came by and explained. He brought the family who are going to take Joseph in. Church people.

They seem nice. He'll be the first kid they've ever fostered. And the wife is a therapist, so she'll be able to help Joseph."

"That's good." Kenna leaned against the side of the bed, today's outfit of stretchy jeans and a T-shirt not complete until she'd pulled out a pair of Converse she hadn't worn in years. "That's really good."

Her effort to feel like herself today might have worked on the outside, but inside she still felt like someone else. Which meant she was a fraud. Pretending she was fine, or at least on the road to recovery.

But nothing she did was going to change what had happened to her.

"Anyway," Megan said, "that's part of why I wanted to talk to you. The doctor brought in a therapist to see me, but what's the point? It isn't like I'll get better."

"You don't know that." Kenna shook her head. "I happen to know from personal experience that things do get better."

"Because you know about being held against your will?" Megan laced her words with sarcasm.

Kenna just looked at her.

The hardness in Megan's expression dissipated. "Oh."

"I know it gets better." Kenna paused. "You just have to keep moving forward."

"That'll be difficult," Megan muttered.

"Yes, it will be. Don't think this is going to be easy. It might be some days. But others, the whole thing will hit you like a freight train. You'll feel like you can't breathe. Like you're right back there, trapped with no way out."

"Doesn't matter. What matters is Joseph, and they're going to take care of him." Megan sniffed. "But you should know, it was a family thing. The reason Mitch and Carl were able to stay in the military as long as they did, even with all the complaints and times they were written up in their personnel files, or whatever they're called."

Kenna's ears pricked. "Someone in their family protected them?"

"Yeah, and for the record they're both psychopaths. I thought Mitch was nice, but he killed Samantha and left."

"The last time he was deployed?"

Megan nodded. "Someone covered it all up because they're family. I think like an uncle, or someone like that. That's why Carl will never go to prison for keeping me for years. It doesn't matter, though. He'll kill me anyway."

From the door, Jax said, "The police can protect you."

"Someone already came here and stuck me with a needle." Megan rubbed the outside of her arm. "It's too late. I'm already dead. I just figured you should know that there's someone in the military, or the government, or whatever, and they're going to fix it all for Carl, so he doesn't face charges or whatever."

Kenna stared at the girl. "Carl came here?" He should still be in prison, not free and coming to this room and... sticking a needle into his victim?

"Not Carl. Another guy did it. He had a nurse badge, but I knew he was one of them. He had the same look in his eyes that Carl always got."

Kenna didn't know what to say.

Jax moved to the end of the bed and showed Megan his phone. "Is this the man who came in here and stuck a needle in you?"

Kenna's sketch. "The ghost."

"That's him. Now it's me who's the ghost," Megan said. "He was here in the middle of the night. He told me not to bother telling the nurse about what he did. He said I'd be fine for a while, but it would come on quickly when he was long gone. Far enough away that no one will catch him. He was happy about it."

Kenna wanted to reach for the girl but wouldn't put it past *Dominatus* to infect her with a virus that would kill anyone who came into contact with her. It was possibly too late for her and Jax—proximity might've already signed their death certificates.

Kenna laid a hand on her belly. "You could have the doctors test for infectious disease, or something else. If he poisoned you, it would show up in tests."

Megan shook her head. "He said it wouldn't. He told me to make peace with the inevitable."

"I'm sorry."

Megan shrugged. "I knew this would happen. Maybe it'll be quick and won't—" Her voice broke. She cleared her throat. "Maybe it won't hurt too much."

Kenna sniffed back the tears gathering. Such a waste of the fresh start this young woman could've had, and the chance to heal from what happened to her. She wanted the words to give Megan some peace. A chance to walk her through regaining her life. Instead, there was nothing inside her, no words forming on her tongue.

"Anyway, thanks for trying." Megan sighed.

Kenna looked at the light above the bed, blinking away tears. What could she say?

Jax put his arm around her shoulder. "We're glad you got out of there, Megan. And that you had the chance to discover what it feels like to be free. Even if it was only for a short time."

She wanted to add something, but all she could think was that inevitably *Dominatus* would come for Joseph. They would destroy his life the way they had with so many others.

All that came out was, "Do you know who the family member was who protected them?"

Megan started to speak and coughed. After two or three coughs, she looked at her hand. Blood coated her fingers.

"We'll get a nurse." Jax led Kenna to the door with an urgency to his movements. As soon as they cleared the door frame, he yelled, "Nurse!" down the hall, loud enough Kenna winced.

She stepped to the side and leaned her head against the wall. "You think she's contagious?"

Jax turned to her and before he could say anything, the uniformed officer sitting beside the door stood and glanced between them. His craggy features gave her the impression of a mouse with two days of stubble on his chin. "What's this?"

Kenna glanced at him. "The young woman you're supposed to be protecting? She'll be dead in a moment. Maybe the fake ID for the nurse who stuck her with a needle was excellent, but you let a killer in her room and she's going to pay the price." She turned and walked away, heard him call after her, but didn't stop.

Jax spoke to him, then jogged to catch up with her at the elevator. When they stepped in, he said, "The cop thinks we're going to make a statement at the police station."

"Wasn't me who lied to him."

Jax shot her a look. "I didn't intentionally lie. I just wasn't about to let you walk off. He could've chased us down and you'd have been in danger from a police officer because you're being stubborn."

"I'm still not going to the police station." She leaned her head back against the wall as the elevator car descended to the lobby.

"I know." He sounded disappointed.

"Regretting quitting the FBI?"

"Don't ask dumb questions."

She looked at him.

"Or if you do, don't be surprised when you don't get a smart answer." He shot her a look that said he'd already resigned himself to the life he was living now. Opting to exchange a career with the FBI for being with her all the time. "What?"

"It would be another dumb question."

Jax closed the distance between them and kissed her. "I'm very glad we're both here, and I have the freedom to work with you. Protect you. Help you. Solve cases with you."

"I get it."

He kissed her again. "Get used to it."

She wasn't sure that would ever happen. "For the record, I'm glad, too. That I'm free and we're together." She laced her fingers with his. "That we're having a baby."

The elevator door opened.

"I wondered if maybe you weren't so happy about the timing," he said. "Given what's going on."

"And how I'm determined to avoid all of it?"

He squeezed her hand, but her phone started to ring in her pocket.

She glanced at the screen. "Amara. Probably about the sketch." She swiped her thumb across the screen and put the phone to her ear. "Hey."

"You have a minute?"

Jax led her down the last part of the hall from the elevator to the lobby and through the expanse of space where they had coffee only yesterday. Nothing was amiss, but she noted he scanned the tables and people sitting chatting. A guy by the reception desk to the right didn't look up from his phone.

Kenna focused on the call and let her husband do the work of protecting them both. "Did you recognize the photo?"

"I've seen him before, but I don't know his name. I'll need access to one of their computer terminals to find out who he is. Maybe at the platform?"

"Worth asking MSI." The security company that had taken over the platform where she was held during the rescue would likely let Amara have a moment with their computers. "Maybe they have access to files we don't know about. But I did hear that the system was erased when it became clear *Dominatus* was going to lose the fight."

"Hang on." Amara relayed the info to someone else.

Bruce.

Kenna didn't like that he was privy to the details, but Amara already knew not to trust implicitly. The two of them might be aunt and niece, even though Kenna had thought for years that Amara was her deceased mother, but they still didn't put total faith in each other. The only person she did that with was Jax, and to a lesser extent Maizie and Ramon. Maybe Stairns. The Rysons were her friends, but she didn't want their little family to be targets, so she hadn't called them in months and hadn't seen them since she and Jax got married.

"Kenna."

She held the warm phone to her ear. "Yes?" Stepping off the curb beside Jax, she remembered the night shortly after they'd met when someone tried to run her over. Jax had been in her orbit since, and now they never needed to be apart.

"I asked if you were ready for the next most pressing issue."

"Hit me with it."

"Moments ago, Maizie received an encrypted packet in her email. She needs a key to get into the packet. I'm working on that."

"What's going on?"

"Our friends from Hann, Anthony & Associates are being rounded up and arrested as the perpetrators of yesterday's bombing in DC." Amara paused. "You know who the target was?"

Kenna nodded. "I know." Jax held the car door for her, and she ducked her head, climbing in. "The Croatian prime minister." She watched Jax round the front of the car to the driver's side.

"Actually, the president," Amara corrected. "Their prime minister is over the executive branch of their government. The president is their commander in chief, basically the boss of their military."

"Sounds complicated."

"The president is the one here to nail down the details of the treaty with our president. Someone tried to take the Croatian guy out."

"What does it have to do with our lawyer friends?" Kenna asked.

The call muted for a second, then connected to the car speakers.

"Three of the lawyers were already arrested," Amara explained. "The taskforce is moving quick. They pinpointed them as the prime suspects and they're rounding them up and making arrests."

Kenna bit her lip for a second. "Did they do it?"

Jax glanced at her but said nothing.

"Of course not!"

"And you'd know that? We haven't heard from them in months."

"You were captive. We made plans without you because we didn't know when you'd be back." Amara paused. "They were the ones who went with Bruce to rescue Jax."

Kenna didn't want to hear how they'd left her in FBI custody and Ramon hadn't been able to save her. "I was there. I know what happened."

"They're being wrongfully accused."

"Then the evidence will bear out the truth of the matter." Kenna squeezed the phone. "They won't be convicted because there isn't going to be a case. If they didn't do it, there's nothing for them to worry about it."

"You know as well as I do that the truth means nothing to these people."

Kenna had been in their facility so long she'd forgotten what the truth even was. Their tactics had turned her mind inside out. She closed her eyes, trying not to remember.

"They'll get their pound of flesh one way or another."

"I'm not getting involved." She'd said it so many times it should be easier, but the words tasted sour on her tongue.

"You know what this is."

"How could I? I'm not part of the organization." No matter how much they'd tried to get her to come over to their side. She wanted to say she'd resisted. Stood strong. But life was never that cut-and-dried. She and her baby had survived—that's what she had to remember. "They leave me alone, and I leave them alone. That was the deal."

Too bad *Dominatus* wasn't in the business of making deals.

"Kenna, your friends are going to die or spend their lives in prison. And those are the best-case scenarios. They'll be scapegoats. Paraded through the media like they're terrorists with no conscience."

Kenna said nothing.

Amara didn't stop. "Did you know an eight-year-old girl died? Her school bus wasn't far from the limo when it blew. The bus flipped, and all three kids on board were tossed around. The driver and one girl died, and the other two are in the hospital."

Kenna clenched her teeth and stared out the window, unsure what to say to resolve the question in her heart and mind. How to find some semblance of peace in the middle of all of this. She had far too many doubts. Maybe they were good, and meant she should make a change, but she couldn't even tell that much. She had no light to guide her.

Amara sighed. "You can do something to help."

Kenna managed to say, "I'm protecting this baby."

"And in the meantime, what kind of world will she be born into?"

In the background, she heard a man's voice.

She tapped the dash screen and ended the call.

Chapter Eleven

Kenna sat back from the toilet bowl, resting on the ice-cold tile floor. Clammy skin. Wearing thin gray sweats and a white long-sleeved T-shirt. She'd peeled off the sweater they gave her but needed it now. As she sat there, the skin on her forearms prickled. She rubbed the sweater sleeves, trying to friction some warmth back into her.

"Here." The nurse—orderly—whoever he was— crouched and held out a paper cup. "It's warm."

She looked in the cup. "Water?"

"Hot water tastes good. But that's just my opinion." He knelt by her foot, smiling politely. As if he wanted to build a rapport with her. "Hopefully, it'll help your stomach settle. If you want, I can ask if there's anything that you could—"

"I'm not taking drugs, so don't bother. Some gum would be nice, though. Or candied ginger. Or a copy of *What to Expect When You're Expecting*. Access to a computer, a pair of headphones, a thriller novel to read, and a cheese stick. It doesn't have to be in that order."

He lifted his hands. Late twenties, shaved head, and some scruff on his chin. More suited to a military unit, or a back-alley gang. Maybe that was too harsh. He didn't move like someone in the military would. "You know there's zero point in me asking for that stuff."

She shifted on the cold tile to lean her back against the shower door. "So...how'd you end up here?" Her tone wasn't so conversational, as it was completely sarcastic.

"If you wanna chat, you should get up. There's a delegation arriving in an hour, and it'd be good if you're cleaned up and presentable."

She huffed. "With any luck, I'll throw up on someone's shoe."

"That wouldn't go well for you." He didn't look at her as he shifted out of his crouch and held out his hand. "Time to get up."

She wanted to throw the drink in his face. Or kick him in the shins. But it felt like all the energy had drained from her limbs. When she needed the fighting spirit, it wasn't there. Kenna had always thought she was the kind who'd go down fighting. Kicking and screaming to the bitter end. Instead, it seemed like when the time came to fight, she couldn't do it.

She looked at his hand. "If I don't have the ability to get up on my own, then I have no business on my feet."

He grunted and stepped back.

She just didn't want to touch him. Or have him touch her.

Kenna braced her hand on the wall and got to her feet, her body sluggish. She'd eaten breakfast, and now it was in the toilet. She could use a cup of coffee because that always made her feel better, but it "wasn't good for the baby." She wanted to hold a steaming mug and inhale the scent of familiarity. Of the RV, and Jax nearby. Even Jolene, their cat.

The rest of it, she couldn't even think about, or she'd break down again.

Instead, she got dressed in clean clothes and two pairs of socks in the canvas shoes, brushed her teeth, and followed the orderly out to the hall. Past *his* room. He looked out the frosted glass at her with those dead eyes.

Kenna pulled her attention from him. They'd made it clear he wasn't to touch her, but she got the feeling that only made her a more alluring target than if they'd said nothing to him.

Two levels above, up the metal stairwell to the open-air floor. The railing went all the way around the platform, and she was willing to admit she'd considered jumping. When they allowed it, she walked laps of the place, going in squares around and around until she thought the monotony would drive her crazy. Trying to exorcise the thoughts and images they'd put in her mind the day before.

She would withstand this.

She had to.

But already, she could feel who she was slipping away. The cracks in her were developing into fissures and widening. *Dominatus* was leaking into the open spaces inside her, and it almost seemed like they would fill her up until that was all she was.

No.

She looked at the sky, as if God was up there watching down on her. All she could see was clouds. Maybe He didn't care. Or this torture was "necessary" for some reason. Kenna didn't have the ability to grasp any concept that would help her. All the reassurances she could think of sounded like hollow platitudes to her mind.

Above the walkway around the perimeter was a flat roof that drained the rainwater between the walkway and the sides of the building so it looked like the whole place was crying every time after it had rained. Or she was. Kenna didn't want to be dramatic about the despair, but it felt like her soul was crying.

A helicopter landed up there.

The orderly took her to the stairs.

"I don't have a coat," she complained, "and it's freezing up there with the wind."

"He asked to see you as soon as he gets here."

Kenna stepped to the side and leaned against the bottom of these stairs, the ones that led up to the helicopter landing pad. She folded her arms, tucking the sweater tight around her, and stared out at the ocean. But wishing for all the things she couldn't have wasn't going to fix her situation.

If she felt God here with her, she would still be here. She needed rescue, or another way out. Not hollow comfort that didn't change anything.

Moments later, the orderly turned and walked away, but she wasn't alone.

Kenna watched the group of half a dozen come down the stairs—Dr. Buzard and a couple of his staff members in their lab coats because that somehow made them important. The man in the center of the group had two burly security guys in suits with earpieces behind him.

He stopped in front of her. "I've been so eager to meet you."

She assessed him, trying to find fault in his face. Remembering when she'd met a senator who was part of

Dominatus who'd decided she was going to marry him. Until she killed him.

She stared him down. "I'd return the sentiment, but it wouldn't be true."

The blow came out of nowhere, an open hand palm strike that clapped her on the cheek and sent her to her knees.

Chapter Twelve

"Want to tell me what's going on?" Jax waited until they were almost back to the RV park before he spoke. Of course, he wanted to talk about it. She wasn't going to begrudge him for caring about her, whether it was easy for her to face this or not.

"The president of Croatia's life is in danger, and somehow that's my business?"

"No, I mean with Bruce." Jax glanced over for a second, then turned the corner into the RV park. Tucked behind a neighborhood, behind fenced yards and single-story houses. Not her favorite destination to stay, but it got them close to the places they needed to be to work the case.

Right now, Megan Tiller's life was ending in that hospital room, and sticking around might mean Kenna and the baby died as well. Or Jax. For all she knew, they could've been exposed to something. Only the truth of what she knew about *Dominatus* kept her from descending into the undertow of fear that she was also a target.

"Bruce." Kenna shook her head. "I just don't want to talk to him." That was true enough. She couldn't even think the rest of it, let alone say it out loud. "I happen to know for a fact that the president of Croatia is part of *Dominatus*. Why would I care that someone is trying to kill him? If they get into a war, that's less people we need to worry about."

"When did you become heartless?"

"Right around the time they kidnapped me and kept me locked up for weeks, performed stress tests on the baby, and repeatedly tried to reprogram my brain to believe what they believe."

Jax jammed his foot on the brake, and the car suddenly came to a stop. She reached out her hand and braced against the glove compartment.

"I'm sorry." Kenna winced. "I didn't want to say that. I don't know why I did." She squeezed her eyes shut for a second. "I don't know if I'm me, or someone else they manipulated me into. I don't know if I'm saying what I want to say, or if they've rewired my brain."

Now that she'd started talking, more was flowing.

He sighed. "You've been quiet since I got you back."

She didn't look at him. "You were there. You know what it was like in that place."

Neither of them moved.

"And they did surgery on me," Jax said, "so I'm supposed to be grateful. Like them fixing your arms." A smidge of bitterness leaked through his tone. "Yes, I know what it was like. I can't possibly understand what you and the baby went through. I have you back—both of you. I'm trying to be grateful for that, but I can't help wondering when something will happen."

"Like I'm going to suddenly turn into a robot. Or lose the—" She couldn't even finish saying it. Kenna laid both hands on her abdomen. "We have to be careful who we trust. Where we go. But how can I live in a bunker for the next thirty years just to keep us all safe? That's not a life. Especially not if at any moment I'm going to cough and there will be blood on my hand and…"

Jax reached over and unclipped her seatbelt. "Let's go inside." He climbed out and came around, opening the door for her. Held her hand, leading her to the RV.

"We need to get another dog." She wanted to be greeted at the door. She needed the energy and love a puppy brought.

Jax smiled at her. "Come on."

He led her to the bedroom, and she kicked off her shoes.

Kenna lay down on the covers and tugged the pillow over, tears leaking from the corner of her eye. "You can't tell me it's going to be fine." She squeezed her eyes shut. "You don't know that."

He gathered her close, his arms around her. "Bruce isn't going to betray us. There's a limited number of people we can trust, but he's on the list."

"They told me…"

Jax rubbed a hand between her shoulder blades, a comforting gesture that enabled her to let go of a full breath. "What did they tell you?"

She opened her eyes and stared at his T-shirt. "He used to be *Dominatus*. He never said that to us. He never even mentioned them. He didn't tell us he had any connection to them." Her breath hitched in her throat, and she had to gasp in air.

Bruce's former partner, the one who'd betrayed him,

had been *Dominatus.* Maybe not back then but definitely recently. But Bruce?

"You're not facing any of this alone, Kenna." He paused a second. "Whatever happens, we all face it as a family."

She squeezed her eyes closed again. "I can see it all, every time I shut my eyes. Every time I sleep. I can hear their voices. I can feel how cold it was, out there on that buoy. I go to sleep wondering if I'm going to wake up back there, and all of this has been a dream."

"They broke you down."

"That's what it feels like." She pushed out a shuddering breath. "Now I'm in pieces and I don't know how to put myself back together."

"What is it, you say?" he asked, his voice gentle. "That you leave a piece of yourself back there, and you have to find a way to move on without it. Your mind thinks, at least in part, that you're still in that place. It's burned into you."

"I want to cut it out."

"Accepting it is there, and it will always be there, is going to help you figure out how to live with it. Because there's no way to get rid of the memories." He kept rubbing his hand across her back, imparting the steady warmth of his strength into her. "Working to where you can make peace with it is the only way you're going to be able to heal the wound. Right now, it's raw. And that's understandable. We're both in pain from what they did to us."

She nodded, desperate with the need to not discount what he was feeling. Sure, she'd been captive for months before Jax had rescued her, but that just meant he'd been searching during that time. He'd faced all the fear of losing her that came with a fruitless search until he finally uncovered the place she was being held. It wasn't about who had suffered more, but about the fact they both had to work through the aftermath.

"Doctor Buzard is dead." She had to say it aloud. "His men. The ghost. They're all dead. No one is coming after me from that group."

"You're worried there are others who might?"

"I have no idea. That's the problem." That, and the fact she could find out if she made a phone call. But fear of being discovered, even though they probably knew exactly where she was, kept her from making that call. "Short of faking our deaths, which might not even work, I don't see how we can ever escape them."

"And that might solve the problem for us, but it doesn't neutralize them."

She sighed. "We can't take them down."

"I know."

Still, it sounded a little like he was placating her.

"They feel like this big insurmountable evil." He squeezed her shoulder. "One we can't possibly go up against. But can we really live with ourselves if we don't at least try? Let's follow this case where it leads."

"Megan is dead, but Joseph is safe."

"Remember the family member in the military? We can tug on that thread, see where it leads."

Kenna's mind filled with images of military uniforms, and she shuddered. She'd been out of it, drifting between awake and unconscious, at the time. "It hurt."

"What did?"

"They hurt me."

Jax slid his arm from behind her, ran his hand across where the baby was protected between them, and lifted it to touch her cheek. "Tell me." His blue eyes had darkened, a roiling mix of anger and sadness that looked like the ocean at night in the middle of a storm.

"I don't remember." She shook her head. "It's just snatches. Flashes. And the pain."

He touched his forehead to hers and stayed there, still and quiet. Holding her.

Kenna closed her eyes, focusing on the feel of him with her and not the wash of terrible things in her mind. Hanging on to him for dear life.

That's what it felt like.

If she lost him, she would lose everything she had, everything she was. Kenna knew in her logical brain that wasn't how it was supposed to be. She needed a firm foundation in the Lord, and that was supposed to be what her life was based on. Jax should be a blessing, like grace upon grace. An add-on to her life, because God already filled her to the brim with everything she needed spiritually.

But when she tried to draw from that well...it was empty.

"It's gone," she whispered.

He shifted then, responding to her quiet statement. Moving so she could see his eyes again. "What's gone?"

"My faith. God. All of it. It's like I'm reaching for it, but there's nothing there."

"They took it from you?"

She wanted to believe that, and not that she had let go of it. Not that God might have withdrawn from her. "I haven't been a Christian long enough to know what's happening. It still feels like panic. Like trying to find something but it's missing."

"So let's find it. Together. Rediscover what you believe and why and start to put that armor back on one piece at a time. When the next attack comes, you'll be better protected."

She knew he was talking about spiritual armor, but how that worked was something that—yes—she was going to have to learn how to put on. In a way she did feel like a child relearning how to tie their shoes, or how to button a coat to keep out the chill.

"What if it just falls apart again next time?" She bit her lip. Apparently, this was a day for her to voice all her worst fears aloud. Speaking the hidden things into the dim light of their private space, where only he could hear. "What if it happens again, and I'm not strong enough?"

"You won't be facing them alone. We're going to be together."

She'd expected him to tell her that she was the strongest person he knew. He'd said that to her before. But in her brokenness, she didn't feel strong. She felt...

Wrecked.

"Promise me I don't have to do this alone."

"I'm not going to let you do any of this by yourself." He kissed one cheek, then her other. "We're in this together from here on out. I promise you that."

Kenna held on tight to her husband.

He shifted far enough away that she knew he was going for his phone. Before she could wonder why, he tapped the screen, and a voice spoke in a soothing, melodic tone.

"*O Lord, You have searched me and known me. You know my sitting down and my rising up...*"

Kenna's eyes drifted shut, and she soaked up the words in the comfort of his arms.

"*Where can I go from Your Spirit? Or where can I flee from Your presence?*"

Chapter Thirteen

Kenna climbed out of the car shortly after four in the afternoon the next day, in a parking lot half a block from the scene of the bombing. The Washington Monument stretched up from above the trees at the end of this street, apartment buildings on one side and trees on the other.

"How long has it been since you were here?" Jax came over, clicking the locks on the car and holding out his hand.

She took it. "Years, I think."

They set off in the direction of the scene while traffic buzzed past them in both directions. Low clouds hung in the sky, and she thought it might rain tonight but didn't mention that aloud. After the past couple of days, small talk about the weather shouldn't come from her. It would seem too much like she was purposely deflecting.

On the drive down from Boston, they had talked through a lot of what happened to her, things she'd determined to keep for herself. Driving allowed Jax to do something rote while he absorbed her story, though a few times she caught him strangling the steering wheel with his grip.

Talking about her time in captivity definitely helped. The others were right about that. But she hadn't wanted to process her experience with anyone but him. Now that she'd told him everything, she expected it to feel like a wound exposed to the air. But it didn't. It was more like its power had diminished. He knew some of the worst things she could remember, and she didn't have to feel like she was hiding what happened on top of everything else they were all dealing with.

He'd helped her by playing more Bible passages and talking to her about how he found peace during the time she'd been missing. About his own crisis of faith and how he'd come back to the Lord.

She couldn't help feeling like a bit of a fraud, with how fast it seemed like she'd lost it. But if he could lose the grip on his own beliefs at the same time, and he'd been a believer for years, then her own crisis of faith might be a little more understandable.

He glanced over at her.

She didn't want to talk about anything heavy, though. "I always thought at some point I'd end up on a taskforce. The FBI would come up against someone I had experience with, and I'd be called here as a consultant to work with them tracking down a dangerous killer."

"Is it weird to wish for the days when the worst we had to deal with was a serial killer?"

"Ah, the good ole days." She chuckled. "Like that?"

"Something like it." He squeezed her hand. "What's the plan here?"

"I just want to look at what happened. See if there's anything to learn." She shrugged one shoulder. "Even if they've cleared away a lot of the evidence already and they're going to release the scene soon, I still want to get a feel for it."

"Agreed. Even poring over the file doesn't give you an impression of what happened the way being at the scene does."

Along with sending over a stolen copy of the federal case file for the bombing, Maizie had sent a copy of the report on Megan Tiller's death. Kenna wasn't sure they could put much stock in the official cause of death when the medical examiner who signed off on the certificate was none other than Eleanor Walsh. Even the statement of the officer on the door wasn't something she'd have sworn to. Cause of death had been listed as a pulmonary embolism, whatever that meant. Certainly nothing suspicious, apparently.

"Okay, um..." He hesitated. "I wasn't going to ask, but what are you thinking about?"

"I'm just thinking," she said. "Trying to get my thoughts straight before we jump in and get to work on this. Like, did I really see the ghost in the lobby? I guess I had to have, since Megan said that's who killed her. But in the moment, I really wondered if it was just my imagination."

"Zeyla and Ramon are tracking down the man you made that sketch of. If there's someone to find, they'll get him."

She nodded, trying to feel reassured. "And the military connection to Mitch and Carl, the duo kidnappers."

Maybe they would never know exactly what had happened, but Jax had made a call to the district attorney's office in Boston and jumped on a video meeting with the DA so he could explain their fears regarding Carl's release and Megan's worry that he would never be charged.

The DA had reassured both Jax and Kenna, who'd been

listening from the passenger seat, that he wasn't going to allow anyone to sway justice. He had been planning a press conference ASAP to tell the world what Carl had done, and how Megan's rescue had cost her life. Even if the DA considered her death accidental, no one could deny that a horrific crime had been committed. Who could stomach Carl being free after that? The more people who heard the truth, the harder it would be to cover it all up. If *Dominatus* wanted to do that.

Jax glanced over. "Could be the connection ended with Mitch's untimely death during his deployment, and they've got no loyalty to Carl whatsoever."

"That'd be nice. But if they killed Megan, there's a chance it's Carl that needs protection now."

He squeezed her hand. "Maizie will figure it out."

A woman in a wool overcoat that hung to her knees stepped out from a building beside them, red hair and a dark-blue watch cap. Navy slacks and flat shoes. As she passed by, she pushed a folded paper into Kenna's hand.

Jax reacted to the proximity of the woman and shifted Kenna to the building side just after the woman passed her. He turned and slowed to a stop. "What was that?"

Kenna hadn't gotten a good look at the woman's face. By the time Kenna turned around, she was gone. A black town car sped away from the curb and disappeared into traffic.

"She handed me something." Kenna showed him the paper, which turned out to be a folded note.

Jax scanned around them and shifted closer, his entire being a protective stance. She touched his sides, not just to reassure him but also to remind herself of what he'd said. He was here, and they wouldn't be separated. She wasn't alone.

He unfolded the paper. "Tell Maizie FD-2769-CM."

Kenna glanced around like she'd be able to see the woman who had slipped her the note. She wasn't going to think about how easily she could've been killed. *They don't want me dead.* That was the only thing that didn't make her lose her mind with fear of what might've been. The thing she couldn't anticipate. The known unknown that kept her up at night.

"I guess we should pass it on." He tugged out his phone.

"Maybe it's the decryption code for the packet she got yesterday." The young woman had been working on other tasks because she'd deemed it "impossible" to crack. "And that was one of the lawyers? Or a friend of theirs?"

"They want our help."

Kenna groaned. "I'm not making anyone any promises."

He nodded, pocketed the phone and the note. Any photo he took would upload immediately to the server Maizie had set up, and she would get a notification. She would see it right away.

"I agree with you about that." He held out his hand again. "We see what we can do. That's all anyone can ask of us."

It occurred to her that he was treating her as if she were fragile. A little more breakable than usual. Which was completely correct.

She wanted to be robust and strong, able to withstand what life threw at them next. But when that happened, she would shatter like she had before. Even taking weeks out and recuperating hadn't enabled her to put the pieces back together. Nor had working a case—not just because that case turned out to be connected to all of this.

Kenna pushed out a breath. "But we're going to work the case."

"Yep." He squeezed her hand. "We can't let the lawyers at Hann, Anthony & Associates go to prison for something they didn't do."

"If they were behind it..."

"Seems more like they're scrambling out of surprise," Jax said. "They saw it coming, but it happened too fast for them to get safe."

Kenna had thought the same thing while watching the news reports on the drive down. A change of scenery, and hours spent watching the world go by, had helped her find at least some of her equilibrium. But she wasn't fixed.

She wasn't even sure it was possible.

"If MSI is behind it," Jax continued, "we might run into a problem."

"Or we find the person, and they intended to do the world a favor, but they just missed." She paused. "How do you shake the hand of someone who killed a child?"

"I should text Bear and ask, but I'm afraid," he admitted. "Taking out *Dominatus* key players is in their wheelhouse right now. They're on a tear trying to do what they can to shut the whole thing down."

"I've been afraid to even think about that." Kenna winced. "He'll probably be mad that we *aren't* doing it."

"He hasn't asked for help, so maybe he gets it. He lost Ally in New Orleans."

"You spent more time with him, rescuing me."

"Doesn't mean I have an 'in' on what their plan is." Jax shook his head. "If we ran into one of them out here, I wouldn't be surprised."

"I guess we need to know if they're behind this." She stopped because they were at the yellow police tape that ringed the area around the black spot where fire had left ash burned into the street and the sidewalk. The other side of the street had been cleared, cars now driving over where the bus had flipped.

People going about their business in a spot where children had died.

She pushed that thought away and watched the three—no, four—FBI agents in tan khakis, polo shirts, and windbreakers walk the scene with gloves on and evidence bags in hand. One final sweep for anything that might have been left behind.

"Huh." The word was little more than a sound of surprise from Jax.

"What is it?" She looked from him over to what had his attention.

A female agent came over, and it was someone she recognized.

"Special Agent..." Kenna began. The name escaped her, but this agent had been there right before Kenna was kidnapped.

The agent stopped in front of the tape, surprise in her dark-brown features. "Jax. Kenna."

"Special Agent Herron." Jax stiffened. "You're working this taskforce?"

Right. That was her name.

Andrette Herron had been working with Jax during the time Kenna was a captive, coerced by their enemy into manipulating what was going on at the FBI. Jax had left the agent to her fate after he found out that her children were being used as pawns. Andrette had worked to ensure their safety then, and Jax had a fight of his own. They hadn't been able to work together without jeopardizing both.

Was that what they were supposed to do now?

"I thought being sent here was a demotion," Herron

replied. "It all happened so fast that I've only been on the ground a day and a half. This is my first visit to the site." She shook her head. "Now that you're here, maybe there's another reason I'm here altogether."

"If there is," Jax said. "I'd like to hear it."

Chapter Fourteen

Kenna took the corner seat in the coffee shop that put her back to the wall. The ability to prevent someone approaching you from behind was worth its weight in gold when you never had any idea when the threat might come. She didn't know if Special Agent Herron was aware of her pregnancy, but she didn't want to be bundled up in her coat with the heating in here cranked to the "Florida in August" setting.

The fed took a seat opposite her, and Jax came over with the drinks. Conversation had taken a hiatus between their walking the two blocks to get here and ordering beverages.

"Thanks." She took the paper cup from Jax and sat with her elbows on the table so as not to draw Agent Herron's attention to her baby bump.

He smiled and took the seat beside her, then faced Agent Herron. "Last time I saw you was the bank. You killed the Kenna lookalike."

"And you weren't surprised I was alive when you saw

me just now?" Kenna lifted her brows, taking a sip of her drink.

Agent Herron took the lid off her drink and stirred it with the wooden stick, holding the tea bag with her fingers. "That is the last time I saw you. Jax, at least." She laid the stick down. "Even after I shot her, I still wasn't sure it was *not* Kenna. Until the medical examiner took a look. They ran the fingerprints, and it didn't come back as you." She glanced at Kenna. "It came back as the suspect in a suspicious death case in Anchorage."

"Given the proximity, I'm not surprised." Kenna set down her cup. That was close to where the platform had been, and after being rescued, she was taken to the nearest hospital which had been the trauma center in Anchorage.

"So we closed that case, and no one claimed the body that I know of."

Jax shifted in his seat. "They probably did. Or ensured it was destroyed."

Agent Herron shrugged.

Jax glanced at Kenna. "Given what I told you about the cemetery, you figure that's right?"

She nodded, remembering what he'd told her about the Buzard killed in the silo in Phoenix. Kenna didn't want to consider the life and demise of her murderous lookalike.

Other women in her position—six months pregnant—were taking classes, painting a room in their house, and putting together a crib. Having a baby shower and receiving gifts. Kenna figured most people didn't need all of the things they amassed that were supposed to make having a newborn easier. There were a few essentials, but they could get by on a whole lot less than baby fever dictated. Although that was really only because it wouldn't all fit in the RV.

She tuned back into the conversation Jax and Agent Herron were having.

"...outside the bar." Jax waited for the fed to respond.

Agent Herron nodded, brushing back the dark whisps of hair at her temple. Giving herself time to think, or come up with a story. "I haven't seen my family in months. That's not a sob story. I don't need your sympathy."

"Because you believe you got yourself into this mess?"

"Either way, me being away doing my job is safer for Henry and the kids."

"So you toe the line?"

Agent Herron shrugged. "I'm complying. For now, at least. What that looks like long term, I don't know. Why they chose me out of all the FBI agents in the country, I have no idea." She lifted one hand. "But my family is safe, and if I see a way to get out of this, I'll take it."

"They're still sending you orders?"

"The last one came through my boss at the Phoenix office." She winced a little saying that.

Jax shifted in his seat, not quite a shrug, but close. "I don't regret walking away. The FBI I left wasn't the one I joined years ago. And I have more important work to do." He reached over and held Kenna's hand.

"Going freelance?" Herron said. "Being a PI?"

As if Jax was going to openly admit they were working to take down the organization who had their boot on Herron's family. Whatever they chose to do was family business, not information to be shared with people they didn't trust.

"Working with Kenna," Jax said. "What can you tell us about the bombing investigation?"

Agent Herron eyed them both. "Can I ask what your interest is in this?"

Kenna wasn't about to reveal that either. "Most likely the same reason you were suddenly assigned to this taskforce."

Herron didn't like that answer, but said, "The powers that be figure it's cut-and-dried. We're finalizing the evidence collection. And later today, we'll probably release the scene. It's over."

Kenna eyed her. "Because you've arrested all the suspects you uncovered—what?—hours after you assembled here?"

"The responding agents were thorough, so we had a lot to work with. I read the file on the plane on the way here, and the work was exemplary." Apparently, Agent Herron didn't seem to see anything amiss with that. "It was clear from the outset who was responsible for the attempt on President Blazevic's life."

"So you rounded them all up, and now it's 'case closed'?" Kenna couldn't keep the tone from her words.

"You have evidence that we're incorrect?" Agent Herron stared at her. "Because from what we've gathered, it's overwhelming that Hann, Anthony & Associates were responsible."

"Convince me," Kenna shot back. It was a little impetuous, challenging a fed like that when Kenna and Jax had no right to the information, but she hoped that Herron's innate sense of justice would win out.

"It *is* fast," the agent admitted, "but the responding feds took statements and everyone described the same suspects watching the explosion."

Kenna wasn't convinced that was indication the truth was to be had. Witness testimony rarely ever matched. For a group to all say the same thing? Seemed suspicious to her.

Herron continued, "We backed that up with footage

from surrounding businesses, and reports from President Blazevic that he was being followed since he landed in the US. They even went so far as to harass him."

Kenna bit her lip.

Jax said, "If they intended to kill him, why harass him beforehand? Seems like no one would've tied them to the incident if they'd left him alone."

"That doesn't mean they aren't the perpetrators," Herron said. "It just means they left evidence and they have motive to want him dead. It's just a tragedy that innocent people were harmed in the process. These women killed *children*."

"That's also a reason I don't believe they did it." Kenna couldn't imagine risking that kind of collateral damage. "There are easier ways to take out a political player. As we all saw months ago."

"You're referring to the deaths of the president and the CIA director?" Herron glanced between them. "You believe this is connected to that incident?"

Kenna shrugged one shoulder.

"Everything is connected," Jax said. "You. Us. Open cases on your boss's desk. An unsolved murder in Boston. So many things that it would be impossible to piece it all together and come up with a master plan. You'd go crazy trying to figure out how it all connects."

"Is this just a theory, or do you actually have evidence?"

Kenna figured it was a fair question. "Call it personal experience."

Herron stared at her.

"Speaking of theories," Kenna said, "what if this whole thing is a setup? The same people who threatened your family want these people shut down. They brought you in with the rest of the taskforce and set up Hann, Anthony &

Associates as the scapegoats for an assassination attempt, but it was all orchestrated by someone else wanting to take out two birds with one stone, as it were."

"Find me evidence to the contrary and I'll look at it." Agent Herron pulled out her phone. "I have to get back to work." She leaned forward. "I'd like to say it was good to see you guys, but my life is generally a lot quieter if you're not around."

Agent Herron said her goodbyes and took off out of the coffee shop.

"Maizie should be in that package by now." Kenna checked her phone but had no new notifications.

If she wanted to, she could look at an app on her home screen and see the location of everyone in their family, even Amara and Bruce. That was the one thing she'd asked of them after her rescue. She could look whenever she wanted to and see where Zeyla and Ramon, Maizie, or Stairns and his wife were. Just an added peace of mind to help her try and keep it together.

Jax got up. "While we're waiting for her to get through the packet, or figure out what that code meant, we have an appointment."

She frowned, but followed him to the door of the coffee shop. "Where?"

"You'll see." He held her hand all the way down the busy sidewalk to the car. "I thought about a psychologist, but didn't think you'd want to see a doctor you didn't know."

"You think I need therapy?"

"We all need therapy." He smiled endearingly at her, as if he thought her objection was adorable, and parked the car. After driving a couple of miles, they'd reached the community outreach center.

She wasn't mad, because he was right. She did need an impartial person to talk to. Someone she could be completely honest with. "What is it?"

"There's a guy here that I trust, and you need some outside perspective. So I made us an appointment, even though he doesn't usually do that kind of thing."

Jax held the door for her, and she looked down the long hall.

The murmur of conversation got louder as they approached the main room of this center, passing a notice-board on the way with a huge sign for free Thanksgiving dinner.

A group of young guys played pool at one of two tables. Several pairs of older men played chess or checkers at tables to one side. A long metal counter to the left was bare now, with people in white aprons and hairnets cleaning up behind the opening.

A man in a wheelchair backed up from the table where he'd been talking to someone and pushed on the wheels of his chair, heading toward them. He had a shaved head, a tattoo on the left side of his neck, as well as sleeves on both forearms, and no legs below his knees.

"Oliver!" The guy smiled wide.

Jax held out his hand.

They clasped each other's forearm and followed up with a back-slapping hug.

"Good to see you, buddy." Jax straightened. "Jesse Lee Peterson, this is my wife." He grinned. "Kenna Banbury."

"Nice to meet you." She shook his hand. "How do you guys know each other?"

Jesse Lee's eyebrows rose, humor in his expression. "Your husband arrested me."

Chapter Fifteen

"It's not friendly, but it's private." Jesse Lee held the door for them, and Kenna went first into the small office with a metal desk and file cabinet.

The place was neat, but it was clear Jesse Lee Peterson used paper more than the ancient computer. On the wall on one side was a cat poster that said Hang In There and a print of a mountainside with Romans chapter 12 verses 1 and 2 on it.

Jax motioned to a pair of nondescript chairs, and she chose one.

Kenna was trying to live in the present and take every moment as it came. She didn't want to think about the past. Not even to recognize the good that had happened. She couldn't think about any of it, or all of it crashed over her. "To be honest, I don't really know what this is about."

Jesse Lee wheeled himself behind the desk where a chair would have been. "It's just a conversation. It can be about whatever you want."

Kenna glanced at her husband, who looked totally unashamed. "I've been bamboozled."

Jax shook his head, a grin on his face. "The story of how Jesse Lee and I met is also the story of the biggest blunder of my life. Want to hear it?" He leaned back in the chair next to her, relaxing for what seemed like the first time in months.

Watching him let go of the undercurrent of tension allowed her to as well. "Go for it."

"Jesse Lee was a suspect in a series of thefts of government property from a corporation that dealt with funds associated with covert operations." Jax cleared his throat. "We figured out the suspect must have scaled the outside wall of the building and entered through a vent in the HVAC system big enough for a small person."

"I couldn't have done it because my shoulders are too wide." Jesse Lee grinned.

Kenna smiled.

"On paper he was the prime suspect. Only when we kicked his door in to arrest him did we realize there's a problem with him having scaled a wall."

"Maybe he's Spiderman?" Kenna winked at her husband. "You still arrested him?"

"If he didn't do it, he likely knew who did. There was a strong enough connection that we brought him in. I figured he just had a partner."

"I didn't," Jesse Lee told her.

"And you didn't do it?"

"Oh, I did it." He chuckled. "But I didn't take the money. Someone in the company was doing that. All I was doing was planting incriminating information in their system, so someone realized that embezzlement was happening."

"Jesse Lee took a deal for exposing the real crime," Jax explained. "He did some jail time, but only a few years."

The other man shrugged. "I didn't have the, uh, respect for the law then that I do now."

Kenna glanced between them. "How does that get you guys from cop and suspect to friends?"

"Prison Bible study." Jesse Lee tapped the Bible Kenna hadn't noticed on his desk. "I got saved. I knew Jax was a Christian, so I wrote him a letter. He responded, and we struck up a friendship for a while. He helped me figure out what to do when I got out, and it's been years but I'm real glad to see you, buddy."

Jax nodded. "Me, too. And we needed a friendly face."

"It's good you were in the neighborhood." Jesse Lee looked at her. "I know a little bit about trauma. I know what it's like to rebuild your life from nothing, more than once. And I know what it's like when it feels as if your faith has slipped away."

She swallowed against the knot in her throat. "Jax told you?"

"Only a rough overview." Jesse Lee leaned back in his wheelchair, lacing his fingers over his abdomen. "Enough to know I'd like to help you, if I can."

"It's not like I don't *want* my faith back." She shook her head. "It's that I don't know *how* to reach that part of me. When I try to grasp it, it's almost like it's gone."

Jesse Lee nodded. "I doubt I'll tell you anything you don't already know. That's not what this is. It's more about reframing what you do know so you can start to see it in a different way." He glanced at Jax. "Maybe both of you, not just you Kenna."

"Even if I fix what's wrong with me, there's still an enemy out there. The fear will still be in me because it's the reality of our lives. We face this stuff every day." She scrunched up her nose, unsure why she felt the need to unburden herself with this person she'd just met. Probably because Jax had found her a safe place to talk where she wouldn't be judged for losing her faith, and as a bonus she could be certain that he wasn't with *Dominatus*.

"As Christians, the point isn't to shy away from reality. Or bury our heads in the sand. Fear can make you smarter. But when it's overwhelming to the point you can't move, then it's no longer a help. It's a hinderance."

"That's what it feels like." *Paralyzing* was the word.

It seemed like she'd been stuck since she was captive and couldn't get herself free of the mire. Every day, it was trying to pull her under.

Kenna didn't want to drown.

"But there are things that are true regardless of how we feel, or the situation we're in. Whatever is happening." He paused. "You still believe God is real, and that He loves you?"

"Yes." She didn't want to say it, but... "It feels like I failed a test."

"And God is surprised at that, or He's disappointed in you?"

Kenna frowned. "Maybe I don't know enough about being a Christian to answer that. My faith is still pretty new. I only became a believer a couple of years ago."

"Some things take a lifetime of learning, and we all go at our own pace. The point is, we keep moving forward. That includes failing and getting back up."

"I feel like I'm still down."

Jesse Lee smiled. "There's a song by a Christian band called 'Dare You to Move,' and one of the lines is, 'I dare you to lift yourself up off the floor.' But the truth is, sometimes we need a hand up. That's what the body of Christ should be. What we're designed to do for each other. Especially when life puts us on the floor."

Kenna sniffed back tears.

"Your belief in God doesn't depend on your circumstances. His love for you doesn't change, even if you can't feel it. What's true is just true. Always was and always will be."

Jax glanced at her. "We've both worked with people who blocked things from their mind during intense trauma. I've done it, and I wonder if you did as well. As a coping mechanism."

"I blocked a lot out of my mind, but I was fully aware of what was happening." She held his gaze. "Basically thinking about anything else, or anyone. Except you. Even with that, I couldn't think about you much. I wouldn't let myself go there, or it was going to swallow me alive."

"And you think that doesn't make you someone of incredible strength?"

"It didn't work."

"No? I think you held your ground through incredibly horrific circumstances. After all, you're here, aren't you? You and the baby are safe."

"Because you rescued me."

"Because God is good," Jax said. "And He has a future for you that you haven't yet realized. It sounds hokey, but if you weren't meant to be here, then you wouldn't have survived."

Jesse Lee said, "When we believe we've sinned, it's on us to repent. Whether Jax and I believe your lost faith is your fault or not, if you're looking for a turnaround in your heart and mind, confess and believe. That's how you were saved, and it's how you get back on track."

"It wasn't a once-and-for-all thing?"

Jesse Lee tipped his head to the side and back, in a kind of nod. "In a way, yes. But we drift. We forget. Or we mess up. Returning to the Lord can be a daily thing, or every minute. Not necessarily saying a 'sinner's prayer' every time, but the act of praying your way back to that close relationship might need to be something you do nearly constantly for a while. As a reminder to you that you need to keep Him close."

Kenna shut her eyes.

"It's going to take you time to heal, but think of it like recovery," Jesse Lee explained. "We do the work, and at first, it's a lot. It's every moment and every second. Then it becomes more automatic. We don't have to think so hard, or cling so closely. Although, that's never a bad thing. It just becomes more natural to *know* you're still abiding in Him."

She glanced from him to Jax. "That's what you do?"

"I learned it in recovery. I guess it's been a while, so I didn't remember. But now, it's so natural."

She put her hand on his arm. "Thank you for bringing me here. You shouldn't feel bad that you didn't think to phrase it like this."

"She's right, bro. This is what the body of Christ is."

Kenna squeezed his arm, and Jax glanced between them. She said, "You and I have zero perspective when it comes to each other."

He smiled. "That's true enough. Maybe I needed to hear it as well, because I need to be reminded what's true regardless of the circumstances."

"We all do. Things are fine when life is peaceful and happy," Jesse Lee said. "What counts is what you do when the storm comes. You two have faced plenty, together and apart. Those are the times when your faith is solidified. When you get to choose to stand on what you believe regardless of what's happening around you, or if you feel Him close."

"But I didn't do that," she said. "Which is why I feel like I...failed."

"We fight against an enemy we can't see. Not just all the visible ones you face." Jesse Lee flipped open his Bible and ruffled the pages. "And it's a slap in the face to the enemy when we repent and admit we can't do it without God's help. We do fail. All of us. Every day, we come up short. But keeping us in our guilt and shame is his biggest tactic. Because we can't get up off the floor if we feel like we deserve to be down there."

Kenna had felt the weight of what happened, more than just the trauma in her heart and mind. She had been carrying around the burden of guilt that she wasn't supposed to carry.

Jesse Lee bent his head to the page. "He who began a good work in you will carry it on to completion." He looked up. "We're all a work in progress, no matter where we're at or what we're going through. How we failed. If we're currently thinking we're a success." He smiled. "We all need to get on our knees, literally or figuratively, and put our lives back on the right track."

Kenna wound her arm around Jax's elbow and laced their fingers together. She leaned her head on his shoulder. "I need to do that. I need to pray."

Not only did she need to repent and allow God to take the guilt she'd been carrying, but she needed Him to flood her life with His love. It was the one thing that was going to give her the peace she so desperately needed.

She had to cling to Him until this was over and forever after that.

It was the only way they were going to survive.

Chapter Sixteen

"Give it to me, I just want to smell it." Kenna reached for his coffee cup.

Jax burst out laughing. "I guess I don't have to ask if you're okay this morning. Or better. You seem more... you."

"Because I want to smell your caffeine?"

He grinned, pulling into the parking lot with one hand on the wheel and holding his mug out of her reach with the other. "Drink your decaf."

"You're mean." She didn't mean that, and they both knew it.

Out the passenger-side window, she looked at the three-story building. White exterior, long walls of windows on each floor. The kind of generic office space any company could rent. Or a government-funded group doing something or other the nature of which Maizie hadn't quite figured out yet.

Kenna did feel a whole lot better today than she had the day before, prior to going to meet Jax's old friend. They'd spent a chunk of time in prayer, talking through her experience and how it worked to get back "on track" with the Lord, as he'd called it.

What she didn't like was how it'd seemed as if her faith might've been just a shallow thing in the two years since she became a Christian. That she hadn't dug in as much as she could've or developed a solid enough foundation to withstand being in captivity. Jesse Lee and Jax had both told her that her loss of faith was an entirely human reaction to what'd happened, and that a lot of people would've reacted the same in a situation like that.

She was trying to give herself more grace about it, at least. To not get sucked under with what she "should've" done or blame herself for the failure to keep hold of her faith.

To simply take the next right step and keep moving forward, being who she wanted to be.

"This is it?" She pointed to the office building.

"This is the address Maizie gave us."

"I need to stretch." She pushed her door open.

It was barely past eight in the morning, but with DC area traffic, it had taken over an hour to get here from their campsite. The other residents in the RV park had been starting to wake up, an older couple out walking their tiny dog around the rows and lanes. Just looking at the empty pool made her cold and this empty parking lot was no different.

Kenna tucked her heavy coat around her. She was glad for a season of not having to worry so much about her health, but the reason why wasn't a good one. Being the subject of medical research wasn't something she'd had on her bucket list, but at least they hadn't been trying to correct an issue. It had all been about gathering information on her progress, and the baby's growth.

She shut the door and leaned against it, scanning the industrial area while Jax came around the hood of the car. She dialed Maizie and held the phone in front of both of them, the audible sound of ringing coming through the speaker on the bottom of the phone.

"Hey." The young woman sounded breathy.

"Everything good?" Kenna frowned. All Maizie had sent so far was an address she'd managed to gather from the information in the packet they'd been given the password for.

"We got a warning about a wildfire a few miles west of here. We're supposed to be getting ready to go, but depending on what happens, they might upgrade us to go now or downgrade us because it changed direction or they squashed it."

"A wildfire?" Jax leaned against Kenna's shoulder and put his arm around her, his elbow on the roof of the car.

"There was a big storm a couple of nights ago, and the lightning started a fire." Maizie's tone was laced with worry. "It's pretty crazy, but Craig said stuff like this happens sometimes. It's just usually earlier in the year, like over summer. He said because it's been so dry this year, that everything is just going up."

Kenna exhaled. "We'll pray for the situation, and for you guys."

Only after she said it did she realize how easily that sentiment had come, and how it wasn't just a platitude. She would pray, because she knew it was the only thing she could do that would be effective in a situation like that.

"Thanks," Maizie said. "Elizabeth and Craig said we should come to DC if we do have to evacuate, so we're in the process of packing up just in case."

"What about Cabot?" Kenna asked, suddenly missing her old dog.

"I'm not sure, because we might have to fly. But there's, uh, someone who can watch her. Someone that"—she cleared her throat—"that I know. He and Cabot get along pretty well."

"It's serious enough he's been to the trailer? Wow."

"I didn't let him come inside. That would've been weird, and he doesn't *exactly* know what I do for you. Just some of the admin stuff. And I showed him the website."

"Are you going to tell your adoptive parents what his name is?"

Maizie was quiet for a moment. "Andrew, but I'm not telling you his last name because you don't need to have him investigated, and I *don't* want Ramon paying him a visit in the middle of the night and scaring the life out of him."

Jax grinned.

Kenna laughed to herself, keeping it silent so Maizie didn't hear. "Of course, we can't approve of anyone in your life without meeting them first." She tried to force all humor out of her tone and sound stern.

Maizie sighed. "Craig told me to tell you about him. But it is pretty new. When he came over, it was for a school project, and we were still just friends back then."

"And now?"

"We're still mostly just friends, but...I don't know. I have no idea how to do this. We talked about it, and we both agreed to take things slow."

"In the middle of a wildfire and the case of our lives?" Kenna said.

Jax squeezed her shoulder. "Happy for you, Maze."

"In the middle of the case of our lives?" she repeated.

"It's a good distraction," Maizie said. "And taking it slow

doesn't mean I'm distracted all the time. He knows I have to work and it's important."

Kenna didn't want to worry that the guy in this young woman's life was an agent of their enemy, but it was a possibility they had to consider. That and the wildfire being a design to force them from their safe place. Were it not for the lightning storm, Kenna might have thought it was intentional.

She closed her eyes for a second and prayed silently, determined to cling to the Lord in every situation. Even ones that didn't seem scary.

"Speaking of work," Jax said while she finished up her prayer, "tell us about this address, and the packet you received. Give us the rundown."

"Okay, here goes," Maizie began. She sounded confident again. Now that the big secret was out, things could blow over and get back to normal. Back to work. "The code unlocked everything, but there's so much we couldn't even print it and divide up who's reading what. Elizabeth and Craig are working through parts of it on their own, listening to it super fast. But it could still take days to get through all of it."

"But you found an address for where they were working." Kenna stared at the building. "This place is so generic you'd never think anything interesting is happening here."

"That's probably the point," Jax said. "We should go inside and look around."

There were a lot of contributing factors that went into how they chose to do that, and he didn't need to explain them all aloud. Kenna had peace about it, because they were here to protect each other. He could go inside alone if it came to it, and if they saw anyone threatening, they'd be out of here in seconds.

She leaned closer into her husband's side. "I'm ready for some action."

He squeezed her shoulder.

"Maizie, what is the packet so far?" she asked. "Beyond the address, what's in the files?"

"There are all kinds of things, it's crazy." Maizie paused. "Elizabeth found personnel records, but they aren't people who exist. We found maps of different metropolitan areas, and what look like escape routes. Then there's a long section of battle plans. An in-depth review of the European Union and projections for the next twenty years, including expanding to several additional nations."

"Like Croatia?"

"Yeah, actually. That country is on the list. How did you know?"

"Just a hunch. I don't suppose there's any indication of *Dominatus* in the files is there?"

"Not in what we've looked at so far. Like, they didn't sign it or anything obvious like that." Maizie paused. "Craig thinks the place was some kind of think tank, but he's trying to piece together what they were working on. Right now, it's all just random tasks that don't make sense unless they add up to something."

"Could be a number of scenarios." Kenna didn't know much about think tanks. "Was it something the government was doing, or a private company?"

"All we know is it's connected to the lawyers. Like maybe they participated, but we still don't know who was paying the bills. We're hoping there's a list of people involved somewhere in the packet, so we know what their role was. And who paid them."

"Hmm," Kenna said. "Seems odd that they jumped on

this. Unless it was a way to further their aim of fighting *Dominatus*."

Jax nodded. "We should go inside and look around. They might've cleared out, but there could be something inside worth finding."

"Maizie, can you send us the photos that are with the personnel records? I'd like to look at all the people and see if I can recognize any of them."

"Okay." Her voice was quiet for that. "I didn't know if you wanted to see them."

"I don't, but it's a good idea."

"I'll send them."

"Keep us updated on the fire, and the file packet, okay?" Kenna stepped away from the car and turned to face Jax.

The street remained empty. She hadn't seen any movement or lights on in the windows of the building, no cars had passed them, and no one was visible around any of the other buildings on the street in this industrial area. Only the drone of morning rush-hour traffic a couple of streets over let her know they weren't completely alone.

"Will do." Maizie signed off.

Kenna stuck her phone in her pocket. "Let's go."

He didn't move. That steady gaze held hers, strength and peace in his expression. "What if I asked you to stay in the car?"

"I would, even though I'd probably complain. Not that I need to be in the middle of the action." She laid a hand on his jacket, over his heart. "I just feel safer near you."

"I know what you mean." He nodded slowly, as if conceding the point within himself. At war in his own mind between work and keeping them both safe. "Let's at least peek in the window. See what we can see. If it looks clear, we could check it out."

She nodded. "Sounds good."

Before she could even turn, the sound of traffic swelled. Multiple vehicles turned the corner at the end of the street. Black SUVs, the kind that could only be government vehicles, sped down the street.

She tucked herself closer to Jax, who straightened away from the car with her in his arms. Ready for what happened next.

The SUVs didn't pass by. Instead, they turned into the empty parking lot where she and Jax stood and screeched to a halt around them and men and women in suits climbed out.

Kenna stayed by Jax's side as he turned to face the approaching agents. No question, that's what they were. Even before she saw the first badge on a belt each of the suited men and a couple of severe-looking women, she knew they were with an agency.

Kenna muttered, "Secret Service."

"That's a new one." Louder, Jax said, "Can we help you?"

The lead agent was older, probably in his fifties. Still trim like maybe he'd never had an extra few pounds in his life but kept his weight as tight as his belt. Hair completely white. No stubble on his chin. Clean-cut, maybe military at some point. "I'm Assistant Director Ranturno." He glanced between them. "Mr. Jaxton, Ms. Banbury."

"It's Mrs. Jaxton." Depending on whether this was a personal or a business contact, anyway. Right now, she wanted as much association with Jax as possible. They had to know who she and Jax were to each other. Plus, it was fun to correct someone who operated on the principle that they knew everything.

"Right." Ranturno nodded. "The president would like a word with the two of you."

Chapter Seventeen

"This way." The woman walking ahead of them wasn't Secret Service. She looked more like some low-level staff person. An assistant, but in the White House of all places.

This woman didn't have to worry about protecting herself from the threat Kenna and Jax presented, because the Secret Service had divested them of every weapon they'd been carrying and their phones before they could even set foot in the door.

Jax hadn't been happy that the government would have unfettered access to their cell phones while they were in this meeting, but there wasn't much they could do beyond accept AD Ranturno's word that wasn't going to happen.

Kenna held on to Jax's hand through the hall with its high ceilings and ornate artwork above the center rail that ran along the wall. Wallpaper under it and cream paint above. It would be impressive if they were here for the tour, but being torn away from what they had been working on and summoned against their will to a secret meeting meant she refused to admit this place was awe-inspiring just on principle.

The assistant gestured. "Follow me." She wore a knee-length skirt, white blouse with a jacket over it, and flat shoes. Pantyhose. A short haircut she could tuck behind her ears and horn-rimmed glasses.

They descended a set of carpeted stairs in the corner of the building. Kenna didn't know enough about the place to know where they were, but she was pretty sure this wasn't part of any normal tour. The artwork grew sparser, and downstairs was a whole lot more utilitarian. This wasn't somewhere the public got to see.

Jax said, "Is it true the White House has as many floors below ground as there are above?"

The assistant glanced back at him but said nothing. "This way."

She kept walking down the hall, making her comment redundant since that's what they were doing. Without taking a turn, because there weren't any until the end. It was a long corridor with closed doors on either side, all labeled with numbers. At the end, the corner took a sharp right angle, and beyond that was a set of double doors. A red light above.

Kenna glanced at her husband and nearly laughed at the look of wonder on his face. Okay, so that was adorable. He was totally geeking out about being in the White House.

She leaned over as they walked. "Maybe we should come back and do the tour," she whispered. "We can pretend to be from out of town."

The assistant stopped at the door and produced a key card from her pocket. After a hard swipe through a card reader, the light turned green. She opened the door for them but stayed in the hall. "Through here."

Jax went first, still holding Kenna's hand.

A few steps in, he stopped. Instinct she didn't understand had her wanting to stay behind him, tucked at his back where she was protected and no one could see her, or get a good angle for attack. The door shut behind her, bumping her forward with the heavy sound.

"Mr. Jaxton." The voice of the president of the United States of America wasn't a voice you'd fail to recognize. She just had that tough, weathered tone to her. The commander in chief because her predecessor had died, and as vice president, she had immediately been sworn into office. "Mrs. Jaxton."

Kenna looked over the shiny wood conference table and at least twelve high-backed leather chairs. The president, Miriam Tetherton, walked from the far end where there was a small cabinet with a water pitcher and glasses and a glass decanter of something that looked like bourbon, over to them, holding her hand out.

But she wasn't alone in the room.

Kenna shifted to Jax's right and met the president's outstretched hand with her own. "Madam President. Not to be rude, it's nice to meet you and all..." Maybe. Depending. "But this isn't a conversation I'm interested in having." She pointed to the man over on the far left of the room. "Not with him."

"Kenna?" Jax glanced from the man to her and Tetherton, wariness in his body language.

"I can understand your reticence." The president clasped her hands together in front of her, showing off the muscle tone in her biceps thanks to the sleeveless dress. Miriam Tetherton looked like a CEO, which fit. Even down here, meeting like this in low light in a secret room, she was going to play boss and politician.

"It's not reticence. It's dislike." She glanced at him. "You knew if I'd known you were here that I never would've gotten in that car. That's why no one informed me." Kenna looked at the president. "We already know you're either with *Dominatus* or you're someone they control so thoroughly they're willing to risk installing you as president, because they're in control either way. So I guess we know what your deal is, but not why we're here."

Tetherton's expression remained neutral. "We all have a part to play."

"I don't." Kenna lifted her hands. "My family has no part. We're nothing to do with any of you. If I thought it would do any good, I'd tell you to pass that on up the chain."

Jax shifted, and she knew he needed an explanation.

Kenna took his hand, holding on tight. "Jax, this is Petyr Blazevic, the Croatian head of their military."

"The treaty." Jax's tone indicated dislike, but it wasn't about politics. "And the bombing."

"He and I have met before, of course. When he visited the platform where I was being held prisoner so they could experiment on me." Kenna glanced at the president, just to see if she had any empathy in her, or a clue as to what was happening.

A slight flex of the skin around her eyes was the only tell.

"Not to be on the nose or anything..." Except Kenna had no problem with that. "But I hope you know what you got yourself into."

The president had a strained look on her face. "Perhaps we could sit."

Kenna glanced at Petyr. He lifted a glass of the alcohol from the decanter and sipped without saying anything. She said, "You want us to hear you out?"

Petyr lowered the glass. "Someone is trying to kill me."

"How do you know it isn't me?" Kenna said.

The president turned to her. "Is it?"

"I've been busy."

Jax squeezed her hand a fraction. "I'd like to hear you both out. I'm guessing Kenna is safe here in this house."

"It's the safest house in the world." The president moved down the table, ushering them over to sit by her and pulled out the chair at the head of the table. "I can assure you we didn't bring you here to do either of you harm. You have nothing to fear here."

Kenna didn't know if she was prepared to believe that. Petyr took a seat on the other side of the table, and Jax sat beside Kenna opposite him.

"First of all, thank you for coming." The president laced her fingers together on the table. "As you can imagine, we're concerned as to the threat level this treaty presents. After the bombing, it's become clear that steps need to be taken to neutralize any potential risk."

Kenna bit back what she wanted to say and kept her lips pressed tight together. The president surely had people for that, Kenna didn't consider it any of her business, and what did they want from her and Jax anyway?

She looked across the table at Petyr. He always wore a similar suit, and today's tie was blue with gold stripes at an angle. His dark hair was slicked back, threaded with gray on the sides. Thick brows and a heavy forehead. Piercing eyes that looked almost black.

The president continued, "We have reason to believe someone is intending to influence the upcoming vote for the new *Imperatoris*."

Jax said, "*Dominatus* is voting in a new leader?"

"Petyr is one of the top contenders." Kenna bent her

knee and put her foot on the chair, trying to appear as casual as possible. Like none of this meant anything to her. Problem was, making that position work meant drawing attention to her growing midsection. "The president can't be in charge because she's female, and *Dominatus* doesn't get with all that progressive stuff. They only want a male in charge, and he can't be a head of state. They're too busy. Commander in chief of the Croatian military is a gray area, unless Petyr quits, which he's thinking about doing if he wins the vote."

"For the greater good." He lifted his glass in a toast. "For the future."

Kenna glanced at Jax. "When he drinks too much, he gets chatty. He told me about all of it during his visit to the platform."

A tendon flexed in Jax's jaw.

Honestly, seeing how much he disliked the entire thing helped keep her steady enough to glance between them. "What do you want? The culprits of the bombing have been arrested, so what is there for me to investigate? Or you'd rather I act as a human shield in case it happens again."

The president gasped.

Petyr slammed his glass against the table hard enough some of the liquid sloshed out. "We would never endanger—"

"One of *your* children." Kenna glared at him. "I have that right, yeah? That's what you were going to say?"

"The sanctity of life is one of our highest values. It's why we do what we do."

The president crossed her arms. "No one in *Dominatus* would dare harm an unborn child. It's simply not done!"

"Glad we got that straight." Kenna swiveled her chair

side to side an inch to try and ease some of the tension she felt.

"I'm relieved to hear it," Jax said, "but I'm not satisfied by any means." He stared across the table at the Croatian man. "Don't take my remaining placid as indication I intend to do nothing."

Petyr inclined his head just a fraction.

The last thing Kenna needed is a rapport between them based on something akin to respect. "You still haven't told us what you want."

"We aren't going to ask you to put your life in harm's way," the president told her. "Of course, we would never ask you that."

"Maybe you should give me a Secret Service detail. Tell them I'm a diplomat." Kenna would find that hilarious, but she also wouldn't trust even the most upright federal agent right now. She'd rather have Ramon and Zeyla any day. The two of them were worth an army.

"Unfortunately, I'm unable to devote additional resources to your protection. As much as I might like to."

"How reassuring *Dominatus* cares about my well-being," Kenna mocked. "That's so nice." She wanted to continue arguing the point about her captivity, or why they wanted her baby safe and what that meant for their future. But she kept her mouth shut so the president would continue.

"We're dealing with a threat from within." President Tetherton flashed a plastic smile. "As you can understand, it's difficult for me to devote resources to an internal manhunt. Especially where the Pentagon is concerned. I'm new to this position, and right now isn't time to start ruffling feathers. Which presents me with a problem that requires an alternate solution." She reached under the table, pulled out a file folder, and pushed it to Kenna. "Take this with you. It's everything I have."

"I don't have time for a case right now. Even if *Dominatus* can afford me, why would do a job for people I despise?"

From across the table, Petyr said, "Because we are the reason you're alive."

"You're also the source of any and all threats. So you wanna run that one by me again? How you're the solution to the threat, or like you've done anything to keep me safe?"

"My English. It isn't stellar." He took a sip of his drink.

"That's a lame excuse, and you understand just fine."

Jax picked up where she left off. "We aren't available right now. We're working another case, and two at once isn't advisable. Not when the lives of people we care about are on the line."

The president said, "The case against the lawyers is open-and-shut. There's nothing to investigate. I'm told—"

"You just admitted there's someone working against you in your own government, and you're going to bank what you believe on what you're told?" Jax glanced at Petyr, then back at the president. "I'm not sure that's wise."

"Be that as it may, you now have differing priorities."

Kenna shook her head. "You guys think we should just jump when you say so. What a shocker."

"I'm flabbergasted." Jax sounded like he'd been forced to watch paint dry.

She almost smiled.

President Tetherton said, "There's time for you to help the lawyers. They aren't going anywhere. This is time sensitive and deserves your undivided attention."

"Because you say so." Kenna flipped open the file just for curiosity's sake. A police report from Baltimore PD, a murder scene. One male deceased. She turned the first page and saw a photo. "Why do I care about the death of a guy who worked in the Pentagon?"

"Someone is killing us. One by one." The president shivered. "I can't bring this to the attention of anyone who works for me without disclosing my...allegiances."

"So you want me to find whoever is murdering *Dominatus* operatives? I'm liable to shake their hand." Kenna put her foot down and stood, pushing the chair back. "This was a waste of time."

"They aren't killing assets. They're killing offspring." The president sat back in her chair. "Which means if there's a list, then you're on it. Who knows...you might even be next."

Chapter Eighteen

"I'm supposed to believe your singular focus is my well-being?"

"Kenna, you already understand our position about the next generation," Petyr said. "If we lose our offspring, then our hold on the world is lost as well."

She stared at him. "That doesn't mean I want anything to do with you. My baby is just a baby. She's not part of your organization, and neither am I. Whether you claim a hold on us or not is irrelevant as far as I'm concerned. We get to choose our own futures."

"Perhaps you should explain that to whoever is trying to kill me."

"Not my fight. It's politics, and I want nothing to do with that." Kenna braced her hands on the back of the chair, pushing it against the table. Jax hadn't stood yet, which meant he wasn't satisfied he had enough information to leave with a complete picture of what was going on. She wasn't sure he'd get that, but she could help. "If you want to take over *Dominatus* as their supreme overlord or whatever, then get rid of the competition and take the throne. Preferably before someone else does the same to you."

"That is what I believe is happening."

Kenna shrugged one shoulder. "Have you made a list of suspects?"

"There's no way to know."

She let out a big breath. "You guys and your secrecy. You know, if you had a membership roster, you'd know who was trying to kill you."

Jax shifted in his seat.

Petyr dipped his head. "I'd be obliged for your assistance."

She wasn't even going to touch that, not coming from him. "I'm busy. Apparently, I have cases."

And a suspect, but she wasn't going to tell them that she had seen the "ghost" young man from the platform where she'd been held in a hospital up north in Boston. Or that he'd killed Megan Tiller. Given their usual tactics, if they got their hands on him again they would bring him back in the fold and then get him to kill on their behalf, which wouldn't solve anyone's problem. It was far better for Amara or someone else in Kenna's family to end his deadly antics. Either by turning him over to the police, which was Kenna's preferred result, or by being forced to take his life.

"I'm not surprised you care nothing for my fate. Despite what we are to each other."

Of course, he was going to bring that up. "Don't."

Petyr flicked a hand in Jax's direction. "Did you tell him?"

"It isn't a secret, but no. You're not some sordid part of my life. You're no part of my life at all." In her defense, she didn't consider him credible and she'd been dealing with a whole lot of huge stuff in her heart and mind. "Despite what you think we are to each other."

"I am your father, Kenna."

She touched Jax's shoulder just to steady herself. "At least you didn't use the word *seed* like last time." She made a gagging motion. "But calling yourself something doesn't make it true, and it doesn't make me care."

"The test was clear."

Clear as mud. "Yeah, *Dominatus* has never faked a DNA test before. It must be real."

"Deny it all you want—"

"Petyr." She cut him off, and Jax reached up to put his hand over hers. "So what if you're my biological sperm donor? You aren't part of my life, you never have been, and you never will be."

"I could keep you safe."

"You'd be using me to keep yourself safe."

"I cannot be certain my enemy would respect our ways. It may be he who is targeting our offspring. Attempting to turn *Dominatus* in a direction we were never meant to go."

"So I save the kids from being killed, you fix your problem and become the leader, and then my focus turns to taking you out. After all, you just became *Imperatoris*." She stared at him.

"So be it."

Kenna shook her head. "You'd accept it simply because you believe I'm your daughter."

"If you wish to end my life, I will not try to stop you."

Jax's fingers flexed around hers. He pushed back his chair and stood, disconnecting them for a second before he took her hand again. "I'd like to say it's been a pleasure, but it's certainly been informative at least."

"I'm not finished." Petyr looked at her. "You insist on having that piece of trash in your association."

She glanced at Jax. "He's talking about Bruce."

The president's sharp intake of breath was audible.

"They don't like him."

"Seems like a good reason to keep him around," Jax said. "Unless there's reason we should be wary of him?" He glanced around.

Petyr said, "He will betray you."

"Then it'll be our fault for trusting him." Kenna shrugged. "And none of your business." She glanced at the president. "Thank you for your time."

As if she'd asked to be here.

The president nodded like a queen to her subjects, the political mask back in place. "Take the file with you."

"I'll be sure to find a shredder on the way out." Jax took the file, and Kenna's hand and they headed for the door.

It opened before they reached it, and two Secret Service agents entered. Two stood in the hall. Those followed Kenna and Jax.

At the turn in the hall, the assistant reappeared. "This way."

Kenna plastered on a smile. "Of course."

Jax waited until they were through the lobby and out the North Portico, with its hanging lantern light above them. Between the two center pillars. He chose the left path. Not until they were out in the open did he say, "If he hadn't been there, were you going to tell me that the Croatian president is the one who claims to be your father?"

She winced.

"Interesting guy."

"You aren't mad I didn't give you all of the information?"

Jax shook his head. "I don't like being blindsided. I don't think anyone does. But were you actually going to tell me between yesterday and everything that happened, with him being here in town and us working the lawyer's case? Or were you going to keep it to yourself and hope the situation just fizzled out and went away?"

He had a point, which was why the questions had been rhetorical.

"Do you have to be understanding?" She wound her arm through his as they walked toward the gated entrance and onto Pennsylvania Avenue, which was closed for traffic and had Secret Service guards at a gate to the left. Beyond that, there was a coffee shop on the northwest corner she'd been to before. "I have to pee, by the way."

Jax chuckled. "You wonder why I just roll with it."

"Maybe you should be mad. But in my defense, it's all scrambled in my brain. Although, I clearly remember him slapping me when I backtalked him."

Jax's arm tensed.

"He's a *great* guy," she drawled in a sarcastic tone. "Definitely grandpa material."

"What's their problem with Bruce?"

"See that's the thing. They're all about harping on the fact he's bad news. That he'll betray me. Blah-blah. Where's the proof?" She rolled her eyes. "They're trying way too hard. Makes me think I can trust him, just because they said I can't."

"So why avoid him?"

Kenna sighed. "I've been avoiding a lot because it was just easier. Or I thought it should be easier. Maybe I have to face him, too."

"We might not trust anyone implicitly, except maybe Maizie. But that doesn't mean he's going to betray us."

She nodded, dragging it out while she thought the situation through. "There's always an agenda. Why tell me Petyr is my biological father, and that Bruce is going to betray me so I can't trust him? What's the reasoning behind that? Add in a lack of caffeine and it's enough to keep a pregnant woman up at night, pacing the RV."

Jax walked her to the coffee shop, and she stood in line with tourists for the bathroom. A small moment of normal life in the middle of the insanity of their chaos. She and Jax weren't the kind of people who'd bring their family to Washington, DC, to do the tourist thing, even if it was worth a trip. They knew far too much about what went on behind closed doors, what power did to people who wielded it, and the darkness beneath the surface of a civilized society to be at peace in a place like this.

She took care of the pressing business and found Jax in the corner by the door, reading the file the president had given them while he sipped from a paper cup. Of coffee. "Turns out I'm not so understanding as you," she grumbled. "I want coffee."

He held out the cup to her. "This is apple cider."

"My hero." She swiped the cup from him and sipped, savoring the tartness and cinnamon flavors. "That's good."

Jax chuckled. "Our rideshare will be a few minutes."

"Back to the car?"

He nodded. "I still want to check out that building. You probably need to look at this file to see if it's that guy."

"At least you didn't say *your friend.*"

"Also, we need to check what Maizie sent so you can look at the photos from the file packet. See if you recognize anyone."

Kenna slumped into the closest chair, holding the paper cup to her lips. "I'm exhausted already."

"Want to pack it in and go to Wyoming?"

She took a sip, contemplating everything. In the middle of the mental recounting of what'd happened the past few days, she remembered to pray again. "There are too many unanswered questions."

"And *Dominatus* is in the middle of it." He focused his gaze on her. "Do you believe what they said about the baby being safe from them?"

"Mostly, I figure she's safe where she is for now." Kenna leaned forward on the chair and put her elbows on her knees. "But what about after she's born? What if one of them decides they want her for whatever sick and twisted reason, and they take her from us?"

"Would Petyr being in charge mean she's safe? If he believes they're related, maybe it's in his best interest that she's unharmed and protected with us."

"It's worth hoping for that." Kenna wished she had a way to be assured of their safety. "All I've got is faith, and right now even that feels fragile."

"There are never any guarantees. I wish there were. I'd have less to worry about." He gave her a soft smile. "I'd also have less of a need to rely on God and trust Him, because I'd be confident it's going to work out. But my confidence would be in people and not Him."

"Understanding and wise."

Jax smiled at her. "Guess you'd better keep me around."

"It's on the list of reasons why I'd be an idiot to let you go."

"So romantic."

Kenna shrugged. "It's the hormones. They're making me mushy."

He leaned in and kissed her, a soft touch of his lips. "Love you."

"Love you, too." She wanted to thank him again, and would, but she uttered it as a prayer.

Thank You.

God had given her Jax as an ever-present support. Even when they were separated, she knew he would've burned the world down to find her—because she'd have done the same in his place.

She needed to trust God for the outcome. After all, it was her only shot at finding peace in the middle of this chaotic situation. No matter what happened next, they'd be together and God would be with them. His hand would be on them.

He would be fighting for them.

Chapter Nineteen

"Did you just break and enter into a building?" Kenna smirked at her husband, when in reality it was kind of hot.

"What is that look?" He eyed her. "Because your FBI agent husband is now a criminal. Am I some kind of dangerous bad boy now?"

She shrugged, trying to keep from laughing. "You're a pretty good distraction."

Better than thinking about everything that was going on. Whether she might be in danger, who in their sphere needed help or someone to get justice for them.

He leaned over and kissed her, then pushed the door open and went into the building where the think tank had operated. "For the record, that was barely a lock. It took almost nothing to get it to open. Which tracks with the idea that they cleared out and there's nothing to find."

He was right. The entrance to the building was empty. An elevator in the center of the far wall beside the stairs, no one behind the desk. Nothing on the desk and not even a chair for someone to sit on.

"Stairs?" she asked.

Jax took her hand. "From the information in the packet, they were housed on the second floor."

"So what was the top floor? And what kind of work were they doing here?"

He stopped at the directory at the bottom of the stairs, screwed to the wall. "Third floor is an accountant's office."

The first floor was listed as a property management company, and the floor the lawyers had been hired to work on read "The Denari Foundation." Whatever that was.

She dialed Maizie's number and put an earbud in her ear. When the young woman picked up, Kenna said, "How's things?"

"We were told we can stand down. They're working on the fire, and hopefully we won't have to evacuate."

"That's good."

"The air is thick outside, and hazy. Everything smells like a giant bonfire."

"Yep." Kenna had been around wildfires before, but usually in California in July and August. Not this late in the year in Colorado. Even if a dry season, a warm start to the winter season, and a lightning storm were to blame, she still had a hard time believing it wasn't coincidental. "Can I ask about the packet?"

"Sure."

"Anything in there about the Denari Foundation?"

"Isn't that from the Bible?" Maizie asked.

Kenna squeezed Jax's hand. "Is Denari from the Bible?"

He glanced at her as they rounded the first landing and headed up to the second floor. "It's currency. The unit of money they used in the Gospels. It might be Roman, but I'd have to look that up."

"It's—"

Maizie said, "I can hear him."

"Okay. Whether it's a good name for a front company, a shell corporation, or some other kind of money laundering thing wrapped up in a charity or not...I have no idea." Kenna let Jax go through the door to the second floor first, hanging back while he made sure it was safe.

She laid a hand on her baby bump, trying to reassure herself they'd be fine. If the ghost was coming after her, there were a lot of people he would have to get through before he touched her. Plenty of protection here to keep her from having to worry about facing danger. But she was going to worry anyway.

She asked Maizie, "Have you heard from Ramon and Zeyla?"

"They were working something until late last night, tracking his movements after visiting Megan Tiller in the hospital. Now that they know you might be on his list, they're on the way to you. Probably stopped to get some sleep."

"Okay." That was reassuring enough she could relax for a moment.

Jax held the door. "Not much more in here than there was downstairs."

Kenna stepped into the open plan office space. "Hardly surprising. I mean, if they were hired to be some kind of think tank and come up with a scenario about whatever this is, then no one is going to want to leave evidence behind."

"You think the scenario was about bombing the Croatian president?" Jax surveyed the room.

Kenna didn't see anyone moving around. They were alone.

There were a few desks separated by cubicles, a conference table at the far end by the window, and a printer in the opposite corner.

She nodded, still thinking on it. "It's absolutely possible they were hired to come up with the scenario. Given the FBI's evidence, they were probably scouting the location of the best place to set off a bomb in good faith, thinking they were working for the right side. Instead, their research was used to implicate them."

"They were framed," Maizie said.

"Exactly."

Jax glanced over.

"We know they worked more than one scenario, though." Kenna paused. "So, what else did they come up with, and is that going to be used against them as well? Or against someone else."

"They're supposed to be part of the resistance," Jax said. "How did they end up getting duped so thoroughly? That's what I want to know."

Maizie responded, "Me too."

Kenna said, "We're all in agreement about that."

Jax walked through the room, stepping on the papers scattered about. "Let's see what we can see here. If there's anything to learn."

She went with him, mostly just for the sake of not being alone and unprotected.

Through the open phone line she heard, "Oh."

"What is it, Maze?"

"The file you uploaded in the car that the President gave you. The dead guy you're supposed to avenge, or whatever."

"Is he in the packet?"

"Yes." Maizie went quiet instead of elaborating.

Kenna pictured her with that crease between her eyebrows, scanning information at hyper-speed the way she did. Not many people in the world could process information like that. Maizie often saw connections no one else did, and it would make her an amazing investigator one day. Not that Kenna had told her as much. She wanted the young woman to find her own path, knowing there were so many careers that would be a lot less dangerous than police work. Her skills would be an asset to so many different fields.

Finally, Maizie said, "Elizbeth and Craig said the personnel records weren't real people, but this guy is a real person. So the image isn't AI even if the rest of the information on him reads more like a fictional dossier."

"What about the others whose photos you have?"

"That's the problem. We didn't find this guy that the president's file says is Steven Braughton because he doesn't have a driver's license that we can find. Or if he does, it's not one anyone can just look up. Maybe it's Top Secret. Like someone found it necessary to hide his identity, or this is his real name and his driver's license will come up as someone else. So maybe they are all real people, and we just can't prove it using any of the usual methods."

Kenna sighed. "How are we supposed to dig up backgrounds on people who don't exist, or who have multiple identities?" She stuck to the wall farthest from the windows, just in case, watching as she moved for the red dot of a laser sight on her or Jax or the wall beside them. Scanning. Staying vigilant. At least making herself feel better if not actually ensuring their safety.

Halfway along, she stopped and leaned against the wall. Jax was looking at papers left on a desk.

"I'll keep digging," Maizie said. "If we find multiple,

that's fine. But starting with this guy is easier because what President Tetherton gave us doesn't yet match up to reality."

"But we know he was a low-level staffer at the Pentagon."

"From the file the president gave you, it seems he works for a branch of the army that deals with logistics. He's a paper pusher, requisitioning more supplies for battalions. In reality, who knows. It seems bland enough it's possible it's a cover for something else. Something the Pentagon doesn't want anyone to know about."

Jax glanced over at her.

Kenna smiled back and said to Maizie, "Stairns?"

"Craig talked my ear off for an hour about clandestine operations and off-book black ops stuff. Sounds like movies."

"I bet." Kenna chuckled. "I mean, I know it happens, but it's nothing I've ever had to deal with. And if I can help it, maybe we don't get involved in clandestine overseas operations."

Jax smiled. "Too late."

She shrugged. "You were co-opted into the resistance by the last president but look where that got him. It didn't do my mom or dad any favors. Zeyla is...whatever Zeyla is. I still have no idea."

"Bruce got burned by the CIA, but he seems to have done okay. He and Amara are working on the ghost thing as well."

Jax looked at Kenna and mouthed, *You didn't tell her?*

She shook her head, because she hadn't explained what *Dominatus* wanted her to believe about Bruce. She had no idea what their agenda was with attempting to convince her that he would betray her. More likely, she should keep him close because they were trying so hard. Either way, Maizie could just make up her own mind.

Kenna also hadn't told anyone about Petyr's assertions that he was her father. As far as she was concerned, it wasn't going to change anything in her life. With the caveat that if any of them touched a hair on her child's head, then they'd have serious problems.

And that wasn't just false bravado.

"Are you guys finding anything there?" Maizie asked.

Jax wandered over. "Just some random papers. Probably nothing we can get anything from, since we have that packet anyway."

"Why did you go there?" Maizie asked.

"The car is outside, so we had to come back and get it," Kenna said. "And the Baltimore police detective investigating Steven Braughton's murder isn't available for another hour and we needed something to do."

"Okay, that makes sense.

Kenna moved to the nearest desk and sat on the edge. She wanted to unzip her coat and peel it off because it was warm in here but also didn't want to stay long enough for that. "And we were here before the Secret Service kidnapped us and still wanted to take a look at the place the lawyers were working."

Maizie said, "How can we prove they didn't do what the FBI is accusing them of?"

"Good question," Jax replied. "We can find evidence it was a setup and take the proof to the US Attorney's office. Fight fire with fire."

Kenna nodded. "Whoever they have as lawyers will be provided with all the evidence they need to make the US Attorney look like an idiot for filing charges. He'll drop it because it won't be worth the fight and put the blame squarely on the FBI for messing up so royally."

Maizie groaned. "Sounds like politics, not justice."

Jax smiled.

Kenna winked. "She gets it."

"I'm so proud." Jax chuckled, then glanced around. "Let's get out of here."

Kenna nodded. "We can get a smoothie on the way to meet the detective. What were the papers you were looking at?"

"Printer toner invoices. Pay stubs. Couple of supply lists, but they're not for anything you'd do in an office." Jax shrugged. "On its own it's nothing. Trying to put it together would give you a load of theories with not much substance to back it up." He frowned. "Maizie, is there anything in the packet that can indicate what they were doing for the think tank, or who hired them for it?"

"I'll dig more into who owns the Denari Foundation. That might tell us. So far, the packet the lawyers handed us doesn't say anything about who was behind it, or the scenario they were supposed to come up with. Right now, it seems like a bunch of different things, but it had them on the street where the bomb detonated in the few days before the attack as well as on the day itself." Maizie made a *hmm* sound. "And it looks like they're scouting the location— because that's exactly what they were doing. There's also a whole dossier about destabilizing a treaty being signed on US soil. But it doesn't say which treaty."

"So all in all, it doesn't look good for them." Jax frowned. "Someone handed the FBI everything they needed to arrest the lawyers for trying to assassinate the Croatian President."

"We should go talk to them," Kenna suggested. "Find out what they can tell us."

"I can find out where they're being held." Maizie paused. "See if you can get in for a visit."

"Do that." Jax shifted his weight from one foot to the other. "We'll meet with the detective about the murder in the meantime."

Chapter Twenty

"Thank you for agreeing to see us." Jax held out his hand. "Oliver Jaxton. This is my wife, Kenna."

The detective seemed wary, his dark gaze shifting between them. An African American man, he wore a smart watch and shined his shoes. He had short hair and a tidy suit that didn't look expensive. There was nothing flashy about him. "Jordan Langley. I'm hoping we can be upfront with each other, so I'll tell you I was given no choice but to offer you both my full cooperation."

Kenna didn't like the sound of that, or her ideas about where those orders might've come from.

Behind Detective Langley, the brand-new apartment building in an area where commuters traveled into DC for work was overshadowed by the gray sky above. A young woman in athleticwear exited, keys in one hand and a dog leash in the other. The tiny Yorkie trotted over to the detective and sniffed his shoes before she tugged the dog along with her.

Jax said, "I'd love to know where the order to cooperate came from."

Detective Langley shrugged. "Want to see the place or not?"

"Thanks," Kenna said. "We appreciate your time, regardless of whether you had any choice in the matter."

The six concrete steps up to the entrance preceded a long hall with mailboxes down one side and a rental office to the left. To the right were the first floor of apartments and the hall split in a T shape like a hotel.

The detective walked them up carpeted stairs to the second floor, and halfway down the hall he used a code on the lockbox before ducking under the police tape and entering the room. "The victim, Steven Braughton, was twenty-six and he'd worked admin at the Pentagon for the past eight months. No roommates, no family we could track down. But I'm guessing he didn't spring out of the ground with no parents."

Kenna nodded. "You think maybe it was a fake identity?"

Detective Langley wandered from the front door down a musty-smelling hallway to the living room. A single recliner, weight bench, a rack of dumbbells and one side table were the only furniture aside from the huge TV on the wall. The kitchen looked just as bare.

Kenna wanted to walk around but needed to see what the cop had to tell them first.

"We dug," Langley said, "but his prints didn't come up with anything else. And neither did running his image through facial recognition."

"And you have to believe the Pentagon did their due diligence on a background check." She glanced around, clocking the cleaned-up spot in the middle of the floor. "So, if there was anything to find, they'd probably have already discovered that he wasn't who he was claiming to be."

Jax chimed in, "Unless the military provided him with the name and background."

"Pretty elaborate." The detective stuck his hands in his pockets. "Why would they do that?"

"Who knows."

Kenna surveyed the floor. "Pretty big pool of blood here." Before it had been cleaned up. "When was he discovered?"

"Hadn't paid his rent, so the manager stopped by. When he didn't answer for a few days in a row, she let herself in." Langley hissed out a breath between clenched teeth. "Nasty stuff."

"Because the killer drained all his blood, or most of it?" She noted three scuff marks at equal points on the floor. "Did he set up some kind of tripod, or stand? Strung the guy up and let him bleed out."

"That's what our techs surmised. No one saw anything, and when we got here the contraption was gone. But they believe the killer set up a device and hung him from it. Slit his throat and a couple of other places and drained his blood onto the floor. Left him lying in it after he died."

"You're right. That is a nasty way to go," Jax said. "Were there signs of torture?"

"None, and he had sticky residue from tape over his mouth left on his cheeks. No duress whatsoever. We believe he knew the killer."

Kenna figured that was one theory. "Or he was resigned to dying. Knew they were coming for him and didn't fight it. What's the point?"

"Would anyone actually do that?" Langley asked. "I figure anyone would fight, even if they're resigned."

Kenna shrugged. "I'd love to talk to his coworkers, or neighbors, or his therapist."

"I did." Langley sounded a little perturbed.

"Good, because we don't have time to do that."

The detective glanced at his watch. "He kept to himself. No friends, and he didn't speak much with his coworkers. Did his job and went home. No indication he was seeing anyone or had a therapist. No cell phone."

Jax wandered to the window. "That you found, or he didn't have one?" He looked back at them.

"By all appearances, he didn't have one." Langley shrugged. "No bill, nothing on his credit card except Door-Dash and all the apps to stream TV and movies on demand. If we was ordering food, he must've had a burner would be my guess."

Kenna looked around, putting her hands on her hips. It didn't matter if this detective found out she was pregnant, and it wasn't like she was keeping it a secret. She needed to stretch out her shoulders and think. Pace a little.

Langley shifted. "What's your interest in this guy?"

She wanted to ask if he knew who she and Jax were, or the kinds of cases she usually worked, but there was nothing about her life lately that was "usual." Instead, she asked him, "Did you come across any other deaths that followed a similar pattern, or did the FBI find any?"

"You think this is one on a list of victims?" His brows raised. "Like a serial killer?"

"More like a hit man," Kenna said. "This guy knew something, or someone wanted to end his life to get him out of the way."

"For reals?" The detective glanced between them. "Like a conspiracy?"

"Trust me," Kenna said. "Stranger things have happened."

She walked down the hall and looked at the bathroom,

then the bedroom. This guy lived a simple life. He didn't accumulate stuff. He didn't have a past. No hobbies, no social media, no life. Just work and his recliner. Sleep. Exercise.

When she reached the living room, she said, "This place seems more like a cover. He hasn't put down roots. He just needs a place to crash while he's on this job. Then when it's over, he moves to the next...assignment."

Langley shrugged. "Great, how does anyone prove that?"

"Probably easier to look for other deaths with a similar MO. Or similar victim profile."

"I'll get right on that." Langley didn't move.

She didn't comment on his belligerence, because in his situation she would've been as skeptical. "Any leads on who did this?"

"No fingerprints, no DNA left behind. Cameras were disabled. No witnesses."

"Sounds like solving it will be an uphill battle." Jax wandered to her side. "And you probably have a stack of open cases on your desk. So we won't keep you from your work."

"I'm not leaving you guys here to lock up." Langley rocked back and forth on those shiny shoes. "How about you tell me what your interest is in this case before I escort you both out."

"We believe Steven Braughton was on a list of victims, possibly one of many." Jax surveyed the markings she'd spotted on the floor. "He's the first we've looked into, and finding the perpetrator isn't currently our primary focus."

Langley eyed them. "Good to know you aren't going to show up at my office with a lead that will hand me the killer."

Kenna said, "Don't rule that out. We do good work."

The detective smiled slightly. "Noted."

Jax said, "We don't believe the murder was connected to Steven's work at the Pentagon, or that it's connected to some vast government conspiracy."

"At least not as far as the usual clandestine operations go," Kenna added. She sort of disagreed with her husband on that one, but Langley didn't need to dig in something involving *Dominatus* and end up getting himself killed. "So watch your back, make sure you're not under surveillance, and just stick to your regular duties."

"Interesting." The detective made a note on his phone.

Jax said, "If you come across any deaths you believe are connected, could you send the information our way?"

Langley nodded.

"Thanks." Kenna returned his nod. "We'd appreciate it."

"What other cases are you working?" He glanced between them, a passive expression on his face.

This guy was a solid cop who didn't let his emotions get mixed up with his work. She wasn't sure how he'd be with a victim and what level of empathy he'd have to draw from, but hoped he had compassion in his arsenal.

Kenna said, "Nothing that intersects with this so far as we know."

Except that the two men in Boston who'd kidnapped teenage girls had a military connection. This case had a military connection. It was only the bombing that didn't fit. Unless it was the piece that made it all go together into some kind of grand plan.

"I suppose that's some kind of answer." Langley herded them to the door and locked it after they'd assembled in the hall. He handed over his business card. "Don't forget to call if you come up with something."

Kenna nodded, and Jax shook the guy's hand.

Langley headed for the stairs, and she looked at the other doors on this floor.

Jax touched her back. "Want to talk to the neighbors?"

"The police would've done it." She shook her head. "I'd rather help the lawyers fight the charges than investigate a murder when I already know who did it."

"Your ghost?"

"He's not *my* anything."

"Sorry. You know what I mean."

Kenna gave him a quick hug. "Let's get to the car. Call Maizie and see what she's come up with."

He pulled out his phone. "I'll call a friend at the FBI and find out who's investigating this. They can tell me if a connection has been made to any other cases."

"Good idea." Kenna didn't imagine it would be easy to do that. "The victims won't fit a pattern in demographics, physical features, or geography. The murders were probably all committed using a different method. Could be there's no way for anyone to connect them."

"Or he left no prints and no DNA at any scene, and that's what we can use to nail him."

Kenna glanced at him, one brow raised. "Wanna let me in on how that works? Because if you can't prove he did it, how can you prove he did it?"

"Exactly." He shrugged, and they headed down the carpeted staircase.

"Right."

Jax chuckled. "I just mean that the absence of evidence is sometimes enough of a connection to at least build a profile of this guy."

"A profile of what? He's good at what he does. That's all we know apart from the body count we're going to gather. Probably won't even be all of them." She could see him in her mind, staring at her through that window. "He's sick and twisted. He also apparently disappears better than anyone I've ever hunted. Someone has to be funding this guy's ability to remain under the radar, or simply protecting him. Someone with serious resources."

"Are we certain it's not Petyr, or President Tetherton?"

"I don't see how we can rule them out. Apart from the fact their fear that all the offspring would be killed seemed genuine enough."

Jax stopped on the top step outside, where it had started to rain a little. He clicked the button on his key fob to start the car engine. Across the street, the headlights flashed and it started.

Someone straightened beside Langley's car, but they were Caucasian and not the detective.

"It's...him." Kenna barely managed to choke the words out.

"Stay here." Jax took off running toward him.

The ghost spun and sprinted away down the street.

Over by the car, Jax yelled, "Langley is down!"

Kenna pulled out her phone to call 911 and headed for the detective.

She found him slumped against his car, a trail of blood down the outside of the car door. He touched a hand to the blood soaking his shirt over his abdomen, blinking in shock.

She peeled off her coat and pressed it against the wound. "Hang on."

Chapter Twenty-One

Kenna glanced down the street where Jax had raced after the killer. She wanted to pull her phone out and call him, but that would only be a distraction in a situation where he needed total focus. *Lord.* She didn't want to contemplate something happening to him. Anytime he was feeling protective, she wasn't going to argue with him needing to ensure her safety. She knew *exactly* what it felt like to swallow back the fear that someone she cared about could be hurt and run down a deadly killer.

Sirens in the distance got louder.

"Cavalry is almost here." Should she get Langley to lie down on the ground? "Stay with me, Detective."

His head lolled to the side, his skin clammy. He caught himself like had to drag his consciousness back to the forefront and lifted his head on a sharp intake of breath.

"There you are." She touched her fingers to his neck and felt his pulse. "Hang in there. We'll get you patched up."

The first cop car sped around the corner, followed by two more and then an ambulance.

"You're gonna be famous in a minute," she said. "The cop who got stabbed by a serial killer and survived."

He eyed her, his expression glassy.

"But you've gotta be alive to enjoy it."

She saw a tiny note of humor in his expression.

"Langley!" The first cop raced over with thundering footsteps and all his gear creaking on his belt. "Step back, ma'am."

"I'm not letting go of pressure on his wound. He's bleeding out." She shifted enough he'd see she was pregnant, which in most people's world made her instantly less of a threat. Clearly not the perpetrator. Where was Jax?

She glanced that way again.

"Let me." He tried to shove her hands aside.

"I've got it. No sense in both of us being covered in blood. The EMTs are almost here."

The cop knelt on Jordan's other side.

Kenna leaned on one hand and used the other to pat the detective's cheek. "Stay with me, Langley. If you're going to fall asleep, I want you to do it where medical professionals can make sure you wake up again."

More sirens on the street. The EMTs raced over with their duffel bags, pushing the cot. They crouched either side of her, and the other officer got out of the way. Kenna said, "Male, forties. Strong pulse. Single stab wound. No other injuries that I know of. It was quick, and I didn't see it happen."

"Got it." The EMT took over putting pressure on with her jacket, but he needed to see the wound. The guy was in his thirties, and moved with competence, instructing his partner. Probably a paramedic, or a guy with years of experience in trauma care.

"Ma'am?" The cop held his hand out. "Let's step aside."

She grabbed his wrist, and he helped her up. Kenna immediately stretched her back and shoulders. "Thanks." She bent and brushed off the knees of her maternity pants and checked again for Jax. "My husband chased after the suspect."

"Recount for me what happened." The officer pulled out a notebook, a frown drawing his thick dark brows together. He didn't like what had happened but, so far at least, didn't seem to have any animosity toward her. Right now, until he had the facts, he seemed to be reserving judgment.

Kenna explained that she and Jax were private investigators looking into a few cases locally, and that Langley had been given permission—as opposed to what he'd told them about being ordered—to talk to them about this case.

As she was talking, she glanced down the street, saying another silent prayer for her husband's protection, and spotted him walking back. She motioned toward Jax. "There he is."

The EMTs lifted Langley onto the stretcher and pushed it toward the ambulance. With an oxygen mask over his face, she couldn't tell if he was awake, but at least no one was doing chest compressions. The guy would need surgery, though. Or so she figured. Hopefully, the knife hadn't nicked anything important that would jeopardize his life.

The officer standing with her said, "Any idea why someone would show up today and stab Detective Langley?"

She watched Jax approach. He shook his head.

She didn't glance at the cop, but said, "It's far more likely that he was targeted because someone has a beef with him than any reason I might know. Other than that, we came here to the scene to take a look and it's possible the killer doesn't want Langley solving it now. He wants to stall the case long enough for it to go cold."

A killer who already got away with his crime, left no fingerprints or DNA evidence behind, and knew enough of what was going on to show up here and stab the detective? She didn't like this at all.

She also didn't want to be a target, not while carrying a baby. But why would the ghost have tried to kill Langley today? Also, why not deal a blow that was certain to end with death? A stab wound to the abdomen was messy and bled a lot, but there were far more expedient ways to kill someone.

Kenna needed to know *why*.

Jax came close enough to give her a quick side hug. "He got into a silver compact, Maryland license plate." He gave the officer the information.

"Nice." Kenna silently thanked the Lord. That was a lot preferable to him actually fighting the killer. Or being kidnapped.

Her arm on his waist tightened, but Jax didn't react to it. He knew how she felt because they had the same fears.

"Are you able to ID this person you saw run from the scene?" The cop glanced between them.

Jax asked Kenna, "You have that picture?"

She dug out her phone, curious that he wanted to let the officer know this tidbit of information. That she'd created a composite image of the killer she'd met on that platform. She pulled it up and showed him. "Was this the man you saw?"

He stared at it, and the cop moved close enough to see as well.

"The hair is longer," Jax said. "He has the same profile, because he glanced back at me and I saw his jawline. But

I'm not sure I'd be able to say yes definitively enough to swear it's him in court."

"That something you do often?" the officer said.

"I used to be an FBI agent in Phoenix."

"And I used to be an FBI agent in Salt Lake City." Kenna smiled. "But a much longer time has passed since I quit."

"All right." The officer nodded. "Here's hoping Langley can confirm it's this guy who stabbed him, or if it was someone else. Can I get a copy of that?"

Kenna nodded. "Give me your email and I'll send it over."

After she'd done that, they exchanged basic information and phone numbers with the officer and were able to leave.

"What is it?" Jax glanced over as they headed for their vehicle. "Do we need a new way to find out if other cases exist that look like they were done by the same guy?"

Kenna chewed over that for a second, thinking it through. "Yeah, probably. I just don't get why he kills Langley. He left him alive. What was the point in that?"

"Because you're the one on his hit list so he came here, and it was a crime of opportunity?" Jax clicked the locks on the car, but it was already open. He held her door for her. "Or do you think Petyr and the president are right about you being safe because you're pregnant?"

She slid into the passenger seat, and he went around, climbing in the driver's side. As he pulled away from the curb and navigated through the sea of cops who'd showed up because one of their own was hurt, she said, "I don't want to think that Langley was targeted because of me."

Jax entered the RV park address into the dash screen of the car and then pulled out, following the directions home.

"Ramon and Zeyla are going to meet us at home so we can regroup."

"We can ask them why the man they're looking for showed up where we are and they didn't." Given a man nearly died, and still wasn't out of the woods, she held off trying to be funny. "I don't want to know how the two of them will deal with this. They're going to take it out on him when they find him, and we need this guy in custody, not dead."

"Maybe it's one of those *Dominatus* lookalikes running around, trying to throw us off."

"Consider me thrown." She shifted in the seat to try and get more comfortable.

Jax squeezed her knee. They drove the rest of the way in silence and within the hour pulled into the RV park. Ramon's car was parked on the lane in front of their RV, leaving the space for them to pull into. Both he and Zeyla sat on the plastic Adirondack chairs beside the front door, and she had Jolene on her lap, stroking the cat in long swipes.

Kenna pushed open the door and tried to climb out gracefully, feeling huge even though she didn't look it. "So you're a cat person." She wandered over, and Jax went in the storage unit under the RV, where he pulled out two folding chairs.

Zeyla shrugged. "Never said I wasn't."

The door to the RV wasn't open.

"Did you pick the lock?" Kenna asked.

"Trade secret."

Jax chuckled, unfolding a chair for Kenna to sit on. "She texted me, and I remotely unlocked the door."

Zeyla shrugged again.

"Sit here." Ramon shot up out of the chair. "I'll take the

uncomfortable seat." He looked like he wanted to pick her up and set her in the chair so she didn't have to expend the energy sitting.

Kenna held on to his arm, much like the cop who'd helped her to her feet and used her hold on him to ease down slowly. She stretched out her feet and let go of a long breath. Then realized she needed to pee again. "Never mind. I'll be back." She levered herself up out of the chair. "Figure out how to resolve all this while I'm in there. We need a plan."

She let herself in the RV and found a sweater, since she'd given her jacket to the detective bleeding out. Kenna set her gun in the lockbox in the closet because she didn't need it on her here with three people around to protect her, then took care of the pressing business that came with there being a baby sitting on her bladder.

Her phone rang before she toweled off her hands, but she got to it before it quit ringing. The number was local, but not one she'd stored in her phone. "Banbury Investigations."

"I told them I was calling my lawyer. They want me to tell them everything, how I planted that bomb, and how I tried to kill the Croatian president."

Kenna knew the voice. It was one of the lawyers from Hann, Anthony & Associates. "And about how you didn't mean to kill a child, but you're so very sorry about the collateral damage."

The caller gasped. "Who wouldn't be sorry? But that doesn't mean I did it."

"I need to know everything about that think tank," Kenna said. "All of it. I need information if I'm going to make connections, and right now I've got a bunch of nothing."

"We sent you that packet."

"Someone needs to fill in the gaps." Kenna braced a hand against the wall in the RV, holding the phone to her ear.

"Then come and see me. I'm sure I'll be easy to find. I'm the one behind bars."

The line went dead.

Chapter Twenty-Two

K enna didn't have any business clothes that accommodated her current situation, so she opted to pull a white button-down shirt on over a T-shirt and leave the buttons open. She had a pair of black slacks with an elastic waist, but no matter what, this was going to be uncomfortable. Thankfully, she still fit in her shoes and didn't have to walk around with swollen feet all the time.

"You'll need to wait in here." The corrections officer opened the door for her.

The room had a single table, a lot like an interrogation room. Door on both sides, four chairs—two on either side.

"Thanks." She'd left her jacket and everything else back at the entrance with security. No one could bring a weapon into a prison, or any electronic device. She'd printed out the image of the ghost she was looking for and had that in her pocket but nothing else.

She spotted movement through the window to her right first and remained standing. Felicity Wuest shuffled down the hall, wearing orange and handcuffed at her hands and feet. Not one of the lawyers she'd had close contact with, but if this woman had information Kenna could use to help her, then this trip would be worth it.

The officer pushed the door open, and Felicity entered, her hair hanging over her shoulders a darker blond than it'd been in Phoenix. No makeup, and she wore glasses with black rims. He tugged back the chair, and she sat.

Kenna said thank you, and he was about to say something when she folded her arms and spoke over him. "I'd like time with my client now."

Both of them waited for him to shut the door.

Felicity lifted her gaze and looked at Kenna. "I didn't know you were pregnant."

"Don't worry about me."

Felicity shuddered. "They killed Lisa *and* Beth."

"I'm sorry." Kenna bit her lip. These were the kind of people who had signed up for a lifelong fight with *Dominatus*. But that didn't mean they wanted to end it gunned down as criminals. "What happened?"

Felicity closed her eyes and shuddered.

"Why don't you start with the think tank?" Kenna slid back a chair and sat across from the younger woman, who probably would've taken the position of paralegal or admin assistant rather than one of the lawyers. She was what someone might think of as the weak link and yet out of the lawyers she was the one who'd survived long enough to be put in prison. "Who invited you all to participate in the think tank?"

"It came from the government. We fully vetted the invitation, met with them and did our due diligence on checking them out. It seemed legit!" She gasped but hadn't raised her voice.

If this got heated, the officer would come in and shut down their conversation.

Kenna patted the center of the table. "You did what you knew to do. We've all been duped by...*them*."

Felicity scrunched up her nose, blinking back tears that moistened her eyes.

"You said the government hired you for it. Was it the military, or just the federal government?" Kenna sat back in her chair.

"The military, or so we thought. It was supposed to be about coming up with scenarios to predict how someone might try and destabilize the country. There was field work, research, and drafting extensive plans. And we had a deadline, so it all had to be done within just a few weeks. The director in charge told us that the president wanted it before the treaty with the Croatians."

Kenna nodded. "Can you describe this director, or tell me who he is?"

"We had no idea who he was and didn't meet him until we showed up, so we were trying to get his fingerprints or a DNA sample from him so we could run it and find out if he was who he said he was. There was no way to find out if the name he gave us was real."

"You didn't manage to get an ID?"

Felicity shook her head. "We couldn't get the sample. Every day they searched us on the way out the door, and we weren't able to take anything out with us. Not even a tissue."

"I might have you describe him for a sketch artist. Would you be willing to do that?"

"Not like I have anything else to do." Felicity tried to roll her shoulders, but the cuffs securing her to the table made that difficult.

"Everything you've told me so far is really helpful."

"I need a real lawyer." Felicity shot her a look. "No offense."

"None taken." She leaned forward a little. "I'll do what I can."

"You're pregnant."

"I'm not going to hide, and I have plenty of people around to protect me and to do the dangerous stuff so I can stay safe." Kenna glanced at the guard in the hall, watching them. She wondered if he could read lips. "I've had enough of being threatened by these people, but I know I can't fight them."

"We thought we were doing good." Felicity shook her head.

"It was a setup for the bombing," Kenna said. "So the feds would come up with enough evidence to detain you all."

"Exactly."

"Do you know all of what was in the packet I received?" Felicity nodded.

"I wouldn't have much without it," Kenna admitted. She didn't want to explain about her White House meeting, or the other job she'd been requested to do. This woman needed to hope that they were doing everything they could, and not that *Dominatus* was manipulating them. But Kenna needed to ask about the pictures in the packet.

She said, "Can you tell me what all those personnel dossiers were? The images are of real people, but it seemed like their details were made up."

Felicity exhaled. "We needed a way to communicate when we realized the situation was turning against us. The images are all embedded with information. You need the right kind of program and a key."

They'd already given over one key, but all it had done

was open the files. "The same key that gave us access to the packet? That key?"

Felicity leaned forward, keeping her voice low. "Backward. The same code, but backward. You should be able to find the real information for each of the people embedded in the files with that."

"Who are they?" Kenna asked. "Is each one part of the new generation?"

"What are you talking about?"

"The offspring *Dominatus* created? Are they the children?" The ones on the ghost's hit list.

"They're images the think tank put together. I don't even know if they're real people, but the notes embedded in them are."

Kenna frowned. "One of them is one of the kids, for sure. I was just at his house. Although now it's a crime scene."

Felicity flinched. "What's going on?"

"He was murdered by a killer who works for *Dominatus*. I know there's a hit list, and you have a list of people and I figured they were connected." But if they weren't...

If the lawyers knew nothing about the offspring, or how they connected, it made no sense.

Felicity stared at the door for a moment, her gaze shifting. As though trying to puzzle this out the same way Kenna was.

"Okay. Here's what we know." Kenna figured they should start from the beginning. "You were hired to come up with a scenario that gave the feds evidence to arrest you."

"An assassination plot that was stage one of a plan to destabilize the country."

"But they're already in charge." The president was part

of *Dominatus.* "So I don't think the president is a target. They won on that count, murdering the previous one and putting her in charge."

"Assassinating the president was never part of the plan." Felicity shook her head. "The scenario had the Canadian prime minister as the next target, followed by the United Kingdom PM."

"Let me guess," Kenna said, "whoever is installed as their replacement is part of *Dominatus,* so now they control three major world powers." She didn't like the sound of that at all.

"That was never their aim before now, so I'm not sure why it would've changed. They were always content to operate in the shadows, to turn things in their favor slowly. And never through such overt means."

"If someone is killing the next generation, it could be another part of the plan." Kenna paused. "Or it's a distraction meant to keep me from figuring out what they're really after."

She wouldn't put it past Petyr or the president to try and distract her with a threat. Especially right now. Even if the ghost was out there killing people, it could still be a deadly plan to keep Kenna and her people occupied so they didn't work out what *Dominatus* was really doing.

Kenna said, "What do you know about the *Imperatoris* vote?"

"They have a few contenders for the top spot," Felicity said. "One is the Croatian president. If he becomes the head of the European Union in the next few years, no one will be surprised. *Dominatus* would have a foothold there as well."

Kenna pushed out a long breath. "I didn't want to get

involved in international politics." She shook her head. "Who wants the Croatian president dead?"

"Anyone running against him for *Imperatoris* would be my guest. They're all in a battle for power, with differing views on how it should be run."

Kenna figured the person who wanted control of most of the governments of the world was the top contender for the suspect behind all of this. The bombing and the lawyers being framed, the murders and anything else going on right now. "Do you have a list of suspects?"

Felicity smirked, but it seemed kind of sad. "That's what they are. And yet I'm the one going to prison for life."

Kenna wanted to tell her to watch her back, but what she needed was evidence that they'd been framed so she could get them released. "How many of you were arrested?"

"Three." Felicity's eyes rimmed with tears. "Someone knows who they all are, but their name will be on the list. If you track them down, how do you know you're not staring the culprit in the face?"

Kenna had friends who would track down each one of the suspects, assassinate them all, and head home to celebrate a job well done. She wasn't going to call Preston Lightwood or anyone with Miami Security International—or what was left of them.

That might have been exactly what the lawyers were also planning. It put Zeyla and Amara's motives into the "suspect" column. All because Kenna had been ignoring the fight and trying to live her life on her terms.

"Would killing anyone vying for *Imperatoris* even solve the problem?" Kenna asked. "Someone else would just fill the void and take control of the organization."

"So instead of someone who parses out information to individual groups, we've got a unifying figure. Let's call him

Hitler for the sake of this scenario." All the upset Felicity had been feeling a second ago was gone now. "What guarantee do any of us have that Hitler is even the worst option to be the new head of *Dominatus*? What if we choose wrong and end up making it all so much more terrifying?"

"Does anyone know who they all are?"

"I suppose they do, among themselves they're aware of who the competition is. I figure that's why one is trying to kill the competition and framing us for the attempt. They've probably got someone else out there pulling off parts two and three of the plan."

"And if they're all taken out, then we have no idea if we've unleashed a worse monster on the world."

Felicity shrugged. "We don't know who's in the wings, holding out for the right time to take over."

"Is Petyr the best option?" Maybe it wouldn't be so bad if the man who considered himself to be her father was the leader of *Dominatus*. It could be awful, but not nearly as horrifying as the alternative possibilities. That was the essence of what Felicity had said.

"I suppose if I'm in here, it doesn't really matter to me. I've got other problems."

"I'll decode the images," Kenna said. "We'll do the work to prove you were all framed. You don't need to spend the rest of your life in here."

Felicity stood, the chains jingling as she rose. "Just donate some books to the prison library. I'll need something to do." She turned to the side and yelled for the guard.

He escorted her out, leaving Kenna alone in the room, trying to figure out this whole mess.

Time to get to work.

Chapter Twenty-Three

Kenna pushed out the front door, already dialing Maizie's number. She blinked at the sun peeking out between gray clouds. The prison parking lot consisted of rows of mid-range cars, nothing fancy, all standard colors. In the center of the lot, Jax walked toward her, while Ramon and Zeyla waited by the two cars parked side by side.

Maizie answered the phone before the first ring. "How did it go?"

"Tell me about the wildfire first, and what's going on there." Kenna tucked the phone between her cheek and shoulder while she put her sweater back on over her business clothes.

"Firefighters came through the property, and Elizabeth made them all coffee. They ate lunch on the lawn."

"Did you talk to them, or stay in the Airstream?"

"I stayed inside, just in case. I would've been fine meeting them but given everything going on we had no idea if one might have been a *Dominatus* plant." Maizie laughed a little. "Cabot ran out and hopped around them all, begging to be petted. I think she got a couple of pieces of sandwich. Seemed like they really liked her."

"That's nice."

Jax stopped in front of her but said nothing. Kenna put the call on speaker and said, "Maizie, can you use the same code we got that unlocked the packet and reverse it? There's information contained in the images that were included. Apparently, they aren't specific people and the dossiers are fake."

Jax frowned. "But we know one was a murder victim."

"Exactly." Kenna didn't know what to make of it. "Maybe she didn't know or couldn't say. But either way, she told me the images weren't part of it. Like they're just stock photos, or AI images, or something." Kenna shook her head. "But they're supposed to be real people? I'm unclear on that, but I do know there is information embedded in the images."

Kenna held out her hand for Jax, and they walked toward the others. "I say we keep trying to figure out who they are anyway, as well as who hired the lawyers. Hopefully as a result of whatever comes from you entering the code backward."

"I'll have to resurrect a program I have that detects steganography. I'll call you when I have the information and upload it to the folder."

"Got it. Thanks, Maze." She hung up and pocketed her phone.

"There's a diner nearby." Ramon didn't look happy, and she had no idea why that was.

Kenna nodded. "Good idea."

She almost told Jax that she would ride with Ramon, just to see if he wanted to open up to her one on one, but didn't. Still, the fear that remained so strong it was almost like she could taste it wouldn't let her be even that far from her husband. So many things could happen in a short drive with him in another car.

"You okay?" He tucked a strand of hair behind her ear.

She looked out the front windshield of the car and saw that they were at the diner already. "I need to pray, but I'm all right."

Jax leaned over and kissed her. "For the record, I'm *not* all right." It seemed he could find the reaction amusing, though. "I thought for sure there would be some kind of prison break while you were in there, or a riot. You'd end up delivering the baby early in a federal prison." He shook his head.

"It's not crazy. My mind won't stop coming up with worst-case scenarios wherein something happens to one of us. It didn't help that you ran after a dangerous killer all by yourself with no backup."

Jax patted his hip. "I have backup. His name is Sig."

"Sounds like a real tough guy." She smiled, so grateful for a moment of levity.

Before she could open the door, Ramon did it for her. "You guys good?"

Kenna climbed out. "I was thinking the same about you."

Zeyla stood by the back corner of the car, frowning. "I don't think I wanna have any babies."

"Now, specifically, or ever in general?" Kenna asked.

"It looks uncomfortable."

Kenna smiled. "Your assessment isn't incorrect, and I'm not even that big."

Ramon said, "The internet says it's normal not to show much when it's your first, and if you have a long torso."

Kenna glanced at Ramon, one brow raised.

He shrugged. "I google."

Zeyla laughed aloud. "I'm going to buy you a baby book so you can read up on the things you shouldn't be asking Kenna about."

Ramon walked ahead of them with Jax, while Zeyla stuck by Kenna. All of them watched the parking lot and the street around them.

Kenna spotted Zeyla checking out the roof of a neighboring building. "So, you don't have a burning desire to take an accelerated course and become a midwife in the next month?"

Zeyla held the door. "Ask Mom. I'd be surprised if she hasn't already done it. Just in case."

"I'm on board with 'just in case' right now. The more variables we can eliminate, the better."

Kenna planned to keep thanking God for every moment of safety, where each of them was injury-free, and she had no pregnancy complications. So many things could crop up, some that would require bed rest or even hospitalization. Not that she couldn't work cases from her bed in the RV, but Kenna intended to enjoy her health for as long as she had it.

The hostess led them to a corner booth, and Kenna sat with her back to the wall. It wasn't even lunchtime, and she was already exhausted. "Today is going to be a nap day."

"Good." Ramon nodded. "While you're doing that, Zeyla and I will work this case."

"I took a look at the photos from the packet." Zeyla looked at her water glass rather than at them. She and Ramon sat with space between them, unlike Kenna and Jax, who took any opportunity to be tucked against each other for solidarity and reassurance.

The two of them, across the table, were different than

they'd been before. They seemed to have reached some kind of consensus. Like new police detective partners, or coworkers forced to team up. Whether that developed into more later, time would tell.

Zeyla continued, "I know at least three of them. I've met them."

"Are they offspring?"

"In the sense that you and I are, probably. They're...in the program."

"Not resistance?"

Zeyla shook her head. "It doesn't pay to be resistance these days. Not since that bombing in Paris, and now with the lawyers all getting rounded up and arrested." She hesitated, then said, "By the way, they asked me to join that think tank as well."

Ramon's head whipped around to her, but he didn't say anything.

Zeyla's confessions seemed like such a tenuous thing, so it was a good call on his part. If Kenna said the wrong thing, or spoke at the wrong time, she could break Zeyla's intention to tell the truth.

"I didn't realize that's what the lawyers were into until Maizie sent me the photos. The name was the same. They emailed a few months ago, and called me a bunch of times." Zeyla shook her head. "Everyone knows I signed up with you guys. I might not be resistance anymore technically, but I'm also not going to give up and do nothing."

Kenna sat back while the server delivered the meals they'd ordered. She'd chosen the first cheeseburger she saw, and it smelled good. She took a bite to try and get her stomach to back down with the hunger pangs and swallowed. "Risky move."

"Signing on with you, or letting people know about it?" Zeyla stabbed a bite of her salmon salad.

Kenna had taken another bite. She shrugged. "Both."

Zeyla nodded, chewing. Ramon glanced at her again. He had a huge roast beef sandwich and a mountain of fries. Jax had ordered a bowl of chili.

Kenna took one of her fries and dipped it in the sauce, swirling it a bit so she could try his lunch. "That's spicy."

He grinned. "It's good."

"Hmm. Maybe I need to dial up the heat when I make chili." And then load it with sour cream for her so she didn't get heartburn as bad.

Jax said, "Maizie is getting us the information from those images. What else do we have? The ghost should be our top priority, right? We need to catch him before he hurts someone else."

They couldn't put that much pressure on their ability to track him down, or they'd feel responsible if he did hurt or kill someone else. She already felt bad enough that he'd targeted Detective Langley.

Zeyla said, "We have a few cases we believe are connected. I don't think he was responsible for anything to do with Samantha Ambrose's death, but I do believe he was tasked with cleanup once we figured out what happened."

Kenna nodded. "Right. Since he showed up at the hospital to kill Megan Tilley."

"He also murdered the boyfriend," Zeyla added. "Carl Allerton was released on bail and found dead less than twelve hours later. Someone slit his throat and left him in an alley."

The server paused by the table, then turned and walked away instead of refilling their water glasses. Jax set his by

Kenna's and took her empty one. He set it at the edge of the table.

"Then he hightailed it to DC to catch Langley on the street," Zeyla continued. "It's almost impressive."

Kenna took a sip. "He's working for someone who wants to take out the competition and secure the vote to be the new *Imperatoris*."

"I know." Zeyla sighed, as if that information was obvious. "I mean, soon as they tried to take out Petyr, it was pretty obvious."

If she knew that, then Kenna had more she wanted to run by her cousin. "Petyr thinks he's my father."

"He wishes." Zeyla's expression turned guarded.

"You don't think it's true."

"I think he can give us a DNA sample to test if he wants to prove it." Zeyla shrugged. "Other than that, I don't trust one single word out of any of their mouths."

"Agreed." But she'd been suckered in plenty of times. Reprogrammed. Twisted around mentally and emotionally until she didn't know which way was up. But if all that led her back to a tighter hold on her faith, on the constant need to trust God more every moment, maybe it wasn't a complete waste.

Her captivity would never be a good thing, but it could be a redeemed thing.

Ramon ran the crust end of his sandwich through the juice on his plate. "If I didn't know he was dead, I'd wonder if it was that Count of Shadows guy. But he's dead."

"Or so we think."

Ramon glanced at Zeyla. "Again with that?"

"We've all come up against one of their lookalikes. Files can be fabricated. Did we really ask for credentials and fully vet them, or were you just kidnapped in a limo and—"

"Been there," Kenna muttered.

Jax shook his head.

"—you couldn't verify it was him," Zeyla finished. "By the time I saw him, he was mist."

"It's the concussion talking." Ramon shoved the last of his sandwich in his mouth, indicating the discussion was over.

Zeyla wiped her mouth a napkin. "Sure, the photo you saw later that Maizie got for you *said* that was Major General Schnell, and it was the same guy. But do we really know for sure that it's him? Maybe it was a decoy."

Ramon eyed her. "How about we go after the dangerous killer we know isn't a decoy first."

"I'm just saying." Zeyla shrugged.

Jax turned to Kenna. "Is that what we were like in the beginning?"

Kenna grinned. "It's more fun on this side of the table."

Chapter Twenty-Four

Her phone rang as she was sliding out of the booth. *Baltimore PD* flashed on her screen. "Kenna Banbury."

Jax held out a hand, and she accepted his assistance getting to her feet.

"This is Lieutenant Parse. I work with Detective Langley."

"How is he?" Kenna walked with her husband and their friends to the entrance of the restaurant, a haze of grease and smoke in the air.

"All patched up. It'll be a long recovery, and he'll ride a desk for a while, but he'll be back to it soon enough. He says that's because of you."

"All I did was put pressure on it."

"Sounds like enough to me," Parse said. "So when Langley told me he scratched the guy who attacked him and to let you know we're running the DNA on a rush, I figured you'd want to know that there's another body."

Kenna stopped before the door. "Someone else was killed?"

"All I know is the victim is older, and he's in a motel. I'll text you the address if you're interested."

"Why hand me a case?"

"Langley said you were asking about other deaths connected to the scene he took you to."

"Are you the superior who ordered him to show us around?"

"We all have our jobs." Parse paused. "Who I am doesn't really matter in the grand scheme. What matters is getting guys like this off the street."

"We agree about that." And now she was pretty sure this lieutenant might be connected to *Dominatus*.

"Figure we agree about more than just that, but who has the time to find out?"

Kenna was tracking with him. She'd never been a cop, but there was still a camaraderie between people who solved crimes. Except for the animosity between the police or feds and the private investigators they considered hacks, she figured they were still all on the same team. If he'd looked her up, or just took his detective's word for it, either way it got her the access she needed.

"The scene is secure?" she asked him. "You know I'm pregnant, right?"

"Cops all over, no sign of the killer. It's secure, and they know you're coming."

That was a little presumptuous. She could go take that nap she'd been thinking about and send Ramon and Zeyla, but Kenna wanted a look at the scene herself, and it wouldn't take long. "We're on our way."

"Sending the address now."

"How long do you think to get the DNA results?"

"Who knows, but Langley said tell you first."

Kenna said, "Tell him thanks." She hung up and turned

to Jax, Ramon, and Zeyla, explaining there was another death connected to the case.

"Field trip." Zeyla pushed the door open and scanned outside for a second, like a bodyguard.

Ramon shook his head, following her out.

Kenna went out with Jax right behind her. "The lieutenant told me that Langley scratched the ghost when he was getting stabbed."

Ramon glanced back at her right as he reached the sidewalk. "It's what I'd do. Even if you're gonna get murdered, you might as well make sure the cops can find out who did it. Except in my case, it would be you guys."

The traffic noise swelled along with thoughts about losing any of them. All of it rushed at her in a way she hadn't been expecting. "Maybe don't get murdered, though. Yeah?"

Zeyla said, "It's not on my bucket list."

"Isn't on mine, either." Ramon lifted his hands, which opened the sides of his jacket so she got a look at the gun holstered on his hip. "So don't worry about that, mama."

Jax just shook his head. "Good to know no one is planning to get murdered."

"I'm more worried about what we can't plan for," Kenna said. "But that's why we pray. So we can cover the things we don't have control over."

Ramon looked like he might have something to say about that, but Zeyla pulled on the door handle of his car. "Let's go."

Kenna buckled her seatbelt. "The cops are putting a rush on the DNA test."

"Great." Jax started the car and pulled out. "If it gets a match to someone in the system and isn't either falsified or squashed by someone who doesn't want the assailant's identity to get out."

"I'm trying to live on the bright side, where there is truth—and time enough to take a nap."

"Sounds good to me."

Kenna shifted in the seat so she could look at him without tweaking her neck. "Are you really all right with everything that's going on?"

"No way. Not at all." He shook his head, his jaw tight. But he wasn't angry. It looked more like frustration. "I'm not okay with murder, or bombings, or kidnappings, or us being involved with any of that."

"Uh, you know what we do for a living, right?"

"You know what I liked? Solving crimes at the kitchen table, from Wyoming."

Kenna smiled. "That was good. I mean, hands on and in person gives you so much more insight into what really happened, and nothing beats interrogating a suspect yourself. But watching the video and reading all the case notes? Why can't we just solve crimes from home?"

"You wouldn't get bored?"

"I don't think that happens with work and a baby, and a crazy extended family. Ramon and Zeyla can do the legwork. If we need Amara, or Bruce, or Maizie, they can pitch in."

"While we stay home?"

"Right now, that sounds *amazing*." She closed her eyes.

"Because you get to take a nap?"

She chuckled. "It sounds...settled. In a way I haven't been in a long time. More settled than even marrying you or knowing we'll be a family of three in a few months."

"I know what you mean." He pulled onto the street. "Guess this is where the murder was."

Two Baltimore Police patrol cars were parked on the side of the street, the officers standing at the hood of one car in conversation. A white van with FORENSICS on the side in big letters across the street indicated evidence collection was currently in process.

Ramon and Zeyla hung back while Kenna and Jax approached the officers and introduced themselves.

One of the officers nodded, set his travel mug on the hood of the car, and headed for the door. "The lieutenant said you were coming."

She followed him up the front walk of the squat house with peeling stucco siding and the odd missing roof tile. The lawn had been maintained and wasn't all weeds like the neighbors, which made it more impressive they'd managed to fight that battle and win. "The body has been taken away already?"

"Murder happened at least four days ago, maybe as much as a week. One of the neighbors saw the mail piling up and knocked on the door. Spotted him when they looked in the window."

"Three notches in the floor and all the blood spilled?"

The officer held the door open. "Guess that's why you're here."

Kenna stepped inside the house and smelled what hadn't yet aired out. Of course, she didn't have anything with her to put under her nose so she didn't have to suffer her stomach roiling every time she got a whiff.

"Oh boy." Jax made a face. "The victim kept the heat cranked. Either that, or the killer cranked it before he left."

The forensic tech in the living room, crouched in one corner, wore a full Tyvek suit and face mask. Currently collecting evidence from beside the couch using tweezers and putting it in a small clear plastic container with a screw top lid.

"What was that?" The officer glanced between her and Jax.

"Turning up the heat messes with time of death." Jax wandered down the hall to the panel on the wall. "It's warm in here. Eighty-four."

"Plenty of folks keep their homes warm." The officer didn't seem curious about the fact.

"Sure," Kenna said. "But it also speeds up decomposition so it has to be considered as a factor. The killer could've turned up the heat when they left and made it look like this person was dead a lot longer than they really were."

She glanced around the living room. There weren't any photos or art on the walls, and only a couch and recliner. One remote. TV somewhere out of sight from where she stood.

Nothing personal whatsoever.

She turned back to the officer. "What can you tell us about the victim?"

"Older male, sixties we figure, but it's hard to tell. Killed in the same manner as the other crime you're investigating."

"Just looking into. Not necessarily trying to solve." Because they already knew who the perpetrator was. The next task was to catch up to him before he killed someone else and get him in police custody. After that, he'd be bound for an institution that knew how to deal with the criminally insane.

The officer frowned. "Anyhow, he was strung up and drained of blood. Left dead in the pool on the floor. No indications he'd been tortured apart from the kill itself. None of the neighbors saw anything."

Jax said, "Any idea what the victim did for a living?"

She was wondering that as well. Whether the guy was employed by the Pentagon.

"No idea. The neighbors never spoke to him, never saw him wearing a uniform, or had any clue what he did. He's lived here a few months, but that's it. Pays cash to the landlord. Nothing personal in the house. All the mail is junk for the previous resident."

"Do you have a photo of him?" Kenna asked. "I doubt I'll know who he is, but I prefer to cross any possibilities off the list that I can."

The officer went to the forensic tech and took the iPad the tech handed him. He swiped through the screens and showed her the crime scene images with the body.

Kenna took the iPad, looking first at the scene. "It matches the other death. Definitely the same killer, because there's no way anyone knows enough to be a copycat." She enlarged the man's face with two fingers.

"Any idea who he is?"

Kenna didn't want to lie. "I've seen him before, but I don't know what his name is." At least not his real one. "Or why he's here. Or why, or who, might want to kill him." She handed the iPad back. "Thank you for your time."

"We'll get out of your hair," Jax said.

Kenna would've stayed a moment longer, but the look on his face indicated that wasn't going to happen. She stepped outside first and spotted Ramon and Zeyla on guard at the end of the front walk, with Ramon chatting up the officer at the curb.

He spotted them coming and his body language immediately changed. He strode over and met them at the end of the walk. "What is it?"

Kenna said, "I was wondering the same thing about you."

"Someone tripped the security system at the RV." Jax put his arm out. She set off for the car, and he put his hand on the small of her back, then hit the button on his keys to start the engine. "Not getting old, is it?"

"You taking care of me?" Kenna stopped by the car. "Ask me again in ten years. Maybe it will have gotten old by then, but I highly doubt it." She touched his cheeks. "I like it that you're here to protect me."

"It has fringe benefits."

She laughed.

Jax smiled, but he looked distracted.

Kenna opened her door. "Who's at the RV?"

"Female." He scanned the street. "She's sitting in one of our chairs out front."

"I'll call Maizie on the way. See if she accessed the information stored in those photos. We need a break in this case, or we're going to keep spinning our wheels and getting nowhere."

Chapter Twenty-Five

"Who was killed?" Maizie's voice came through the car speakers.

Kenna leaned her head back and closed her eyes. "What?"

"At the house, that scene," Maizie said. "Who died?"

"One of those retired guys. I don't know which number he was. Four. Two. One of them was killed." She shook her head. "That was months ago, so it has to be one of the others."

"Two of them showed up to take my blood."

She opened her eyes and looked at Jax. "Right. You told me that."

"Something about needing the father's genetic profile." He gripped the steering wheel, but they weren't going anywhere fast in this inching-along traffic.

Jax probably wished he had lights and sirens, as he had during his days as an FBI agent. It certainly made getting somewhere fast a lot easier. But right now, that wasn't an option, so whoever was waiting for them at the RV would have to wait long enough for them to get there.

He shook his head. "They could've asked. Instead, they decided to just take it."

Ah, so he wasn't super upset that the guy was dead?

Kenna shrugged. "They wanted to see how your genetics contributed to the outcome."

He reached over and held her hand.

"One of the retired guys was on the hit list," she continued. "Which means whoever is out there trying to run *Dominatus* is either working against whoever they're working for, or he's getting rid of that guy and maybe the rest of them as well in order to tie up loose ends. And none of this makes any sense. Still."

"Because you don't know what I know," Maizie said.

Kenna's brows rose. "You retrieved the information from those photos?"

"Score one for steganography. It's a great way to embed information in an image. The file ends up way larger than one that is simply a JPEG."

"More files to pore over?"

"Craig is loving it, but Elizabeth is bored out of her mind. I found her on the couch, snoring under a pile of papers." The young woman chuckled. "She said it's because she isn't a 'spring chicken' anymore. But I have no idea what that's supposed to mean."

"Me either." Kenna smiled to herself. "Maybe I'll find out when I'm old."

"What we have now, on top of the contents of the packet, is everything the lawyers found out about the Count of Shadows and the network of military personnel he was commanding. He had an entire list of *Dominatus* assets in the army, and a bunch of other branches. Craig explained the whole Marines under the navy, Delta Force is army, something else about space soldiers. He lost me pretty quickly, but it looks like this Major General Schnell guy was the guy they had in the military."

"He's dead. Ramon was there." Kenna frowned. "Did someone else assume command and they're moving the plan forward? Or maybe they're cleaning up loose ends, like you said."

"They also found three decommissioned army bases in the US and two overseas that his people utilize. One was discovered thanks to Ramon and Zeyla, but I'm checking into the others."

"Great," she grumbled, closing her eyes. "Send everything to us and them. We can make a plan and divide up tasks." And she could take a nap first.

She didn't like the idea of someone out for blood. But when had life ever turned out the way she liked? She could answer *with Jax* on that one, but it was far from perfect. He likely hadn't anticipated any of this would happen and also wasn't complaining. Neither of them were. They were both making the best of the situation.

When the lawyers were exonerated and the ghost had been neutralized, they'd get out of here.

Kenna heard the murmur of talking, but her mind didn't want to decipher what was being said. She let out a long breath and didn't bother opening her eyes.

Not until the motion of the car came to a stop and she woke up.

"Hey."

"We're here?"

He nodded in response to her obvious question, since they were in the space beside the RV. But she couldn't get out of the car and go crawl into bed. Not with that woman sitting in a plastic chair.

Kenna groaned. "I don't wanna talk to her."

"Who is she?" Jax said. "I figured it was one of the lawyers."

Kenna shook her head. The woman sat in the chair, staring at her. She had blond hair that hung over the shoulders of her big coat with the fluffy hood. Leggings and boots with fluffy edging around the top. Midfifties. "She's a nurse. From the platform."

Jax stiffened.

Kenna's door opened, and Ramon crouched there, letting the cold air in. "I'm not talking to her. She's *Dominatus*."

Jax quickly relayed what she'd told him.

Ramon dug in his pocket. "Comms." He took two from the case and handed it over.

The car door shut.

Kenna and Jax shoved earbuds in. Ramon and Zeyla did the same, and she heard him say, "Got me?" with his attention on his phone, where an app controlled the whole system over Bluetooth.

Jax said, "We hear you."

"I'm here to speak to Kenna." The woman tore her gaze from the windshield through which she could see Kenna and Jax, and looked at Ramon. Then Zeyla. Her expression hardened.

Zeyla stuck one foot out and put her hand on her hip.

Jax muttered, "Uh-oh."

Kenna watched the interplay. The nurse didn't move.

"Tell us your name." Ramon stood with his arms straight, his hands never too far from a weapon.

"You can call me Nurse Smith." Her tone resonated with an attitude. She wanted what she wanted, and she was gonna get it.

Good luck with that.

Even better, Kenna didn't put stock in luck at all. She had hope instead—and that hope had a solid foundation.

Zeyla muttered something Kenna didn't catch.

"Is she getting out of the car, or do I make an appointment or something?" Nurse Smith looked from them, to where Kenna sat in the front seat of the car, then back.

Jax slid his gun from its holster but switched hands with it and reached over to hold hers.

Kenna checked the campsite around them. At least what she could see of it. No sense missing a threat that approached.

"Say what you have to say, then get out of here." Ramon didn't ask how she even knew where to find Kenna and Jax's home on wheels.

Right now, Kenna would like to be anywhere but here. Preferably back in Wyoming. There was nowhere that *Dominatus* couldn't find them if they wanted to, but it felt safe there to her. Maybe it was all a delusion, or wishful thinking. It wasn't that God had seen fit to provide them a place that was safe, although He absolutely could. She just liked the landscape in Wyoming, where the openness made it seem like she could see the threat coming.

More wishful thinking?

She would much rather trust God, no matter what the outcome. Kenna and Jax had no peace of mind in this, and yet they had the peace of God. The knowledge He had it all in His hands because they'd yielded their lives to Him and allowed Him to be in control of it all.

Nurse Smith looked to the side. They were far enough away that Kenna couldn't assess the nuances of her expression, and it wasn't like this woman had ever been her friend. But she looked scared. "I didn't have anywhere else to go, okay? I need to talk to Kenna."

"What's going on?" Zeyla shrugged. "Thought you had a sweet gig going at that platform. What happened to that?"

"You know what happened." Smith shook her head. "I wasn't there. I was with the rest of the team on the island when it all went wrong. I escaped before one of you people could gun me down like some kind of animal."

Kenna bit the inside of her lip. That was *exactly* how most of them had treated her.

"So you ran." Zeyla shifted her stance. "And you've been running since."

"I tried to get back in. To rendezvous at one of the research facilities. No one would let me in."

"We want to know where they are and who works there. Everything about their operation." Ramon's tone didn't invite any argument.

"In exchange for what?" Smith huffed. "I'm running for my life here. People are dying!"

Zeyla said, "You think Kenna can protect you?"

"What else was I supposed to do?"

"So you came here with nothing to offer, and you want a pregnant woman to protect you?" Zeyla's tone spoke volumes. Sort of like she thought Kenna being pregnant was the worst outcome, but probably it was just for show. Or it was about this woman's intentions. Zeyla might even be worried that something could happen to Kenna and as a result it had come out sounding like that.

Smith brushed hair back from her face. "I can tell you stuff." Her gaze searched the area. "I can give you information."

"Who's trying to kill you?" Zeyla asked.

"Kenna knows. He was there."

"They knew what he is," Kenna said, "and they encouraged it."

Ramon addressed Smith. "Seems like if some guy you know is trying to kill you, then all you've got to do is go to the police with what you know. Tell them who he is, and they'll put you in protective custody."

"You think the police can do anything?" She barked a laugh.

"The FBI then. Don't your people have sympathizers in the Bureau?" Ramon shrugged. "Surely they can arrange for protection."

"They're not my people anymore. I'm on my own." Smith paused. "That much is clear from the fact they're the ones who *sent him to kill me.*"

Zeyla said, "I'm still not clear on how this is our problem. He's after you, not us."

Kenna wondered if she was going to give them the line about the assassin being after the "offspring" the way the president and Petyr had tried to convince her that she would be on the hit list.

Zeyla continued, "Seems more like you're here to see what we know. Maybe you're trying to earn your way back in." She folded her arms. "Just think what they're going to offer you if you bring Kenna Banbury back to them. They'll open the door if you have her."

Smith stared at her.

"I should kill you right here." Zeyla slid her gun from her holster, and all of them flinched. "But someone could be watching."

Kenna let out a breath, staring at the scene through the window.

Jax said, "We need the killer's name. Or a way to find him."

Ramon didn't turn from staring at Smith. "I have a better idea. We use her as bait to draw him out." He lifted his chin. "Yeah, I like that a lot. She goes back to her business, we follow her, and when he shows up to kill her, we'll take care of the problem."

"You can't do this." Smith reacted as if certain that meant they'd kill her as well or let the ghost take care of her before they caught him. "I can tell you..." She swore. "You can't just let them kill me!"

"We don't owe you anything." Zeyla shrugged. "Kenna doesn't owe you anything. You shouldn't have come here."

"He'll find you like I did!"

Ramon dragged her out of the chair by her elbow. "Get lost."

"Kenna! I can help you!"

Jax's hand tightened around hers.

Zeyla marched Nurse Smith to the lane that ran between rows of RVs while she yelled for Kenna. A few people came out of their RVs to watch. Thankfully, Zeyla kept it legal, acting as a bodyguard and not drawing the kind of attention that might get her arrested.

Zeyla would probably walk her all the way to the gate.

Ramon glanced at Jax. "Unlock the RV. I'll clear it before you guys go inside. Then Kenna can take her nap."

Kenna swiped at the tear that fell from the corner of her eye.

Jax tugged her over and kissed the same spot.

Chapter Twenty-Six

Kenna pushed back the covers and sat up, trying not to think too much in the moments when her brain was sloughing off the fog of sleep. She used the facilities in the tiny bathroom and secured her hair with a hair tie in a messy bun that flopped on the back of her head. Water on her face. Teeth brushed for good measure.

She drank a whole cup of water and left it on the sink before getting dressed, even though she'd rather have stayed in sweats all day.

Jax stood at the stove in track pants and a sleeveless athletic shirt. The warmth of his body was more than usual, which told her he'd done pushups and sit-ups on the floor in here, where there was barely room for him to splay his elbows out—but he made it work.

"Let's run away together." She slid her arms around his waist.

He chuckled. "Yes, she is." After a second, he said, "Bye, Maze." He tapped one earbud and set it on the counter, putting the other beside it.

"Sorry."

He turned the heat down on what he was making. "Don't ever apologize for that." He slid his arms around her and kissed her like he needed to make a statement. She couldn't begin to understand what the statement was—all she knew was that he made it well.

Kenna took a moment to revel in everything she wanted being right here in her arms. No matter what happened in the outside world she had this, right now. Everything out there could be burning to the ground for all she cared. Well, except for her family. But she sort of forgot about them in this moment and wasn't sure she was prepared to apologize for thinking about her husband only.

In this kiss she forgot about everything but Jax and the baby between them—the child they'd made together. That kind of made the moment sweeter. The evidence of what they meant to each other in the form of a person they would share forever.

Kenna drew back, breathless. "I think you made your point."

"Good." Jax didn't pull away. "The answer is yes, always."

"I want an update, but Bible first." A nap had turned into a quiet dinner, and that had turned into a movie and an early bedtime. When the phone hadn't rung through any of it, she'd wondered if Jax told the rest of their family to leave the two of them alone but didn't ask. Instead, she just decided to enjoy the quiet evening.

Sure, the fate of the world was at stake. But she was pregnant.

Kenna slid into the booth, and Jax set a mug in front of her. "Hot chocolate."

She tugged it over and sipped, flipped her phone right side up, and opened the app that she used to listen to the

Bible. She hit Play on the psalm of the day, chapter 91, and checked the quick view on her notifications just to make sure it was just updates, and nothing crazy had happened.

Then she sat back in the seat and let the words wash over her.

After a few verses, Jax joined in, saying, "A thousand may fall at your side, and ten thousand at your right hand, but it shall not come near you."

Kenna closed her eyes and prayed through the words, asking for that kind of protection. The Lord, her refuge, would be where she lived. Her dwelling place.

Not physically, but spiritually she would be with Him. Secure in a place where she was protected and where this baby was safe, because God had set angels over them.

She'd never heard that before, and even if she understood how it worked or she didn't, she found comfort in it. It was the reassurance her heart needed to face the day.

Jax set a plate in front of her. Sausage and potato with a fried egg on top, along with plenty of "greens" because he seemed to think they were a necessity.

"My hero."

He laughed. "You won't starve."

Too many memories clouded Kenna's mind. She closed her eyes as Jax prayed for their food. He asked for protection and that the whole team would find favor in their work. When she opened her eyes the memories from that platform didn't seem as strong. After she took a bite and swallowed, she said, "Okay, give me the updates."

"They're probably all on your phone. In the group chats." He smiled, squirting ketchup beside his potatoes. "So, you can read it all for yourself, but I'll hit the highlights and catch you up." As Jolene hopped up on the seat beside her and curled up to lick her paw, he continued, "Zeyla spent most of the night following that nurse." His expression betrayed how he felt about one of Kenna's captors, even if she was lower-level staff on the platform. "No ghost sightings, and word is, she's still alive. On the move. Keeping a low profile."

"Zeyla's still on her?"

"She's getting bored, so I doubt it will last long," Jax said. "Meanwhile, Ramon was here all night, watching the perimeter. He had his computer, so he just monitored things from the car and worked through what Maizie sent him. When I woke up, I relieved him, and he went to get some sleep."

"Did he find anything?"

"A couple of places near enough they're worth checking out. He was working on how we can do that when they're secure facilities."

Kenna had a few ideas, most of which she didn't even like, so she knew he wouldn't either. "The president might be able to get us enough access we can talk the rest of the way in."

"*We* as in the team in general, or *we* as in me and my pregnant wife?"

Kenna scrunched up her nose, because she knew which she preferred. She drank her hot chocolate instead of answering.

Sure, she wanted to be the one to work the case. She might not usually prefer to be the one who sat in the car, or hung back, but right now she really was fine with it. Either way, the situation was in God's hands. Whether it was her out in front, with her family around her, or if Ramon and Zeyla took the lead and faced the danger head on. The team would get a result regardless—especially if they all worked together.

"What about the name of the person behind this?" Kenna asked. "Do we know that?"

Jax shook his head. "It still keeps coming back as Schnell."

"He's dead. Ramon was there." Kenna set down her mug. "Sorry to state the obvious."

"You're right." Jax shrugged. "I made some calls this morning and found out that the major general was at an extended retreat for a few weeks, on personal leave. Most people think he was in rehab, which is interesting enough for a high-level military figure that sincere effort was made to keep it quiet."

"Is there rehab for if you're dead?" Kenna knew it was ridiculous, but what about an evil secret society wasn't?

"No, but if you've got a genetic match or someone willing to undergo plastic surgery to look like you, why not get a replacement when one of the versions is eliminated?"

She tapped her fork against the table, but Jolene didn't like being disturbed, so she quit. "More like you send the disposable double out to do your dirty work, let him be the one who gets killed, and when you return to work later, it's the real you. But why the weeks of rehab?"

"He got hurt?" Jax shrugged. "Or the double is the replacement, and he needed training."

"What does Ramon think?"

Jax laid his fork down and took a sip of coffee. "He's not happy to know the general is still out there. What he ran into was some pretty sick stuff."

Kenna had visited Ramon in the hospital right after it happened, but wasn't even sure that she'd believed then what she told him. Now she did, because she'd righted her faith on the foundation it had slipped from.

Jax continued, "Ramon wants a face off. He wants to

find the evidence and confront the guy about his connection to *Dominatus.*"

"Is the general—the real one or the replacement—the one trying to take out Petyr and the other contenders for *Imperatoris*?" She didn't like the idea of confronting anyone, and she didn't want her family in danger. Her version of "nesting" was wanting everyone to get into a bunker and shut the door so they could all be safe.

Nope. That wasn't how this day was going to go. Her fears weren't going to dictate what happened today.

She said, "I vote we ask Petyr to confirm if the general might be the one trying to kill him. Find out what he has to say."

Jax's brow rose. "You have his number?"

"Can't be that hard to get it." She wanted to shrug off his question, but the guy was a political leader who believed he was her father. Kenna sighed. "Why can't Stairns turn out to be secretly my biological dad? I'd even take Bruce right now."

Jax's expression softened. "Maybe all three men should submit to a DNA test. While we're getting a sample from Petyr, we can ask about Major General Schnell."

"It's expedient. It's pretty safe. I like it." She shoved a bite of potato into her mouth, enjoying the flavors—and the fact her pregnancy nausea was a thing of the past.

But that just reminded her of what Jax had missed. The experiences they could've shared, good and bad, because Jax was the father of her child. And she would always know who her dad was.

He smiled. "I'll run the plan by Ramon. See what he says."

"Did he take a look at the guy currently pretending to be the general?"

"I'll find that out as well. He's been steering clear of that side of things, focusing on what Maizie sent over. Looking at structural plans for military bases and satellite images she's managed to get." Jax winced. "I don't want to know how."

Kenna's mind seemed to have spiraled several steps ahead, to secret military bases and clandestine operations. "Maybe Bruce or Stairns could pretend to be a couple of those retired guys that were experimented on."

Jax shook his head, processing it all. "I still don't understand how they were old and didn't look it, or what they could do. It's unreal to think those people are walking around in the world."

"Good thing the government isn't interested in breeding super soldiers, or we'd be in trouble."

Jax stared at her.

"Nah, nah. Don't even think it. I don't want to know." Kenna clapped her hands over her ears. "Our baby isn't one of them. They just wanted to know what she could do. They didn't do anything to her, because I stabbed one of them when they tried, and Buzard told them to back off."

Jax didn't blink.

She lowered her hands. "What?"

"You protected our baby in the middle of that?"

"Wouldn't you have? I wasn't going to let them touch her!" She could have told him the rest of what *Dominatus* had wanted to do to her baby. The fact one of the medical personnel had been working on an incubator so that they could surgically remove her baby from her—womb intact—and keep her alive, experimenting on her until she was ready to be "born." Nope. She wasn't going to tell him that, or the other terrible things that ran through her nightmares like a horror movie she couldn't forget.

Jax smiled. "I think you're amazing."

"Don't make me cry. We have butts to kick." Kenna felt the moisture gather anyway. She sniffed. "It's over. They don't get what they want, because this is *our* life."

"Let's make sure we ruin *all* their plans, not just that one."

"I like the way you think, Mr. Jaxton." She grabbed her bowl and shifted the cat out of the way so she could put it in the sink. "Let's get to work."

Chapter Twenty-Seven

Jax's phone chimed. Kenna's vibrated across the table before she could even stand up. The same alert—movement on the sensors and cameras outside. He tapped the screen, and a second later, someone knocked on the door.

"It's just me." Zeyla pulled at the handle, evidently impatient to get in.

Jax got up and unlocked the door so she could enter.

"Hey." Zeyla looked flushed, but not tired at all from being up all night.

"Everything okay?" Kenna asked.

"I had an idea. I need to borrow some clothes."

Her cousin was an...edgier version of herself. They had very different clothing and hairstyles, but their basic build was similar even if Zeyla was a little shorter than Kenna.

"And I need coffee." Zeyla grabbed a mug from the little shelf above the coffee pot. "This isn't decaf, is it?" She looked over her shoulder.

"I have hot chocolate."

Zeyla made a face. "Awesome." Her tone indicated it was anything but awesome.

Kenna smiled over the rim of her mug, and Jax returned it.

He said, "There's coffee in the French press."

Kenna ignored that. "What do you need clothes for?"

"You have an appointment at this pregnancy center. They take walk-ins, but I figured if we book ahead, it'll hit on someone's radar."

Kenna had an appointment, but Zeyla wanted to borrow clothes? That didn't amount to too many options, and none of them involved Kenna being in danger. Or facing down a medical professional who may or may not be an agent of *Dominatus*. "How long is the ruse that you're pregnant going to hold up?"

"Long enough." Zeyla shrugged, drinking half the mug of hot coffee in a few gulps.

"For what?" Jax asked.

"Hopefully long enough for kidnappers to show up." Zeyla lifted her brows. "I have an idea about that as well." She looked at Kenna. "You good if I take Jax with me? To keep up the ruse."

Jax said, "I'll ask Ramon to trade."

Kenna bit her lip. She didn't want to get in between the team and a chance at a solution, or at least a break in the case. Zeyla clearly had a plan. Kenna didn't need her fears to stall that plan and prevent this whole thing from being over sooner rather than later.

She needed to memorize Psalm 91, just in case. At least so that she could recall more Scripture than she'd been able to previously. But the *just in case* part was about the chance she might once again be a captive of their enemy. Or that the baby might be. If the worst happened, she wanted to be able to recite Scripture to keep a hold on her hope even when things got darkest.

"I can stay here if you want me to," Jax offered.

Kenna shook her head. "It's okay. If the plan is for me to see a doctor, it's way more convincing if you're there." Unless he didn't want to leave her as much as she didn't want to leave him. "If Ramon is here, and rested, it'll be okay. It's a workable plan."

Jax glanced aside at Zeyla. "What's the plan?"

"Kenna sees a doctor we found randomly, trying to roll the dice that it's not one of their doctors."

That had happened before, so it was a valid concern.

Zeyla continued, "The form I filled out online said you just want to check everything is okay with the baby so far. No concerns, but you'd love an ultrasound."

"I would love an ultrasound."

Jax's expression softened.

"Those three-dimensional ones are weird. The baby always looks like a mutant. It's *not* cute."

Jax grinned.

"Right?!" Zeyla said. "And you're supposed to tell people it's so amazing, their baby is beautiful. Okay, so the technology is amazing, because you can see what the kid looks like before they're born. But what if they're ugly? It's like, *Sorry you didn't pass this class. Enjoy your unfortunate life.*"

Kenna turned to her cousin and stared at her.

"What?"

"So you're gonna be *that* auntie? The one who says the kid is cute, but really you're just lying."

Zeyla stilled, the coffee mug close to her mouth. "You two will probably make a cute baby." She shrugged. "I mean, the odds are good your kid will be cute. But what if it's like one of those cute puppies that grows up to be an ugly dog?"

Kenna said, "You'd better be good at presents."

Zeyla's expression shifted, and now she looked affronted. "Mom already got a storage unit. She's filling it with baby stuff for you guys. I pitched in."

Jax frowned

Kenna said, "Really?"

"We're family, aren't we?" Zeyla drank the rest of her coffee, then upended her mug in the tiny RV kitchen sink. "Can I rummage in your closet?"

Kenna nodded. "Maternity stuff is in the drawers, so just go for what's hung up." She turned on the seat and spoke toward the bedroom end of the RV. "What are you going to do about your hair?"

"Huh," Zeyla called back. "Maybe I'll hit a costume shop and get a wig or something."

Her mind still wanted to hang on the idea of Amara with a storage unit of gifts for Kenna and Jax. Of course, her aunt was excited to be a grandma to this baby, but with their enemy and Amara being caught up in the fight along with the rest of them, how could she have carved out time for gifts—or basic supplies?

Kenna and Jax had bought a baby carrier just so they had something for the baby after she was born, but nothing else yet. The basics were diapers and wipes, clothes, and a couple of blankets. Aside from that, it was just a lot of stuff people accumulated, and you didn't know what was necessity and what was frivolous until after the baby was too old to utilize it anymore. Their plan was to flex as needed, buy what was a "need" in the moment, and be grateful for all of it. Every second they had health and life, and freedom, was a second they could be thankful to God for what they had.

"Have you heard from your mom in the last day or so?" Kenna asked.

Zeyla called back from the bedroom, "I can ask her where the storage unit is if you want to look at what she got, but I think it's in Kansas."

Jax frowned. "Why Kansas?"

"It's the center of the continental US, so you don't get stuck across the country three days from where you need to be. You're only a day's drive, or thereabouts." Hangers clacked together.

Kenna figured the logic on that was sound enough. But that didn't mean she was going to move there. "What time is the appointment?"

"Two ten this afternoon."

"Okay. I want to go and see Detective Langley this morning, and I'll be back here in time for you to make that appointment."

Zeyla reappeared holding a pair of Kenna's jeans and a heavy red-and-white lumberjack shirt that was lined. The jeans could probably pass as maternity if Zeyla didn't show the waistband.

"How are you going to pretend to be pregnant?" Kenna asked.

"I guess I need a pillow or something I can stuff up the shirt." Zeyla headed for the door. "I'll text you guys with the plan. Thanks for the coffee!" The door clicked shut.

Jax turned to Kenna. "You want to talk to Detective Langley?"

She nodded. "I'd reassure you that hospitals are pretty safe places, but has that really been our experience?"

"It's at least a good place to be in case someone is injured, or you and the baby have a problem."

They weren't going to be spending much time there, but she agreed on principle.

Kenna nodded. "Let's go."

Half an hour later, Jax knocked on the door to Detective Langley's room.

"Come in." The muffled voice was male, and when Jax opened the door, only Langley occupied the space.

The detective sat up. "Hey, guys."

"Jordan." Jax held out his hand, and they shook. "Good to see you looking awake."

Kenna nodded. "You do look a whole lot better than the last time I saw you."

The detective smiled. "The alternative isn't great." He had on a hospital gown and an ID bracelet, but wasn't hooked up to any machines or medicines.

"How soon until they let you out?" Kenna settled into the chair against the wall beside the little cabinet and countertop, above which was a small TV on a shelf.

"Hopefully later today. I'm all stitched up, no infections, and I can go back to work in a week. I just can't do anything but sit at my desk. And no lifting anything heavier than a piece of paper."

Jax chuckled. "I've been there. You'll be back to work soon enough." He paused a second, then asked, "Did you see the face of the man who attacked you?"

"I scratched his neck."

"I heard about that." Jax nodded. "Good for you."

"Maybe I got a look at his face. But mostly I just remember the sneer, and teeth."

He enjoyed it. Kenna wasn't surprised. But unlike his usual drawn-out kills, where he got to enjoy spilling blood and causing someone terror, this had been quick. "It was different with you. Fast."

"He still managed to enjoy it," Langley said.

She nodded. "Because he takes pride in his work."

The two men looked at her.

She shook her head, mostly to try and shake off the memories. "Don't worry about it." She found the image in her phone and showed Langley. "Was this him?"

"I got his DNA. I don't need to ID him."

"His name is Simon Newton, and he's a dangerous killer. If he isn't in the system, then your colleagues need you to ID him from this photo so they can hunt him down before he hurts someone else."

"He's the one killing people?"

Kenna nodded. "Did he say anything at all?"

She couldn't let go of the idea that hurting Langley had been about sending a message. To her, to Jax. To someone else, or all of them and the police department. He was a hired gun, though. Or a hired knife. The person that whoever wanted to be in charge of *Dominatus* at the expense of everyone else sent to take out those who got in his way.

Either Langley was a player who needed to be removed from the board, or he was a pawn. If he meant nothing to Simon, then the assassin would never have bothered to hurt him.

"Not that I remember."

Jax said, "Any idea why he'd hurt you?"

"You mean tried to kill me, right? Because that's what he did."

Kenna shook her head, but it was Jax who pointed out what they knew. "If he wanted you dead, you would be. He severely injured you, but he didn't kill you."

"Because he's the kind of sicko who likes to see people suffer."

"Yes, unless death needs to be expedient," Kenna said. "We've known him to poison people and leave them to succumb while he's miles away. Or chase a person for hours and then draw their death out for days."

Surprise registered on Langley's face.

Of course, he mattered as a human being. Everyone had intrinsic value. She just didn't know if he mattered to *Dominatus*.

"Sorry, but we have to know how you fit into this whole thing," she continued. "Or if you were just in the wrong place at the right time."

Langley picked up his cell phone. "Guess I'm the chump who got targeted. But I'm also the chump who's going to catch this guy."

Jax shifted, empathy in his body language. "Detective—"

Langley cut him off. "Can't do that without a hit on that scumbag's DNA."

"You have the results?" Kenna asked. "Your lieutenant told me the department put a rush on it."

"That happens when someone tries to kill a cop." Langley frowned. "They're retesting the results because they think there was an error."

"What kind of error?" Jax asked.

"They're a match with some guy in the army. But he was killed in action six years ago."

Chapter Twenty-Eight

Kenna laid two slices of cheese on one sandwich and one on the other, both of them on top of a mountain of turkey. Lettuce, and then the other slice of bread. "Here." She laid the plate in front of Ramon but didn't sit.

He had his own laptop open on the table, and hers was backed up against the window. The feed on the screen was from Jax's lapel camera so they could watch the whole scene at the doctor's office.

"You really think this is going to work?" She sipped from her can of caffeine-free soda.

"Zeyla comes up with pretty good plans. I don't always agree with her methods, but you can't deny the results." Ramon clicked the mouse, then continued typing. "There's nothing on this Simon Newton guy who was a soldier, and in his afterlife evidently decided to be a killer for *Dominatus*."

"He really died in action?" Around the same time Megan's boyfriend had, which was interesting. Her gaze, and her attention, drifted to Jax. She didn't want to be there; she wanted to be here. She wanted him here, but also she wanted to solve the case.

Unfortunately, she couldn't have both without outsourcing the legwork.

Ramon didn't lift his gaze from his computer. "I'm guessing no, he isn't dead. Since he's still running around being a murdering psycho."

On the screen of Kenna's laptop, Jax parked the car.

"How long do we have?" he asked Zeyla.

"Fifteen minutes," she answered.

"Let's go."

Ramon glanced at her screen, then back at what he was doing. Jax and Zeyla couldn't hear them, and Kenna didn't want to distract them with a phone call. It was enough to watch what they were doing so she knew they were safe while she stayed here.

Meanwhile, she wanted some progress on this hunt. "What the police got back was DNA on file for an army private Simon Newton."

Simon says.

Just thinking it made her want to shudder.

Ramon stared at the screen. "Maizie can't dig into it because they'll know we're onto them."

On the screen, Jax told the receptionist that Kenna Banbury was there for her appointment. Which only made her wonder if that ruse was even going to work. After all, it wasn't like she'd go see a doctor under her real name. Was *Dominatus* or whoever the target was right now actually going to fall for this?

Jax and Zeyla went to sit in the waiting area.

She looked at Ramon. "I want to know if there's a connection between Simon Newton and the other army guy we know who was killed in action. Mitch Caudelle. And Carl Allerton."

Ramon lifted his gaze from the laptop to look at her. "You think there's a connection?"

"It happened around the same time. Maybe they were deployed together?" Kenna shrugged. "Simon might've killed Mitch and faked his own death, or the whole group was declared dead and Major General Schnell recruited his own hit squad."

"You think Mitch is alive as well?"

"I have no idea," Kenna said. "But it's worth figuring out."

"I'll have Stairns dig into it. He still has some military connections he can ask." Ramon typed rapidly on the keyboard.

"It's been a long time since he served." Was he really going to be able to get them information? Though, maybe that was better than Maizie trying to hack secure government servers that were also possibly controlled by *Dominatus*.

Ramon shrugged. "He wants something to do so he can feel involved."

On her laptop, a nurse walked Zeyla and Jax through a doorway into a long hall and had Zeyla record her weight before she took them to a room. Kenna tuned out the blood pressure reading and the initial questions about how things were going, and what the reason for their visit was.

She did want to get an ultrasound. Who didn't need the reassurance that everything was all right? But she regularly felt the baby kicking around, and she felt fine. Keeping active, sleeping well, eating nutritious food, and drinking plenty of water counted for a whole lot in the vein of healthy living. There were always factors that couldn't be accounted for, but she'd just never had that many health problems. The few times they'd taken her blood pressure on the platform, during her captivity, it had gone from being on the low end to being normal, not even the usual higher reading that pregnancy brought. Or the raised pressure that would result from being kidnapped and subject to experiments.

Maybe it was a function of her birth and her connection to the *Dominatus* breeding program that gave her the blessing of good health. But she wasn't going to thank them for it.

"If you want to see a doctor and get checked out for real," Ramon said, "your mom can make that happen."

"She isn't my mom."

"Your aunt. Whatever. Amara is determined to be this baby's grandma. Might as well take her on as your mom. Unless you have a better offer?"

"There's a whole lot of water under that bridge." Apparently, the water ran through a storage unit she hadn't known existed that was full of baby stuff. "She's still part of my life."

Ramon stretched his arms above his head. "You don't get to turn this back on me and tell me to go find a family, because I'm working on taking my own advice. But I don't think you should discount the people around you. They care about you."

"I know that." She sipped from her can and watched Zeyla pace the small doctor's office room from the vantage point of Jax's lapel camera. "I'm not ruling it out."

"You're also not letting them in."

"I've done a lot of work to deal with what happened. Most of it in the last week. Give me a second to get my footing back on the right track."

"She's here for you."

Kenna glanced at him. "In the sense that she's not actually here, right?"

"You know Amara. She's a behind-the-scenes person." Ramon smiled. "I wanna see Zeyla being an aunty, though. Because that's gonna be hilarious."

"I know who to call if someone needs to pace up and down with the baby in the small hours of the morning."

Ramon chuckled. "She has a good heart. She's just never lived a life where she babysat, or had friends who have siblings, or ever had a mother in the traditional sense. Amara made sure she was alive, and in return got another foot soldier for her war. Once the fight is over, they can both learn how to be family in the sense you and I know."

"Do we?" Kenna shrugged. "I have no idea what I'm doing. What I am doing, I'm probably doing wrong."

"Says who?"

"Someone. Somewhere," Kenna said. "But it's my life, and I get to live it how I want."

"Let's find a door to knock on so we can inform *Dominatus* of that fact. Make sure they understand they're going to leave you guys and the baby *alone*." He put extra emphasis on that last word.

"Thanks." She took a bite of her sandwich, even though she wasn't that hungry. She probably wouldn't have an appetite until—

The door to the medical office opened, and a doctor in slacks and a buttoned shirt came in, stethoscope around his neck but no lab coat.

"You know what?" Zeyla turned to him. "I actually changed my mind."

Jax stood. "What's that?"

"I don't wanna have this visit today." She rushed past the doctor. "Sorry for wasting your time."

He sputtered, but Zeyla was already out the door.

Kenna sat at the RV dinette table so she could see the image more closely. It wobbled as Jax followed Zeyla down the hall toward an illuminated EXIT sign.

"What is it?" he asked her.

"I got a weird vibe before he even came in. Something isn't right."

"So you bail on the mission? I thought you wanted to get kidnapped."

Kenna frowned at their conversation.

Zeyla pushed on the bar across the door, and the screen washed with bright sunlight as they stepped outside. "Who knows what's going to draw them out—"

"FBI! Freeze!"

Jax and Zeyla pulled up short, surrounded by agents with weapons pointed squarely at them. Zeyla glanced at Jax. "See what I mean? Not right."

"Stand down!" Special Agent Herron walked between two agents, approaching them. She eyed Zeyla. "Another lookalike?"

Zeyla tugged off the wig to reveal her hair pinned back underneath, holding the fake Kenna-do up with her hands. "I wasn't even pretending that hard. Why are you guys here?"

Ramon reached over and hit the mute button on the laptop. "You can hear about how they talked their way out of that later. I have something."

Kenna tore her attention from the screen, at least assured that Jax was safe for the moment. The agents with their weapons were standing down. Realizing that whatever the reason they'd shown up was done now. Likely they were there to round up another of the lawyers, but this operation was a bust.

"What do you have?" Kenna asked. If he told her fast, she could listen to the conversation after.

"The unit Mitch Caudelle was in is the same as Simon Newton. There were three other guys in their team, and they weren't anything special on paper. No secret assignments. Nothing out of the ordinary. Just a fire team or whatever they call them. At least according to what Stairns' contact was able to dig up, they were just average grunts who did what they were told."

The nature of which always depended on who was giving the orders.

"Just because there's nothing overly suspicious about it doesn't mean that's the truth," Kenna said. "It isn't like covert ops is listed as that in their records." She snuck a glance at Jax and Zeyla and saw they were still in conversation with the special agent.

They'd tried to draw out *Dominatus* and wound up facing the taskforce hunting the lawyers.

Whatever Zeyla's plan had been aiming at, Kenna guessed it wasn't that.

"I say we track down the other three guys and find out what they're up to."

Kenna looked from the laptop screen to Ramon. "Get a psychological profile as well. Because if they're anything like Simon or Mitch we need to get them on the radar of local police wherever we find them."

Ramon nodded. "On it."

Kenna pushed out a long breath, the baby kicking against her abdomen. Her husband on the laptop screen, facing down a crowd of FBI agents who all wanted answers.

She wouldn't be surprised if they were arrested. Or at least taken to the FBI office for questioning.

Talk your way out of it and come home. She switched to prayer, asking God that they would find favor rather than sitting here and willing them to make it for themselves.

She worked through all the things they had leads on, and all the possible options in front of them. If they could follow a supposedly dead soldier into a secret base, that was a big win. Coming back out alive would be another story. It seemed as if they had a nascent idea forming. The beginning of a plan.

Kenna slid over her phone and decided to take Ramon's advice.

She called her mom.

When Amara picked up, Kenna said, "I have an idea."

Chapter Twenty-Nine

Kenna walked up the stone steps, lifting the hem of her red dress with one hand. Jax set his on the small of her back.

The building in front of them had been lit up like a beacon under the black of the night sky and orchestral music poured from every door and window. People milled around just inside the entrance dressed as she and Jax were in their evening finest for this event.

Flanking the doors outside were armed guards in army green dress uniforms. Soldiers for the country of Croatia, protecting their embassy on US soil.

Kenna showed the severe-looking lady at the entrance the QR code on her phone that Petyr had sent and checked over her shoulder. Amara and Bruce followed them up the steps. Bruce had his hand under Amara's elbow. She looked like a queen with a black velvet dress and her hair piled on her head. Kenna wasn't sure she pulled that look off the way Amara did, and not because she'd needed a specific dress that accounted for her and Jax's plus one.

"Are you sure about this idea?" Jax whispered in her ear.

"Beats spending a night being questioned by the FBI."

He smirked. "True." His gaze drifted to her no-straps, split in the leg, "Look at me, I'm pregnant" fancy evening dress, and sort of glazed over. Apparently, Zeyla had done all right picking her outfit for the night.

Kenna had opted for flat sandals, even though Zeyla thought that was the cardinal sin. "They hassled you for long enough today."

All because someone had called in an anonymous tip that one of the as-yet-unaccounted-for lawyers would be at the pregnancy center. Zeyla had explained that the ruse was for the FBI to show up and catch *Dominatus* assets in the act of kidnapping "Kenna" and arrest them. Too bad that hadn't happened. It had been a decent plan, and Zeyla had said she even saw a van she believed was the retrieval team speed away from the scene.

No one could've anticipated that the FBI would arrive early and jump the gun.

Amara and Bruce reached them. Kenna told the security lady, "They're with me." But Petyr split the crowd, approaching at a fast stride. Wearing a dark suit and bow tie, his hair slicked back.

"No, I don't think so." Petyr waved his hands, which summoned black tie guards. Not the ceremonial kind who flanked the door like set pieces in the display of Croatian elegance. These were the kind of thugs she would expect to see in an alley, only they were dressed for a gala. He motioned to Bruce. "He isn't coming in."

Kenna faced off with him. "They're with me."

His jaw flexed. The head of state who believed he was

her father didn't want to back down. But was he going to turn it into a scene in the lobby of his embassy?

"Unless you want to tell me what your problem is with Bruce, he comes in."

"Both of them stay outside." Petyr looked over her shoulder and hadn't yet actually acknowledged her presence.

"They're coming in." She was pregnant. She wanted backup. "End of discussion."

He stared at Bruce.

Kenna stared at the side of his face, waiting for him to relent. Finally, she added, "Petyr."

One of his thugs reacted to that. They were either unused to hearing him be addressed by his first name or hadn't been briefed on who she was. That was interesting.

"We just wanna talk."

He looked at her then, those dark eyes. Trying to appear magnanimous because people were starting to stare at him. "There is no 'we' in this. There is only you and I."

Kenna shook her head. "Doesn't work like that." She tipped her head to the side, which made the hairdo Zeyla had given her flop a bit. Hopefully, she hadn't ruined it. "You remember Jax, don't you? And Amara. Maybe you two have met. She's my mother. Or, at least, the closest I'll get to one. I had a father. His name was Malcom Banbury, but he died tragically many years ago. I'm not sure what your problem is with Bruce, but I've known him a while now and he's saved my life several times."

"I have guests to attend to," Petyr said. "I'll find you shortly."

He walked away before she could respond to that.

"Welp," Bruce said. "That went well."

Kenna slid her arm in Jax's elbow, and they headed across the lobby for the main ballroom. A server passed them with a full tray of champagne glasses, and Jax asked the guy for soda water. She scouted out a good location amid crowd, but not near to anyone who looked chatty.

The last thing they were here to do was mingle with the Croatian ambassador's guests. Unless any of them happened to be former US soldiers listed as killed in action.

When she'd found the ideal spot, she turned to Amara and Bruce. "One of you needs to tell me why *they* seem to be fine with Amara and Zeyla being in my life but have a huge problem with washed-up ex-CIA officers." She whispered the last part, so no one overheard.

Bruce smirked. "True enough."

Kenna waited. Even Jax seemed content to hold out for the answer, in between accepting two glasses of iced fizzy water. Amara sipped from her champagne glass, and Bruce looked longingly at the bar for a second.

"Talk now. Drink after." She lifted her chin.

He usually wore Hawaiian shirts with enough buttons open at the top to reveal he was well endowed with gray chest hair. Even in winter. Today, he had on a suit that she'd guess was rented, but she couldn't be sure. His cheeks moved—working his mouth around, trying to decide what to share.

"Bruce, why do they keep telling me to get rid of you?"

He took the bait on that one and ran with it. "Because I'm an asset to your team, obviously."

"Or something," Jax quipped.

Kenna ignored both of their attempts to brush off the heaviness of this conversation. *Dominatus* insisted Bruce would betray her. They'd repeatedly told her not to trust him. As far as she was concerned, that likely meant she should keep him close. But fear had her pushing him away the past few months, attempting self-preservation in a situation where she had zero control. "You need to tell me, or I'll think what they are advising might have merit. Enough to ask you to step away."

Amara shifted to face Bruce. "Just spit it out."

Kenna shouldn't be surprised that Amara knew whatever it was. She watched Bruce and realized that she'd always known there were things he was keeping from her. Months ago, he'd been determined to take down the man who had betrayed him. It turned out that guy worked for *Dominatus*. He was dead now, but did Bruce consider that the man's comeuppance? Or was he using the betrayal as fuel to go after the whole organization now?

Bruce said, "You know who my partner was. How he screwed me over."

Not the expression she would have used, but he had colorful ways of putting things on occasion.

Kenna nodded. "I know what happened."

Even if most of it had been while she was a captive, Jax had caught her up. And right now, her husband put his hand on the small of her back. She leaned against him, not just for support in standing up.

"After it all imploded and I was burned and left for dead in England, I was approached by a guy. He had me do some odd jobs for a buddy of his. I needed cash. I had a certain skillset and no paperwork, so it wasn't like work was easy to come by." Bruce reached up and scratched his jaw.

A nervous move she hadn't seen him make often.

"After a while I realized who I was working for," he continued. "At first, I didn't want to care. When I asked questions and dug below the surface, I realized I was working for *Dominatus*. Not the same part as my partner.

They probably didn't even know each other existed. But I'd become the thing I hated the most."

Kenna looked at the ballroom of people milling around, chatting each other up, or dancing to the orchestra's mellow tunes. Had she brought her family into the lion's den hoping to stir the nest enough she got some answers, or at least cooperation?

"I got out, but it almost killed me. I hit rock bottom and once I'd crawled out of that hole, I had to rebuild it all from scratch. For years, I lived on almost nothing, moving from place to place and getting paid under the table. Until an old friend reached out on a message board from decades before and told me someone needed my help."

She could still remember him pulling up outside the empty house she'd been hiding in. The target of a *Dominatus* assassin she had killed. Bruce had walked into the middle of it like the sunshine in that gray British world. Like a piece of home on foreign soil.

Stairns' former friend had taken her to his home and welcomed her team. He'd treated Maizie with nothing but respect since they met and had become another reason the young woman was learning how to trust the men in her life.

"I meant what I said about you saving me." Kenna walked to him, opened her arms, and gave Bruce a long overdue hug. "And you have no idea what it meant to me that you dropped everything and showed up to help."

His arms tightened for a second before he stepped back and let her go. "Wasn't much to drop. And in the end, it got me my life back."

"You didn't know that at the time." He'd been there to help, not looking for a ticket out.

He tipped his head to the side, conceding her point.

"Why does he have a thing about being my father?" Kenna wasn't sure why she asked, except that Bruce was much more of a father figure to her than anyone other than Stairns. Both men were mentors, friends, and the kind of man she wished was here to support her the way a dad might.

"Why do they do anything, or say anything, other than that it serves their purpose?"

"Any chance you gave a donation at a *Dominatus* sperm bank a lot of years ago?"

Bruce's expression softened, but something like grief touched his gaze. "I wish." He leaned in and kissed her cheek, his rough hand gentle on her elbow. "Doesn't change anything as far as I'm concerned. That baby has a set of grandparents. Three if you count Jax's folks, and Elizabeth and Craig."

Kenna looked up and sniffed, trying to will away the tickle of moisture in her eyes. "I refuse to cry when I'm dressed like this."

"Sometimes you don't get a choice about that. It just happens."

Amara eased up to his side, winding her arm through Bruce's. "He's right about us females. Besides, no one here cares if you cry. They just don't want you to be upset."

"Because I'm very obviously pregnant in this dress." Kenna didn't need the world tiptoeing around her. She could still kick doors in!

Jax slid his arm around her back. "I forgot what I was going to say. I looked at you and got tongue-tied. Why are we here again?"

"I thought you were a professional?" She had to razz him a little, even if she thought it was adorable that he thought she looked good.

"That's why we're here," Amara said. "Because this is family business."

Kenna nodded. "Thanks for coming."

Bruce said, "Wouldn't miss it, girlie."

"Now that we're done with our heart-to-heart, can we get to work?"

Chapter Thirty

"I appreciate you giving me some of your time." Kenna sat on the chair Petyr had pulled out for her. She glanced over her shoulder and politely smiled at him.

Jax stood not too far away on guard. Giving them the chance to speak. Kenna was prepared to be polite, as long as he gave her what she wanted.

Petyr settled into the chair across from her, and a waiter delivered two fingers of whiskey in a crystal glass, then set a glass of water in front of her.

She was thirsty, but she wasn't going to drink it. For a second, she wondered if Jax might take a sip for her. Thankfully, he didn't. She didn't want to find out it was poisoned that way.

Petyr smoothed down his tie. "How has it been, working the case? Searching for our mutual associate."

"He's killed more people than we thought initially, not only 'offspring' and not only the man who's murder file you gave us. Who knows what the total is." Kenna didn't even want to think about Simon, let alone draw his attention.

"Surely, you have some resources available to you that could enable me to track him down."

"In the interest of our mutual survival..." He drew a paper from the inside pocket of his suit jacket. "This is the motel where he's been staying, but every time my people have dropped by, he's out. They sit in front, but he never shows, and yet inside it appears he's spent time there."

"Thank you for the information." She took the paper from him and put it on the table in front of her. "I appreciate the assistance."

Petyr eyed her over the rim of his glass.

An elderly couple passed by them, and the husband said something to Petyr in a language Kenna didn't speak. Presumably Croatian. Petyr nodded but didn't respond otherwise.

When he turned back to her, he said, "Are we only here to talk about business?"

"Seems to me like that business puts us on either side of a chasm. There's no way to cross it without compromising what we believe. Or becoming what we despise."

He sipped his drink.

"The only way I see that changing is if you provide me with a DNA sample, like a cheek swab. Let me test it."

"What difference would it make? I know what I know."

"It makes a difference to me." Kenna tilted her shoulders to the left a little to give the kicking little girl a bit more room so she might not come up against the hard resistance of Kenna's rib cage. She glanced at Jax. "To us, and to the rest of our family. Not just the baby Jax and I are having, but our *entire* family."

"There's nothing I can say that would satisfy you." He set the glass on the table, his forearm on the edge. Fingers around the drink. "Any interest or curiosity in the young woman you adopted will be misconstrued. You already know my opinion of the company you keep here. Any other person in your periphery will immediately be viewed as a potential victim if I bring them up. When I only wish to get to know you and those you hold dear." His gaze drifted over in the direction where Bruce had remained with Amara, and she was pretty sure she saw a slight curl in his lips.

"You don't have a problem with Amara or Zeyla the way you do with Bruce. Why is that?" Seemed to her it was backward. Surely, it meant Kenna should be more wary of Amara because *Dominatus* had no problem with her.

"She's given up a lot of her more...problematic activities."

"And as such, she doesn't represent as much of a threat?" Kenna hoped that was a mistake on their part.

"We all have our ends, and those who stand in our way. Perhaps, if given the chance, I could usher my people into a new era."

"Global control?" She wasn't sure it wasn't the goal of any of the candidates for *Imperatoris* to take over Canada, the UK, Europe, and the US in one go. Whether that presented a threat to innocent people under their rule likely depended on who was voted in.

"Am I to apologize for wishing to be king?"

He'd been born in the wrong country if he wanted that. "You already have a whole lot of power."

"There is always more."

"What do you know about Major General Schnell?"

Petyr blinked, and the skin around his eyes contracted.

"Could he be the one who tried to kill you?"

He muttered a word in Croatian she probably didn't want translated.

"Is he alive?" Kenna asked. "Because if you know where I might find him, I can put a stop to the present threat."

"We have rules." Before she could respond, he continued, "But in this case, his actions are permitted. As yours would be."

"So, because he has other people do it, the rules of engagement permit him trying to take out you and probably everyone else who threatens him being voted in as *Imperatoris*."

Petyr hissed in a breath.

She wasn't going to apologize for saying that aloud and potentially jeopardizing the secrecy of it. "This is about innocent lives. People caught in the crossfire. Too many have lost their lives for what *Dominatus* wants. It has to stop. Here and now, this needs to end."

"Then ensure I gain the vote, and you will be safe." He sat back and sipped his drink, so satisfied with his plan. Except that put more innocent lives at risk.

He wanted her to bargain for her family's future with his bid for power. As if that was the surest way he had to become the leader.

"What I do isn't for you," she stated.

"The end result is the same," Petyr said. "Your safety and my leadership are intertwined."

He seemed to genuinely believe he was her best bet at a future that didn't involve more grief and terror than she'd ever experienced before in her life. Which was saying something.

"I don't want any part of this." She couldn't care less than she did about who was in charge, except that he was right. Kenna didn't want to admit that much, however. Why let him know that he was right and might be her safest bet? If she was interested in gambling with her future, that was.

She would rather trust God for the outcome.

"Let the chips fall where they may." She shrugged her bare shoulders, suddenly aware she'd come to this event in her finest just for this. "Or help me eliminate a dangerous threat, both to you and to innocent people."

Rather than leave the fight up to her and claim mutual benefit when her family inevitably succeeded—which always meant lives at risk—he had to participate in this.

"Help you how?" he asked.

Kenna found herself back on solid footing, rather than off balance by this man who hid his lethality behind a veneer of civility. She doubted she was cut from his cloth, even if she were genetically related to him. She'd been raised by the man she called Dad, and he'd never been a foreign dignitary.

Malcom Banbury was a man who fought for his brand of justice.

"Major General Schnell was killed weeks ago in Washington using military arms," she began.

Ramon had been injured in that attack. In fact, it was a miracle both he and Zeyla were alive given their proximity when the missile, or RPG, or whatever it had been, hit the ground right were Schnell had been standing.

"And yet, he's currently showing up for appearances on news outlets, holding Pentagon press conferences, and performing his duties." She paused for a second. "So was the general who was killed the double, or is the man who is alive the replacement?"

"I doubt a man of the general's caliber would allow himself to be caught, let alone killed."

"So the original is alive and well." Kenna didn't like the sound of that. Ramon and Zeyla were going to flip when they discovered the man they went up against wasn't even the real Schnell. "And commanding a small team of men who were also reported deceased. Former soldiers, one of whom is Simon Newton. The killer you tasked me to find."

Petyr nodded.

"Tell me where to find the rest of the team, and Major General Schnell."

"The rules of engagement prohibit me from revealing his whereabouts."

"And yet he tried to kill you," Kenna pointed out.

"Unless I can prove he gave the order, he did not."

Innocent until proven guilty. No man-made institution would ever be perfect when run by humans, who were flawed. But in the courts, it was a way to ensure justice had to be found without a doubt rather than guilt being presumed. Interestingly they'd also adopted that tenet.

"What about the team?" Kenna asked. "Are they off limits?"

She figured there was a reason he and the president had only told her about one deceased man, Steven Braughton. Probably because she'd met his killer, and working the case might lead her to not only Simon Newton but also the rest of his associates.

Did they work together, or was each one a hired gun who did everything alone?

She didn't like the sound of multiple assassins out there.

Petyr shook his head. "I cannot be seen to be actively pursuing assets. The council would deem me a threat to *Dominatus.* I would be eliminated."

"I need carte blanche access to any military instillation my people want to enter. No questions asked, just complete access to anything we need."

"And what makes you think I can provide that?"

"Your access to the president is considerably less

conspicuous than mine." Kenna let him absorb that. "Tell her I need all-access passes for the person who presents the pass, no matter who it is." She couldn't provide specific names to be pre-authorized, since she had no idea what the plan was going to be. "And you need to tell me where to find the general and his men."

"You need access, and you don't know where you're going?"

Kenna rolled her eyes. "As if that ever stopped me from ending the threat."

"I'll get you what you need."

"Thanks." She spotted Amara at the edge of her vision, motioning her away from Petyr, and started to stand.

"And a DNA sample."

Kenna straightened, and then Jax was beside her, holding her hand. "Thank you."

Petyr inclined his head.

Kenna and Jax walked away, back over to Amara and Bruce. "We're leaving?" she asked.

Bruce gave a sharp nod. Amara said, "Something isn't right."

"I'm going to run to the bathroom before we go." Otherwise, she'd end up making them pull over to a twenty-four-hour chain pharmacy, and the facilities here would be a whole lot nicer.

Jax walked her to the hallway off the lobby, where she found the restroom.

She kissed his cheek. "I'll be right back."

He probably wanted to ask her about the conversation she'd just had with the Croatian president, but they'd have time to chew over that after. "I'll be over there." He pointed toward the door.

Kenna chose a stall and had just locked the door when

she heard the creak of the restroom door opening and a female voice, muttering, as she crossed the tile floor. Instinct Kenna didn't fully comprehend, but also wasn't going to question, had her lifting her feet off the floor.

The woman sighed. "It's me."

Kenna sat still and listened to the phone call, all her nerve endings alert.

"He's drinking it now. I'll give him ten minutes and then lead him out the side entrance." Pause. "I said you'd be paid the rest, didn't I? Just do what I told you to do."

She knew that voice.

Kenna slid her cell phone from the runner's armband she'd fastened around her thigh and sent Amara a message.

Chapter Thirty-One

The bathroom door creaked open again. Kenna flushed the toilet and let herself out of the stall. "Don't mind me. Just need to wash my hands."

The woman to her left was...

"Nurse *Smith*." Kenna hung a right, walked behind Amara, and washed her hands while the two women faced off. She needed to go tell Petyr that he'd already been dosed with something.

Assuming he was the target.

Kenna pulled two paper towels from the dispenser. "Who were you here to kidnap, and who's working with you?"

Nurse Smith just stood there. Faced with Amara, Kenna wasn't exactly surprised to see the woman was frozen with no idea what to do.

Amara was deadly even without a weapon in her hands.

Smith started to lift her phone, her attention shifting. Hoping to quickly send a message?

Before Kenna could object, Amara flicked out her hand. A tiny blade embedded itself in Smith's shoulder, almost to the hilt. She gasped and stumbled back a step but didn't go down. And she didn't pull the knife out.

"Better to hand over the phone," Kenna said.

The nurse had hung up with whoever she was talking to before Amara came in. Someone within the embassy staff, or even on Petyr's personal security detail, maybe. And here they'd thought they were going to leave in the next few minutes. Amara and Bruce and their instincts had already known something was wrong.

Unless there was more to come.

Kenna leaned against the wall by the door. Her phone buzzed with a text from Jax. She replied back,

> Clear

She was safe, and he was safe to enter. But the door didn't open.

"Who was the target?" Kenna asked again.

Nurse Smith sneered at them, stiff now because of the pain. Blood seeped into her blouse over her shoulder. "Doesn't matter. We can get to anyone at any time. We're everywhere."

Amara didn't react. But then, the brainwashed assets of *Dominatus* were nothing new to her. This woman was low level. Probably only here so she could work her way back into their good graces. Taking a job just to prove she was useful. But in an organization that regularly tossed aside anyone who wasn't, and who barely considered the foot soldier to be part of them, Kenna wasn't hopeful for her long-term chances.

All *Dominatus* cared about was power. The only people who mattered were those at the top. Everyone else fell in line, or they were eliminated.

"Petyr?" Kenna tilted her head.

Smith's eyes flared.

Amara repeated, "Petyr," as if that alone confirmed Kenna was right. "Too bad you failed."

"Question is, who is in on it with you? Are they *Dominatus* as well? Or did you recruit them?" Kenna gave Smith a second, but she said nothing, so she continued, "I see we're going to stand here in this bathroom for the rest of the night. Until the drug you put in that drink has run its course and your partner believes you've changed your mind and left him. Or her. I guess it could be a woman helping you. Someone strong enough to help you carry him to the car after he passes out. Am I right so far?"

Smith just stared at her.

Kenna would've waltzed over there and taken the phone, had she not been pregnant. "I'll talk to Petyr. Make sure he's safe. We need to know who the partner is."

Amara nodded. "Send Bruce in."

Kenna pushed the door open and found Jax and Bruce right outside. She looked at Bruce. "We need the phone, the plan, and the partner's name."

He nodded and headed into the bathroom, leaving her with Jax.

"Good?" He touched her elbows, worry on his face.

She nodded. "Good thing I had to pee, because if we'd just left, he would've been kidnapped and probably killed."

"Petyr is the target?"

"If he's the one looking drunk like he's gonna pass out," Kenna said. "I guess it might be hard to tell in a crowd already well into their cups...but we need to figure out who she dosed."

Jax took her hand. "I'm resisting the urge to accompany you to every bathroom from now on. Just in case."

She squeezed his hand but neither of them let go. "I

wouldn't blame you, but I'm not sure you need quite *that* much information about how things are going with me."

She heard a breathy exhale out of his nose that was almost a laugh. They stopped at the archway that separated the lobby from the ballroom and glanced around. She scanned the crowd looking for Petyr, or the ambassador, or anyone stumbling and looking drunk enough they might've been drugged.

"I don't see him," Jax said.

"Neither do I." Kenna twisted around and found the hostess with her black pants and white shirt, tight bun, and earpiece. "Could you help us?"

"Yes?" The woman had heavily accented English.

"We're looking for President Blazevic. We believe someone might've drugged his drink and they're going to attempt to kidnap him."

The woman flinched, twisted around, and lifted a hand to her ear. She spoke in Croatian as she strode fast through the ballroom.

"Does that mean it's taken care of?" Kenna looked at Jax.

His attention drifted over her shoulder. "They're out of the bathroom."

They met Amara, Bruce, and their new friend by the entrance. Smith had Amara's wrap around her shoulders, but the pale face was a dead giveaway that something was wrong with her.

Amara said, "We're going to take a ride in the car with our ill friend." She glanced at an embassy staffer who approached. "She isn't feeling well, so we're going to leave."

The guy nodded. "I'll have your car retrieved."

Amara smiled like she was an older actress, still in her prime. A starlet. "Thank you so much."

Kenna and Jax followed them out. "Can we continue the ruse and catch whoever she was supposed to meet?"

Jax glanced over, but a yell from their right interrupted whatever he was going to say. She glanced over and saw Petyr collapse to the floor. Kenna flinched toward him, the innate instinct to help someone there before she caught herself and stayed where she was.

Amara shoved Smith into the car and got in with her before anyone saw the blood on the woman's shoulder or asked too many questions.

Jax said, "I'll see if they figured out who she was working with."

Two of the thugs caught Petyr, who stumbled toward the car. The crowd was comprised of half a dozen plus a woman in a dark-green dress with very pale skin and black hair, who fussed around them all. If they were trying not to draw anyone's attention, it wasn't working, though there was a chance some inside hadn't seen any commotion.

"Hang on." Bruce lifted the phone and hit a button. The sound of ringing was low, but audible.

Across at the group, one of the thugs backed up. Kenna watched to see if he'd reach for his phone, but he merely stood there. Instead, the woman they'd alerted to the problem took her phone off a clip on her belt and put it to her ear.

"*Zdravo.*"

Bruce whispered, "That means hello."

He and Jax both headed over there, while the woman got annoyed that the caller hadn't yet responded. Kenna leaned against the car to watch the conversation unfold. Saying a quiet prayer no guns would be drawn and no one hurt. *Nice and easy.*

They alerted the security thugs to the fact that this

employee was part of the conspiracy to kidnap and likely kill their president. The woman in the green dress whirled around and slapped the staffer in the face. She stumbled back, and two thugs grabbed her.

Jax said something else to them, and he and Bruce came back over.

"Not the way I thought this evening would go," Kenna muttered.

Bruce exchanged the phone for keys. "Follow us?"

Jax nodded. "We'll be right behind you."

Kenna would rather hear firsthand what Nurse Smith had to say, but it was safer for her to be in a different vehicle. Jax drove, and they followed Bruce's car to an industrial area with plenty of empty parking lots. Bruce threaded through the complex, then through the trailer park behind it. The street switched to gravel, and he pulled into what looked like an old industrial plant.

The parking lot asphalt was cracked, with weeds growing through the openings. Bruce turned to the left and parked at an angle. Jax did the same, leaving space between the two cars. The place seemed deserted, but Kenna had been caught off guard by that before.

"I'll stay put." She palmed her phone. "I want to call Maizie anyway and check on Petyr."

Jax leaned over and kissed her, then climbed out.

Being in the car wouldn't necessarily protect her from a well-placed shot by a high-powered rifle, but if she was going to worry about that, then she really wouldn't ever leave her bunker. She couldn't live in fear of things she would never see coming.

Lord, protect us.

She tapped her phone on her knee, unsure how she was

going to ascertain if Petyr was all right. It wasn't like she had his number.

Maizie was easier to contact.

"Banbury—hey."

"Hi, Maze." She put it on speaker and dropped the phone to her lap so she could see what was going on through the windshield.

Jax had his arms crossed facing off with the nurse. Smith looked belligerent, even with the blood all over her shoulder. Bruce and Amara stood on either side of her.

"Anything from the files you've been going through?"

Maizie groaned. "Besides a headache?"

"Sorry." Kenna didn't envy the young woman's job sometimes. Just the protected place where she lived, and the world that was hers inside that Airstream. Maizie was slowly emerging from it. Testing the waters of the outside.

"I switched to hacking satellites instead, because it's way better than reading pages and pages of personnel reports and operation plans."

Kenna smiled to herself. "Don't get caught." Kenna watched the tense conversation continue, and another car pulled into the lot. She twisted around. "Uh-oh." She checked the others had spotted this new player but quickly realized she knew the car.

"What?"

"Ramon and Zeyla are here. No worries."

"Okay." Maizie sounded relieved.

"You were worried?"

"Of course. You're out there fighting them, and you're pregnant. And I'm sitting here, and I never know what's happening."

Kenna bit her lip. "I need to finish this. Hopefully, the baby doesn't decide to come before I know it's done." Being vulnerable like that sounded like the worst thing imaginable. The thing that put the taste of fear on her tongue. "When she does get here, maybe you could come and visit us. Or we'll bring the RV to Stairns' house, and we can all spend some time together."

"I'd like that."

"So would I. After all, she needs to see her big sister."

Maizie was quiet a moment. "Thanks."

Jax broke off the conversation and came over, leaving Nurse Smith with the now four of them standing around her. He got in, and Kenna saw Amara shove Smith into the trunk of the car this time.

She showed him the phone. "Maizie."

He nodded. "She was supposed to take Petyr to an address in West Virginia, but on Maps it's just a gas station. They still want to keep up the ruse and try to catch whoever she was going there to meet, so we're rolling out."

Kenna leaned back. "Sounds good to me."

Chapter Thirty-Two

Jax pulled off the highway at the correct exit. "I see the gas station."

Kenna scanned the whole terrain out the window, tugging Jax's coat tighter around her. Hills around them. Not much light at this time of night. No buildings other than this out-of-the-way gas station that looked boarded up, like it had been shut down a long time ago. "We're late."

"Good. That way we stay out of it."

"Okay, good point." They'd driven the speed limit, as opposed to Bruce and Ramon, who'd gotten here way ahead of Kenna and Jax. "Looks like they're around back."

"Hard to not see someone coming when it's so open like this."

Kenna looked up. "There are so many stars out here." She loved places like this. Just without the operational threat, and the fight underway to rid the world of *Dominatus.*

The west side of the highway had a dark hill on the left of the winding road that disappeared around the shadowed peak. On the other side, only headlights and a couple of street lights around the gas station helped her see what was happening. Jax pulled in, then made a sharp left and stopped with his side of the car hugging the strip of sidewalk.

Around the back of the gas station, muzzle flash erupted several times in rapid succession. Kenna flipped down the glove compartment and slid a pistol from its holster, flicking off the safety.

Jax opened the door. "Stay here."

As if he had to tell her that. She wasn't getting out of the car, but she definitely planned to defend herself if it came to it.

Jax raced across the rutted parking lot toward the fray, ducked down behind one of their cars, and took aim. She slid down in the seat, just in case, and covered them all with as much prayer as she could muster up. Relying on God and not putting her baby in danger weren't mutually exclusive. She had to trust Him all the time. It just happened that right now it wasn't only about her and her husband, it was also about their daughter.

Zeyla raced to the right, in the dark, all the way around the front of the building. Coming around behind the attackers.

Kenna's phone rang, a number she didn't recognize.

She put her elbow on the center console and leaned as best she could, trying to make it comfortable and prevent herself from being a target. She slid her thumb across the screen. "I'm a little busy right now, so if this isn't important, you should call back later."

A pause filled the line, and then, "Please hold for the president."

Kenna spoke to no one in particular. "I guess that's one way to find out if Petyr survived."

"He did, indeed." President Tetherton sounded annoyed. "Thanks to you."

"You're welcome?"

"I thought you might like to know that he is currently at the White House under the care of my personal doctor."

"Good for him." Kenna didn't want to sound sarcastic. "Did he get roofied?"

"After a fashion. We are testing to ascertain precisely what substance was used. Not that it matters, as I believe you have the suspect in custody?"

"After a fashion." Kenna peered out the windshield without lifting up too much. Looked like Ramon was fighting someone hand to hand, getting his workout in for the evening. The other guy was bigger than him, so her friend might even break a sweat.

The phone was warm against her ear.

"Have you spoken to him?" Kenna asked. "I asked him to pass on a request."

"I'm told he won't wake until tomorrow. We'll discuss it then. I'm about to enter a meeting."

Kenna looked at the dash clock. The president was working at this hour? She wondered what the meeting was about, but figured it was probably not her business.

"As I said, I just wanted to thank you for your actions. You likely saved his life, and this treaty."

Kenna just loved helping *Dominatus* advance their agenda to control the world. Not. "If you really want to say thanks, there is something you can do."

"I'll make no promises."

"It's fine if you just listen, because someone needs to know."

"Go ahead." It sounded like Tetherton had stopped moving.

Kenna tried to move on the seat, but it only made her more uncomfortable. "Have the taskforce investigating the bombing re-examine everything and address the possibility that Hann, Anthony & Associates were set up. That they were hired for that think tank purely as a trap so there would be enough evidence of their guilt that it's considered open-and-shut."

"You want the FBI to publicly apologize as well?"

Because she thought Kenna was asking for the impossible? "I know you want the threat eliminated. Congratulations, because several of them are dead. They realized they were being set up and defended themselves, which got them killed. I'll convince the rest of them to leave you alone. To just go live their lives and forget trying to take you down."

"This is what you talked to Petyr about?"

"No," Kenna said, "that was a different favor."

"You ask for much, Kenna Banbury." The president sighed. "But I live in a world where favors are currency."

"You'll have them look at the case again?" She'd figured asking the president to just release the lawyers was too much. The FBI would have to explain their actions. An escape would launch a manhunt. Justice was always the best end to injustice.

The president said, "I'll send that request to the task-force director."

"That's all I ask."

"Until tomorrow." That wasn't a salutation, just a reminder there'd be another request as soon as Peytr woke up.

"We'll take down the threat targeting you and your friends." Kenna paused. "But it's something we need your help with."

"I thought you were more than capable."

"You're the ones who made a point to tell me how highly you regard the unborn. You want my daughter to be in danger?"

President Tetherton scoffed. "Of course not."

"Then I'll need your help to pull this off without someone getting killed." Kenna took a breath. "Someone in *your* military that you're the commander in chief of is recruiting soldiers, declaring them dead, and sending them out to kill people. You hold the highest office in this country, which means you have the authority to stop this."

"You understand our ways."

"I know you're a pawn like the rest of us. Guys like Petyr and Schnell are the ones with the power. Unless we stand up to them." Kenna didn't want to make this about women's lib, but in the *Dominatus* hierarchy, women had less worth than the men. Why not encourage the president to use the reality of the position they'd put her in to do some good for once?

"So nice talking with you, Ms. Banbury."

"Think about what I said. You can change—"

The call ended.

Kenna's door opened. She brought the gun up, already ready to fire, but saw it was Ramon.

"Whoa, mama."

She lowered the gun and shifted in the seat. "How's things?"

"We're all good. The bad guys, not so much." Ramon backed up, standing holding the door open. "Coast is clear."

She brought the gun with her and followed Ramon across the parking lot to where they had two men sat on the ground with their hands secured behind their backs. Her eyes had adjusted to the dim light enough that she could make out their features but not all the injuries and swelling on their faces.

Jax and Zeyla stood on either side of the men, enough room they'd simply shoot one if he tried to make a break for it or tried to hurt one of them.

One of the men leaned slightly to the side and spat on the ground.

"I'd rather be at home in my sweats than standing here in this dress talking to you." Kenna kept the sides of the coat out in front, which let the cold in but didn't outline the baby bump. "But here we all are."

Amara and Bruce dragged Smith out of their trunk, also tied up, screaming obscenities at the top of her lungs. Bruce shoved her in the direction of the two men, and she stumbled to the ground with a yelp. The man she nearly landed on lifted his legs and kicked at her with his boots, sending her rolling back.

"Phones?" Kenna glanced around.

Jax said, "On the hood."

Kenna wandered over, half listening to Jax begin questioning the men. She sent Maizie a text so she'd know what to expect, then called the teen first from one phone and then the other. From each call, Maizie could connect to the phones remotely and see where they'd been thanks to the location services phones had these days. She could also see who they'd been talking to, which would hopefully lead to where their orders were coming from.

One of the men cried out.

Kenna glanced over her shoulder. They both just sat there, neither one saying anything. Determined not to divulge what they knew, or who was giving them orders. She called back to Jax, "Do we know these guys?"

"They're the ones from the team," he replied. "Killed in

action. Part of the same team as Simon Newton and Mitch Caudelle."

"But not either of them? That's a shame."

Megan would still be danger if Simon hadn't already killed her. Whatever she meant at some point to Mitch didn't apparently, leading to him being the one who took revenge on her—or rescued her.

"Wait a second." Kenna turned around. Her phone rang, but Maizie would have to wait. "Z."

Zeyla looked at her.

Kenna tossed over her cell phone. "Find out what she wants."

Amara said, "What's going on?"

"Yeah." Ramon lifted his chin. "What?"

"I think I know how we find Mitch." She turned to Jax. "When we discovered Megan and the child..."

"Joseph."

"Right." That was his name. "We figured he'd be safe with extended family. We didn't know Mitch was still alive."

Jax said, "Megan was discovered, and Carl was arrested. Both of them are dead now." He paused. "We need to warn social services and the police in Boston that Joseph might be in danger."

"It might even be too late." She couldn't believe she hadn't connected those dots. Now that she had, the ideas it brought were terrifying.

Amara squeezed Kenna's shoulder. "I'll make some calls. Ensure the child is safe."

"Thank you."

Zeyla wandered back over. "Maizie got in the phones. They're communicating in a group chat on a secure app. One member of the group isn't local, he's 'taking care of something' and another is on a job tonight. These two are here."

"Mitch and Simon."

"What's the job tonight?" Jax asked.

Zeyla glanced at him. "Another hit."

Kenna knew that had to be Simon. "Who's the target?"

"An FBI agent."

Jax froze. "Andrette Herron?"

Zeyla shifted. "Yeah, how'd you know?"

"Good guess." He coughed. "I mean, stellar detective work."

Ramon snorted. "You guys go save your friend. We'll take care of these three."

"All right."

Kenna turned to Jax. "What do you mean 'all right'? We have no idea what they're going to do with these three."

Zeyla said, "Maizie knows where they've all been recently. Same location. One of the decommissioned military bases we have information on. Guess that's their hideout." She shifted as if antsy to get to work.

"We need a plan," Kenna pointed out.

"Save your friend," Ramon said. "We'll have a plan by the time you're done."

Chapter Thirty-Three

Kenna was *still* in the dress when they pulled into the parking lot of an extended stay motel that looked pretty nice. The kind of spot with suites that had kitchens, and federal agents on long-term assignment could charge their travel expenses to the government dime.

"Nice digs," she told her husband. "Took too long to get here, though." She didn't like their odds of finding Andrette alive in her room, but she had hope that God could do anything.

A single police car was parked at the curb in front of the main entrance, the motel stretching two stories either side of the tall doorway. Plenty of windows lit up, curtains drawn. Dawn would be lighting the sky in just a few hours. Kenna had slept part of the way, but both of them needed rest. Hopefully, the peaceful sleep of having saved a life.

"You're gonna check in with everyone?" Jax asked.

"Yeah, I'll sit in the lobby. You make sure your friend is alive." She leaned over and kissed him.

The dome light illuminated as he got out, washing her in yellow light.

Kenna was ready to get out of the car and stretch her legs but brought her gun with her. She tucked it into the pocket and left her hand in there as well. Loose hold on the grip, just in case, and walked to the entrance with him.

The air held a chill, and ice had collected in what would be puddles in cooler weather. Jax had the car warm since she'd been cold falling asleep, but now she was glad for the low temperature. As long as it didn't rain while she was standing here.

Inside the sliding doors, she said, "Go" and he raced to the elevator, knowing he would've been up there much faster if it wasn't for her.

She found an alcove where the desk person couldn't watch her and called Maizie, put her earbuds in, and tucked the phone in her other pocket. When the young woman answered, she said, "Catch me up." Scanning all directions around her. Checking no one lurked in the shadows outside, ready to pounce. Sure, she'd been left alone in this lobby, but she was also standing beside a fire alarm she could pull. She had her hand on her gun.

"You good?"

Kenna said, "Sure."

Just because Jax was dealing with the cops and she was here didn't mean anything would happen.

Eventually they'd have to do things separately. Today was just a taste, and she could admit she didn't prefer it. So she knew that "eventually" wasn't going to come that fast.

"At least make it sound convincing," Maizie said.

"The police are here. Jax is checking on his friend. I'm fine, but ready to get out of this dress. Feels like I've been wearing it for days." Kenna paused. "Now catch me up."

"They're working on a plan. Neither of those men is going to play along with a ruse that could get Ramon and

Zeyla into a military facility, so that idea got tossed out pretty quickly." Maizie paused, sounding distracted. "Their phone location histories have them all at the same facility often over the past few months."

"A decommissioned base?"

"It's in West Virginia. Craig says if you didn't know where to find it, you'd never stumble across it. He wants Amara to come here and 'watch' me and Elizabeth so he can be there helping you, but neither of us liked that idea."

"We'll figure out how to do this," Kenna said. "I might have an angle on access, but it won't happen for a few hours. If it does at all."

"I'll tell Zeyla."

"What about Joseph?"

"Amara called Boston authorities." The tone of Maizie's voice rose. "They showed up at Joseph's grandparents and found Mitch in the process of beating them to death."

"Whoa."

"I know. It was crazy. Apparently, Joseph was upstairs screaming. They took the grandparents to the hospital, and the kid is getting checked out. Mitch is under arrest. Hope you don't mind, but I told them I was from Banbury Investigations and explained they should consider him extremely dangerous and capable of anything. That he's someone we've been investigating, and he's committed a number of serious crimes."

"All true," Kenna said. "Good thinking, Maze."

"Thanks."

Kenna took a couple of steps and sat on a cushy chair someone had placed in this alcove beside a small end table. "What's going to happen to the nurse and those two guys?"

"They're part of the team that was killed in action supposedly. Craig is on the phone with a contact of his that he trusts, but Ramon said if we turn them over to the military police, then we risk *Dominatus* letting them out again. Or moving them to another secret division where they keep doing what they're doing."

"The alternative is murder." Kenna had seen enough bloodshed in her life that she didn't want to be even vicariously responsible for the end of someone's life like that.

She spotted movement over by the elevator and stiffened for a second before realizing it was Jax.

"Anything else?" she asked.

"Plenty," Maizie said, "but it can wait if you have to go."

"I'll call back." Kenna hung up and waited for Jax to walk all the way to her before she held out her hand. He assisted her to her feet, and she hugged him. "How is Andrette?"

"They took her to the hospital half an hour ago. She'd lost a lot of blood, but there was no sign of Simon."

"Do you want to speak to her? Maybe he told her where he'd be going next."

Jax didn't answer right away. "We already caught two tonight. I shouldn't be disappointed we didn't get three."

"We did." She told him about Mitch, about Joseph's grandparents being alive and the child safe.

Relief washed over Jax's face. "That's great."

"We got three out of four. That's pretty good odds." She squeezed his side. "Once we have a plan, we can get on wrapping this up and shutting down Schnell." She said the name quieter than the rest. "And then hopefully Simon as well."

Jax nodded. "That sounds good." His gaze scanned her face.

"What is it?"

"I want to pack up the RV and get out of town." He

hesitated, like he wasn't sure how she would react. "After tonight...I want us gone from here."

"Wherever we go, there's a real threat that they'll find us."

"But I'll feel better being able to see it coming."

She nodded. "I know exactly how you feel."

"That's why we have a team, right? So they can help us?"

"And carry the whole load?" Kenna paused. "I know they'd jump at being in danger so we're safe. Asking them to do it, that's another story."

"The plan to take down Schnell isn't going to involve you going into that military facility, so we don't have to worry about asking if one of them can take your place. It won't even occur to them."

Kenna shook her head. "Who'd have thought it would come to this? That my life would be at a place where the biggest baddest threat of my life is one I don't fight alone, but the people I care about put their lives on the line for me."

Jax kissed her forehead. "That's what family does."

"Let's go home and then unhook our home and drive it *home*." She'd had a taste of being alone, even though it was barely a few minutes, and she didn't like it. She wanted her husband by her side. It wasn't something she would demand, but as long as Jax felt the same, this is where they would be.

Together.

The entrance doors slid open, and they went outside.

Jax shook his head. "It's freezing here."

"Too much time in Phoenix?"

"And an entire childhood in California."

Kenna shuddered. "Utah weather is my speed. Florida is a nightmare."

He chuckled. "I'll keep my thoughts about Florida to myself, but even in Salt Lake City I tried to escape somewhere warmer in the winter."

"You're destined to turn us into snow bunnies. Summers up north, winter in the mild south."

"I can handle that if you can."

Kenna glanced at him, content to lean on him for their protection. Just in case. "I think you're giving up a whole lot more than me in this equation."

"You've given up plenty in your life. Just like with the team, it's time someone makes the sacrifice for you so you don't have to."

She thought it was sweet he viewed it like that but had no intention of just taking forever. Theirs was a give-and-take family. There would be times where she repaid the favor and stepped up to the plate. Not because anyone owed anyone else in their marriage, or with their family. It wasn't about proving they were good enough or being worthy of love and belonging. It was just about the loyalty and affection they all had for each other.

He beeped the locks on the car.

Kenna flinched, but the engine turned over and it sat there idling. "I really thought it was going to explode for a second."

"We have a bigger problem," Jax whispered, slowing their pace. He drew his weapon and moved Kenna behind him. "What do you want, Simon?"

Kenna should just hunker down behind her husband, but she had to see. She slid her hand into her pocket with the gun. No, she should call 911. No, the gun was a better idea. She looked around Jax's shoulder and saw him.

Simon stood about fifteen feet away. "You interrupted my work."

Unlike on the platform out at sea, where they had met, he didn't wear white scrubs. He wore dark clothing, pants not jeans, and had a heavy overcoat on. Leather gloves. No eyebrows. Likely no hair on his arms.

But she hadn't noticed him being bald when he stabbed Langley in the street. So did he wear a head covering to ensure he left no evidence behind?

She didn't see a gun in his hand, but that didn't mean he didn't have one. *Two against one, buddy.*

Jax said, "Put your hands on your head and get on your knees."

Simon cracked a smile. "A citizen's arrest?" He laughed. "I have more authority here than you."

"You're a killer, Simon," Jax said. "We bring killers to justice."

"Is that you, Kenna? I can't see you hiding back there."

She made sure no one was to sneak up behind them. But Simon only ever worked alone. "Don't worry about me. Worry about what happens to killers who return to the scene of the crime and get caught."

More laughter.

"Put your hands up," Jax said, his gun trained on Simon.

Kenna dug out her phone with her off hand and dialed 911. Maizie would see it, but it was enough for the police to follow her to this location—preferably from as close as inside the building behind her. She moved to look around Jax's shoulder.

Simon moved fast, bringing out a gun. Already firing before he could even aim.

Jax fired back.

She felt the bullet slam into Jax's chest, and everything

in her tensed in a wrenching grief. He grunted and started to fall. Simon barely rocked back.

Kenna squeezed the trigger on her gun and fired over and over.

Simon's body jerked as he fell to the ground.

She lowered the pocket of her jacket. Someone was yelling—maybe it was her. She collapsed to the ground beside Jax and rolled him to his back.

His head lolled to the side, a single bullet embedded in his shirt.

She choked back a sob. "Right. You're wearing that vest." She could hardly breathe.

"Ma'am!" The cop raced over. "Ma'am, are you all right?"

She lifted her hands. "My husband has been shot."

Chapter Thirty-Four

Jax slumped onto the bed in the RV with a groan. Jolene hopped up and curled up near his feet.

Kenna winced, standing by the door that slid across and separated the bedroom from the rest of the RV. "Do you need anything? An ice pack?"

She doubted the over-the-counter medication he had taken was even taking the edge off the pain from the giant blue bruise in the center of his chest. Just looking at him made her chest tighten in sympathy.

"Ice...pack." He groaned out the words, his eyes closed.

Kenna had given him a hand changing out of his gala event clothes, and he looked more comfortable now, but all that movement had to hurt. She grabbed an ice pack out of the stack in the freezer compartment and took it to him. Her phone buzzed in the pocket of her sweats, a notification for their security system. Before she could grab her pistol off the kitchen counter, the door opened.

"Just me!" Zeyla pushed the door open and came in, grinning. "Don't shoot."

"Too soon." Kenna shook her head, leaving the gun where it was.

Her cousin looked around. "He's good, right? The vest he was wearing stopped it?"

Kenna nodded back toward the bedroom. "He isn't dead."

"Dead would feel better than this!" Jax called out.

"It's too soon for that as well," Kenna yelled back. But the fact that any of them were joking about it was a minor miracle in their lives.

Zeyla pressed her lips together like she was trying not to laugh. "I know exactly how getting hit in the vest feels, among other things. Like we all do. I'm sorry you got hurt, Jax."

Kenna waved at the fridge. "You know where the drinks are. Help yourself."

Zeyla stayed by the door, putting one elbow on the headrest of the passenger seat, while Kenna sat in one of the two recliners between the dinette and the front cab of the RV. "You good?"

She nodded. "There was a lot to explain to the police. They didn't exactly believe me that Simon was the one who tried to murder Andrette, but I had enough information on my phone to prove I'd been investigating his crimes. They also called Langley, and he backed me up."

Zeyla shook her head. "Good riddance. I'm glad you shot him."

"So am I!"

Kenna smiled in Jax's direction. "I'm glad no one is hurt." *Thank You.* "God protected us."

It hadn't taken more than an hour to get things squared away with the police so they could leave the scene. They weren't happy that Jax didn't want more than a cursory assessment from the ambulance crew but couldn't argue with his legal right to be miserable at home instead of at the hospital.

"Jax is laid up in bed." Zeyla shook her head. "How is that protected?"

"He was wearing a vest. I wasn't hit. Simon is dead, not either of us." She could go on, but that pretty much covered it and she was tired. Kenna flipped the footrest of the recliner up and sighed. "Tell me what else is going on. You drew the short straw and got protection?"

Zeyla made a face. "I volunteered." She rolled her eyes. "Everyone *flipped* when Maizie said you called 911, and the report was multiple gunshot victims. One deceased."

Kenna winced. "Sorry you all were worried."

She'd wanted to call them all and explain, but the cop wouldn't allow her to use her phone. When she'd finally looked, she had so many missed calls and notifications it had been overwhelming. She'd sent a quick text on the group thread with everyone and drove Jax back to the RV park.

Zeyla grabbed a can of soda. "Nothing to be sorry for. Like I said, good riddance."

Kenna stared at her, marveling that this woman appeared so tough and no-nonsense but cared about all of them the same way. She'd known it was possible that deep down Zeyla loved them all like family. It was just that her cousin didn't show affection the way most people did.

Zeyla had been groomed as an operative, targeted by the enemy, trained for war, and likely hadn't known peace and family during her growing up years. She was also the biological daughter of the man Kenna considered her father, Malcom Banbury. As far as she was concerned, that made her more of a sister than cousin.

Kenna smiled. "Thanks for coming here."

Zeyla waved. "Whatever. No big deal."

"I want to get everything unhooked and get on the road."

"You're leaving?" When Kenna nodded, she said, "Good idea. We've got this." Then paused. "Well, the others have it. I'm with you."

At any other time, Kenna would reassure Zeyla that it was possible something interesting might happen, but now she hoped it was boring. "Can you go outside and unhook everything?" She explained how it worked enough Zeyla would get the gist.

"I'll do that." Zeyla nodded. "You wanna leave soon?"

"As soon as we're good to go, I'll drive. Might be after I sleep a bit, but I'd rather be ready."

"Did you get anything from the president yet? Maizie hasn't called me back, but I'm hoping when she does, we'll have what we need." Zeyla sipped her soda.

Kenna shook her head. "Once Petyr wakes up and explains what I asked for, it shouldn't be long. But we can't count on it, I don't think. Not with everything that's happened tonight."

"Hopefully, you will before Ramon and Bruce have to figure out how to get in that military facility. They're doing reconnaissance, but it's hard to see more than the exterior of all the buildings. If your stuff from the president comes through, they'll be able to walk on base. At least, we hope so."

"Us, too." Fatigue washed over her. She'd have to balance pushing through and resting for the sake of all the stress on her body lately. The exertion. Still, she wasn't the one with a giant bruise on her chest. She was the one who'd been protected.

For the sake of letting Jax rest, she could drive, and she

would worry about being tired later. "I'm ready to get out of here."

Zeyla jogged her knee up and down, her weight braced on her straight leg. "What about the general? Can we tell the FBI that one of the lawyers is hiding on the base, get them to raid it?"

"You'd need physical evidence, or they won't go in hard."

"We need SWAT teams with rifles and helicopters that swoop down. They all rappel to the ground and karate chop everyone down there."

"Have you thought about applying for one of those teams?"

"MSI asked me." She shrugged one shoulder. "I'm good with you guys."

Kenna lifted her fingers. "I'm not trying to get rid of you. I'm just thinking about life after *Dominatus*."

Zeyla stared at Kenna for a second, then shook her head. "I've never actually thought about life after they're done." She looked down at her boots, then back up at Kenna. "I have no idea what I'll do."

"I highly recommend kicking in doors and saving people." She glanced toward the rear of the RV. "And marriage. And children."

"Maybe." Zeyla pushed off the seat and straightened, her expressiveness shutting down over something Kenna had said. "I'll go unhook the rig. Did I say that right?"

"Yes, you said it right." Kenna smiled, the shutdown in her cousin gone now. At least as far as Kenna referred to it, Zeyla was correct. Then again, she didn't even know whether she was right. She just lived her life.

She laid a hand over the baby. *Look where it brought me.*

God had been with her every step, whether she knew

Him at the time or not. He was with her now. Tonight. Every moment. In it all. No matter what happened.

She closed her eyes and prayed in the quiet while Jax rested and her sister got them going on their way. When the door snapped shut with Zeyla inside, Kenna opened her eyes. The flinch was just a reaction, the fear that would always be there. Because life could be scary.

"Ramon is on the phone." Zeyla handed over her cell.

Kenna's was near enough she could reach it, but she took Zeyla's and held it to her ear. "Hey, what's the latest?"

"Chopper and a bunch of guys took off a short while ago. Other than that, it's been pretty quiet. Maizie isn't answering her phone." Ramon sounded frustrated. "We need a way on this base, or we'll never get her access to their system."

She needed to check in with Maizie. Make sure everything was all right. "As much as I love the idea of exposing him all over the internet, are we sure the world is ready to learn it?"

Zeyla crumbled her empty soda can. "Who cares. Do it anyway."

Ramon spoke, too, but Kenna was too distracted by Zeyla to hear what he said.

Kenna still fought the need to run as far from *Dominatus* as she could. At the same time, there were more innocents to save from them. Her family members were willing and ready to put their lives on the line while she couldn't. Jax was laid up. Which meant she was the boss, whether she'd intended things that way or not. All of their futures hung on what they could accomplish, and the price they'd have to pay to do it.

Ramon said, "I don't think we'll be able to sneak into this place."

"We need video evidence enough to send to the FBI." Kenna chewed on that. "Imagine you stumbled across this place. What would you think it is?"

"Militia." Ramon didn't hesitate.

"Okay, so we call it in. Anonymous tip. There's a militia in that abandoned military base. Maybe you saw them loading barrels onto a truck that pulled out. People walking around in Tyvek suits with face masks. Some kind of chemical warfare. Just enough to get the FBI to come and take a look around before they realize the evidence was AI generated."

No doubt Kenna and her people would get in trouble once the ruse was discovered, but would it get the result? And would they all stay out of jail?

Maybe the president could pardon them. Tell everyone they'd had good intentions, and that law enforcement *wanted* people to report real suspicious activity. Revamp the whole "see something, say something" campaign.

It could work.

But when had she started thinking about everything like a politician?

Zeyla shoved open the door and poked her head out into the early morning light. "Helicopter going over." She ducked back in, shaking her head. "I'm becoming paranoid."

Kenna blew out a breath. "Far as I can tell, a little paranoia is helpful."

"What's going on there?" Ramon asked.

"Just a helicopter. Sit tight and take some photos and video. See what Maizie can do with a little augmentation to get us something actionable for the FBI. *Someone* needs to realize there's a bunch of people using that military base. And it's not the military." At least not officially. "And find out if Stairns has any contacts in the military police."

"Got it." Ramon hung up.

Kenna handed Zeyla's phone back. "I'll call the president and nudge about those passes. We've got to keep working all our options until we get a result." She dialed the number the president had called her from.

"I'm gonna check what's going on outside." Zeyla pocketed her phone.

The sound of a helicopter overhead hadn't retreated. In fact, it had grown louder, as though the craft was above them.

Zeyla pushed the door open. Someone with a black gloved hand grabbed the door and pulled it the rest of the way. Zeyla was grabbed and tossed out of the RV by her arm.

"Hey!" Kenna pushed the footrest of the chair in as men in black stormed into her home.

Her phone fell to the floor, the call connected.

Kenna screamed, "Help us!"

Chapter Thirty-Five

"You don't need to point that thing at me!" Kenna yelled, keeping her hands up. She'd managed to grab her phone from the floor, pretending to fall to her hands and knees on the carpet so she could grab it. Now it was stuck in the back of her pants, and no one had searched her.

In fact, these men were being oddly accommodating.

Jax, however, had emerged from the bedroom in time to see her on her hands and knees. Now, as he stepped slowly out of the RV, he had a cut on his forehead dripping blood down the side of his face. His *very pale* face.

"You don't need to hurt any of us." Kenna looked around at these men in their black fatigues, helmets, and bulletproof vests. Rifles pointed at her and her family.

Zeyla struggled, facedown on the asphalt.

"We'll cooperate." The taste of fear was back. Kenna tried to think. *I will say of the LORD, "He is my refuge and my—"*

"Get her up," one of the men commanded. "I want all of them on the chopper. We're airborne in two minutes."

Kenna knew the odds of survival after a person

was taken from one location to another diminished drastically. Her only consolation was that the president had the resources to track them. She'd said she cared about the baby and didn't want her harmed. Petyr was with her, and on the same page about the baby's safety.

The idea she was looking to *Dominatus* for help didn't sit right, but if that was all she had...

No, it wouldn't ever be all she had. Not even the hope inherent in knowing Ramon, Bruce, and Amara were on site at the facility.

Was that where they were being taken?

Kenna had two potential assists. But the reality was, this could end very, very badly. She had so many points of vulnerability that could be used to force her to do anything they wanted.

She bit the inside of her lip. *Surely He will save you...*

Sure, there were ways she could be rescued, or someone might intervene on their behalf, but she had to put all her hope in God and not people.

One of the men grabbed her arm and started to walk her to the helicopter they had landed in the middle of the RV park. Problem for them was that people had emerged from their vehicles to find out what was going on so early in the morning. Now these guys were being filmed kidnapping three people.

"That one is pregnant!" A woman had her phone up, recording the whole scene.

Kenna winced. If these guys opened fire on the few people outside and confiscated the phones, that could end the exposure of their actions. However, if that woman was live streaming and not just recording, then the word was already out.

"Let's go!" the commander yelled from behind them, ignoring the citizens watching this display.

The guy holding on to Kenna started walking faster. He pushed her up the steps into the helicopter, not hurting her but also not giving her any choice but to comply. She sank into one seat, and Jax sat beside her. They clasped each other's hands. Zeyla came in and shrugged off the person holding on to her. She took the seat on the other side of Kenna and held her other hand.

Men climbed in and surrounded them, taking seats opposite and on either side.

The chopper lifted off the ground, and wind whipped through the vehicle's open sides. Zeyla tensed. Kenna whispered to herself because the noise of the helicopter was so loud no one would be able to hear her talking. "If you say, 'The LORD is my refuge,' and you make the Most High your dwelling, no harm will overtake you, no disaster will come near your tent. For He will command His angels concerning you to guard you in all your ways—"

The man across from her smirked and shook his head, then looked away.

Whatever his thoughts were concerning her beliefs were none of his business. This time as a captive of *Dominatus*, she'd lean on the Lord. She'd stay where she was because she had already made Him her dwelling place. She could rest, protected by Him.

Sure, their lives were on the line. The danger was real.

Other *Dominatus* agents might just be their only way out of this, if rescue was in the cards. Her life had been tossed upside down in the past few years.

She closed her eyes and continued to recite Psalm 91, determined to make the Most High her dwelling, and to continue to do that no matter what happened.

They flew over buildings, residential areas, and parks. She knew they were headed west because the sunrise was behind them. The air chilled, and skin prickled on her arms. Jax's head lolled to the side and rested on hers, but she knew he wasn't asleep. He was injured.

Kenna didn't know how much time passed on the journey. Eventually, they descended into a clearing centered in tall pine trees that would disguise any secret compound. *Please be the same place Ramon is staking out.*

That would be a God-thing, and she would thank Him for the blessing. All the more so if this situation resolved itself in a way that ended the threat. God could do that whenever and however He wanted. People didn't always understand, but Kenna was learning to find contentment regardless. There was so much to learn about her faith, and how it all worked, and hopefully that would be a path she walked through—a long life full of family and happiness.

Not a short one of suffering that ended with pain.

Jax's strong fingers had slacked around hers. Zeyla's remained tight enough to squeeze the bones in Kenna's hand together. How her cousin was doing, or what plan she'd concocted in her head, Kenna wasn't going to worry about. No matter what, they were together in this.

Past the high fence with razor wire atop it, the buildings were concrete and square, single story—at ground level anyway. Who knew what hidden things this place housed.

A couple of Quonset huts had their doors open. Leaves and the odd flattened cardboard box had collected at the base of a wall, blown there by the wind. No one had mowed the grass around the asphalt in a long time, but it was green in a way that a lot of places couldn't achieve without constant sprinklers.

Overhead the sky remained gray, even though dawn

had risen while they were flying. Had the phone GPS enabled them to be tracked? Preferably by someone currently putting a rescue plan together.

Kenna recited more of her psalm, centering herself on the truth that God would protect her no matter what. That in yielding her life to Him, she allowed Him to be sovereign over what happened to her. Same with Jax. Zeyla still needed to surrender her life to the Lord, but with her history, giving up that fight and admitting defeat wouldn't come without a fight. The woman could be stubborn.

Probably their whole family was.

The helicopter set down, and they all swayed with the motion. In front, as the pilot toggled switches, the engine cut off and the rotors began to slow.

The men around them were more visible in the daylight, and she caught tiredness in some of their features. She didn't want to have any empathy for them. Maybe it came with her renewed faith, but she wanted to pray for them to know God like she did. Not that she had it figured out, or that them getting "saved" would fix this situation, but they should know Him, because facing that truth and making a decision was important for anyone.

The guy who was in charge, at least of this group, waved at them. "Everyone out. Let's go."

Zeyla let go of her hand.

"Hey." Kenna patted Jax's arm, but he didn't open his eyes. "Get a medic. He might be hurt." She didn't care that she was giving orders to one of their kidnappers. Not in the slightest.

Kenna kept patting his arm as Zeyla moved around her and crouched on the other side of Jax, concern on her face.

"Jax. Wake up." Kenna patted his cheek, her fingers coming away wet with blood.

The in-charge guy grabbed Zeyla's arm and dragged her out. "Let's go!" He yelled the words at max volume, and she flinched.

Jax flinched as well, coming awake in a second and launching out of the seat.

"Whoa. Jax. Jax." She grabbed the waistband of his pants, pulling him back to the seat so he didn't hurt himself.

That was when she realized the phone was still in the back of her waistband.

Kenna reached back, slid it out, and pushed it down between the seats out of sight. *Please.* She prayed the president sent an entire army. *The* army would be great. Or the national guard. State police. The Secret Service. Any kind of mass group of honest people who'd sworn an oath to serve and protect the citizens of this country. She wasn't fussy how that came, but rescue would be great.

"Come on." She helped Jax out while he swayed, but he found his feet. "He needs a medic."

Jax blinked like his eyes had to adjust to the daylight and lifted a hand to shield his gaze from the glare. He brushed at his forehead, staining his fingers with blood.

"He has a concussion." Kenna didn't know how she knew that, but it was likely true. At the least, he had a bad-enough head injury he was dazed. She got his arm across her shoulders. "Just point me to your medical facility, and I'll take him there myself."

Some of the men had dispersed, wandering off to the buildings. Or milling around as if the excitement was over.

Zeyla stood about twenty feet to her left with two guards, a look of defiance on her face. As if she wanted to jump into action. And tear the heads off everyone standing around them. Kenna could understand the sentiment, and the fury she held in her for these people who had ruined so much of her life. Taken so much from her.

But that wasn't how this was going to end.

Kenna continued, "After Jax gets medical attention, I want to speak to whoever is in charge." She lifted her chin. "It's Major General Schnell, right? He's the commander of this...outfit?"

"You think you give orders around here?" The guy unclipped his helmet to reveal gray hair smashed down, plenty of sweat, and a frown.

It's worth a try. She was a big proponent of bluffing. "He's here, isn't he?" And if Ramon was at the fence, he could get the general on video, and the nails on his coffin would secure his demise. "He's the one behind all this, right?"

"Let's go." He motioned for her to walk ahead of him.

Jax came with her, steadier on his feet than she'd have expected. It made her wonder if he was faking his diminished capacity. They held on to each other, following the commander to the nearest building.

"It's such a nice day," Kenna said. "We should have our meeting outside."

From behind them, the commander didn't say anything.

Jax squeezed her shoulder as they were pushed inside. That had been worth trying as well. She didn't like the idea of being inside.

It would feel far too much like being trapped.

When the door clanged shut behind them, she realized she was right.

Chapter Thirty-Six

The room was a hall with an arched ceiling and the width of a school gymnasium. On either side were rows of tables, though she spotted no kitchen facilities. In fact, the far end had a dais built into that wall, a raised platform with the curtains drawn across where the stage would be visible.

She didn't want to know what went on here, but back in the day, it would have been a place for performers to entertain the troops.

Just in front of the stage, a buffet of platters was set up on a long table covered with a white tablecloth. And she spotted carafes and mugs. Actually, it kind of smelled like hashbrowns in here.

Jax shifted to stand slightly in front of her, on her left side.

Behind her, Zeyla said, "Get off me," then came to stand in front of her on the right-hand side.

Kenna whispered, "I think they found my Kryptonite."

Jax twisted his entire body around to look at her, alertness in his gaze. "What's that?"

"Breakfast."

Zeyla jerked as if trying to contain a laugh. She cleared her throat. "I think we're late."

A man emerged from a side door on the far left. The uniform of a high-ranking soldier, dark hair with a little gray. In his sixties at least.

"The Count of Shadows." Zeyla breathed out the words like a threat.

Kenna wasn't sure if her cousin planned to be the threat, or if this man was.

"Come in, come in." The man waved them over, but it wasn't a request. These were orders, and he was accustomed to being followed. "There are enough seats for all of you."

Kenna called out, "I'd rather not eat tainted food today or any day."

"Nonsense." The general waved over a couple of his soldiers, who stood against the wall at intervals wearing fatigues and boots. Standing at attention. Mostly men, but a couple of women.

Two stepped away from the wall, and both men came over, taking a plate from one end of the table and selecting something from each platter as if they were at a buffet.

One of them spoke to the general, but Kenna was too far away to hear it. Their commanding officer nodded. "Of course."

The soldier set his plate down and poured two cups of coffee.

Zeyla turned her head slightly toward Kenna and Jax and spoke in a low voice. "Is this supposed to convince us it's not poisoned?"

Kenna wasn't sure about this display, but didn't want to stand by the door all day. "Let's go."

"You think we should hear him out?" Jax asked.

"He seems to have gone to a lot of trouble." She could see the general heard her, but that was the point.

"No trouble at all. My staff are happy to provide for distinguished guests." The general settled into a chair on one side of the table, a single place setting on that long side.

There were two place settings on her side, but Zeyla dragged over a chair from another long table with no cloth and no food, and made a big noise about scraping it over to sit by Kenna. She shifted and pulled out a gun everyone seemed surprised to find her in possession of, holding it loosely in her hand on her lap. Pointed vaguely in the general's direction.

The general held up his hand to someone behind Kenna. "We aren't here to fight. No one is going to harm anyone." He looked at Zeyla. "This is just breakfast."

Zeyla said, "You could've sent us an invitation."

"You and I both know it would have been ignored." He stared at her.

Zeyla set the gun on the table, reached forward, and grabbed two strips of bacon that stuck together. She folded them and shoved them in her mouth, then grabbed a piece of toast from the pile on a platter. She spoke around her mouthful. "If you don't plan to murder us, and this isn't about torture, what do you want?"

On Kenna's other side, Jax shifted in his seat. His head had to be killing him, but he seemed okay.

The general looked from Zeyla to Kenna.

Something in his eyes she didn't like struck a chord, and she decided that at best this could be a negotiation. "Years ago, I met a man who took a baby and raised her. Before she was twelve, he married her and called her his wife. He tormented her and tortured her. Is that the kind of man you are?"

Jax looked like he was about to jump out of his chair.

"I believe I'm more of a...visionary," the general replied.

Zeyla scraped the chair forward, close enough to the table that she could pour herself a cup of coffee. "Like posing dead girls in display cases for your sick friends to enjoy. That kind of visionary?"

"I've discovered there's a market for everything. Some businesses are more lucrative than others." He paused. "But what my double chose as his hobby had nothing to do with me. His businesses did well, but they were niche."

"And you didn't stop it." Zeyla scraped her chair back and crossed her legs, drinking her coffee. "Because you needed the money?"

The general turned to Kenna. "You've destroyed my team. If you want to continue, I'll take yours as replacement."

Behind her, the doors crashed open.

Kenna twisted to look over her shoulder and saw several of the gunmen shove Ramon and Bruce in the door. They forced the two men onto their knees and stood behind them, rifles pointed at the back of their heads.

Zeyla said, "Let them go, and I'll stay. I'm worth at least four of your guys."

Ramon's head whipped up and he glared at Zeyla, but even from where she sat, Kenna could see there was fear in his eyes.

"We're not part of your war," Jax said. "If your soldiers came at us, we only defended ourselves."

"That's how Simon ended up dead," Kenna added. "He left me no choice."

The general sneered. "You're the one who suggested an invitation."

And that was what Simon was supposed to be? The general's attempt at inviting them here? Kenna shook her head, but there were no words.

Jax said, "We're not part of your war. None of us."

"Our lives have nothing to do with you." Kenna lifted her chin.

The general studied her with the assessing gaze of a scientist staring at a lab rat. "Many years ago, I provided my DNA to *Dominatus* for the advancing of the next generation. That DNA was used to create exactly one of our offspring."

Don't say it.

"I'm your father, Kenna."

Her stomach clenched. *I don't think so.* "That sounds familiar. Where have I heard that?" She tapped her chin with one finger. "Right. You tried to kill him with that limo bomb so you could take over as *Imperatoris*. Which I believe is against the rules, isn't it?"

"I make my own rules." He spread his hands, indicating the kingdom he reigned over. But she spotted a slight question in his gaze.

Which made her wonder who really set the bomb. "Sometimes the best thing we can do in life is realize how small and insignificant we are. In the grand scheme of the world and all human history, we're just a speck."

Zeyla had reached for another piece of toast. Probably cold now, which Kenna thought always tasted nasty. She frowned at Kenna, as if astounded by her statement.

"That is not the way of *Dominatus*," the general said. "We are all of human history. And your grand scheme."

Kenna shook her head. "*We* aren't going to play along

with whatever this is. You people need to stop trying to ruin my life."

"You don't know what you are." His gaze drifted to Zeyla, as if she was responsible somehow. "You still fail to understand the significance this child represents."

"I don't care who you think she is." She looked from him to Zeyla. "Any of you."

The general said, "That child will start a war. But it's one I am prepared to fight." He slapped the gold buttons on his chest.

"Fight amongst yourselves," Jax said. "It has nothing to do with us."

Kenna nodded. "All of you need to leave us alone."

She wanted desperately to walk out of here. With all of them—Jax and Zeyla, Ramon and Bruce. Where was Amara? If Kenna, or one of them, could get to a computer terminal and enter a back door for Maizie to hack their system, they could spill all of *Dominatus'* secrets on the internet for the world to see. Exposing everything would allow people with integrity to eliminate those in power for their own selfish gain. Charges would be brought, corruption extinguished, and the world would move on in the fallout.

A young man, probably midtwenties, strode in wearing a crisp uniform. He bent and whispered in the general's ear.

"Excellent." The general nodded, and the man gave a salute. "Our other guests are here."

People around them cleared plates, bringing additional chairs to the table. Zeyla hopped up and picked up another mug. "Jax, want some coffee?"

"Fine." He sounded about as happy with this situation as Kenna.

Outside she heard the heavy beat of helicopter rotors,

although the sound was much quieter in here than it would be if they were in the open air. She wanted this to be the cavalry. Were they about to get rescued? Should she excuse herself to the bathroom and find a computer?

Jax slid out his phone, his breathing choppy. She couldn't imagine how much his chest and his head hurt. He tapped on the screen, then looked at her and mouthed, *No signal.*

Kenna prayed that wasn't a hurdle for Maizie, or anyone else looking for them. Then she prayed Amara would be victorious in whatever she was doing, imagining all kinds of sabotage that made Kenna feel better.

Moments later, with additional seats at the table, the doors opened again.

When Kenna turned in the chair, moving her knees to the side, she spotted Ramon and Bruce on one wall sitting on the floor. Both of them looked unhappy to say the least, but they were standing down right now. Letting this situation play out.

Two Secret Service agents entered, took up flanking positions on either side of the door, and stood at attention. The president came next, followed by Petyr and his entourage of people in office attire. Their footsteps echoed up to the ceiling as they walked down the aisle to the table. Secret Service agents fanned out, and a couple of aides stood to one side. One had an iPad—did it work here? That might help.

"Major General Schnell." The president seemed annoyed, but she pulled out her own chair and sat on Jax's left.

Petyr went to the right and found a chair on the other side of Zeyla.

"My esteemed colleagues," Schnell began.

"Just get to the point," Petyr cut in. "We're here to sign the treaty, not listen to you drone on."

"Very well." Schnell stood.

Kenna glanced between them, leaning forward in her chair to look at the president. Then, turning to Petyr, she opened her hands. "Why are we here?"

President Tetherton said, "The treaty requires witness signatures. Yours and mine."

Jax frowned. "I thought the treaty was between the US and Croatia."

Tetherton shook her head, sitting straight in her chair. Poised and unflustered. Kenna wanted to shake her. "It's between Europe"—she pointed to Petyr—"and the US." Then shifted to the general.

Kenna's jaw clenched. "This is a *Dominatus* treaty?"

"As the mother of the first offspring of the next generation, you have a part to play in history."

I hate everything you just said. Kenna nearly got up and walked out the door. "I see you didn't take my advice."

Schnell said, "If the two of you are finished, we'll get down to business."

Chapter Thirty-Seven

Kenna stepped out of the bathroom and found Jax in the hallway, leaning against the wall. "How is your head?" She checked there was no one else within earshot and stepped into his arms.

He shrugged, sliding his arms around her waist. "How are you?"

She made sure she didn't press against his chest. "Wondering why they're bothering me, and then wondering why I bother?"

"Pretty much." He looked exhausted. "At least the RV is still in one piece."

"We need a phone, or a computer terminal." She glanced around, then spoke so quietly she was almost mouthing the words. "If we can let Maizie in their system, she can expose all of this insanity. Or MSI can swoop in and..."

She didn't want to say *take them all out* aloud. After all, she'd be speaking of murdering the president. That kind of talk would get all of them put in jail.

Kenna dipped her head and laid her forehead on his

shoulder instead of his sternum, where he'd been shot. "I've been ignoring MSI for weeks, trying not to get dragged into a plan that puts people in danger. Refusing to give them intel and trying to stay out of it. Now here we are." She shook her head. "Right back in the middle of it, whether we like it or not."

He hummed agreement, and she felt the rumble under her cheek. "It feels like a bunch of murderers decided they're going to rule the world," he said. "But as long as they're not trying to kill us, I'm prepared to stand down."

She figured that didn't mean he would back off. "Maybe we should tell them to write that clause into the treaty wording."

He said, "They should add in that you're in charge of *Dominatus* if something happens to the rest of them."

Now there was a horrible idea. But it was also kind of intriguing. She hadn't wanted anything to do with these people. The idea that she might be in charge of the whole thing someday wouldn't mean she was in any less danger than she was already. She would be able to steer the ship in the direction she chose, and she'd have resources to enact that plan.

The temptation to decide people's fates that came with so much power was something that could corrupt anyone. It would be much better to shut down the entire organization. Dismantle them from the inside and make sure they were never again connected as a group.

The end.

Kenna looked up. "What I don't get is, wasn't there supposed to be a vote? That's how they get a new *Imperatoris*, right?"

Jax shifted, his attention over her shoulder.

"In this case," the president said, "they agreed to supersede the vote and rule as a group. For the betterment of the world."

Kenna turned to her, not letting go of Jax. "And where do you fit into that?"

The president looked down her nose at them. "Peace is a good thing. As is order."

"You think that's going to keep you safe? It's like negotiating with terrorists." Or what Jax had said. "Convincing a murderer you believe him when he says he won't do it again."

"You fail to understand the constraints of my position, Kenna."

Kenna could see it plainly, considering this woman existed constantly surrounded by armed Secret Service agents. "It's you who isn't thinking big enough."

"You want me to overthrow them? Take control?" The president shook her head, almost laughing. "That is not the way the world works, Kenna. Despite what people choose to believe, we're still the same savages we've always been. The strong are the ones in control. Everyone else is a pawn, or a victim."

"Good thing you didn't explain that during the presidential race. I don't think you and your running mate would've won." A lot of people had voted for her predecessor because of his family values, and even Kenna hadn't known the vice president was an asset for *Dominatus*.

The former president had tried to go up against them. Now he was dead, and his vice president had assumed his role. In the end *Dominatus* got what they wanted.

"Now you know the truth."

Kenna stared at the president, unsure if she believed that. Did these people ever tell the truth? "That remains to be seen. What did you mean, the firstborn of all the offspring?"

"Your child is the first of a new generation."

"But she isn't one of *your* children." Jax was the father, not some *Dominatus* sperm donor. Kenna didn't want to think about all these guys purporting they were her father. She pushed those thoughts away. This child would know exactly who she was, and it had nothing to do with *Dominatus*.

"You fail to understand," the president said. "No child has been born to one of us in this generation."

"Any of the kids born around when I was, or after? No one's had a baby?"

"You are the first." President Tetherton sighed. "Many believe this generation was born sterile. Until you."

Jax pulled Kenna closer. "I'm not part of *Dominatus*. Maybe that's why we conceived."

That would make a lot of things make sense. Like why Buzard had those men retrieve a sample of Jax's blood. He might've been trying to figure out a solution to an infertility problem.

The president nodded, a single bow of her head. "That may very well be the case."

"We aren't research subjects for you to figure out." Kenna was emphatic about that. "Don't ask. Don't come calling. No more kidnapping or co-opting, or anything. All of you are going to leave us alone."

"The life you carry means we continue. That's something we have to explore—"

"I'm not part of your sick agenda." Kenna let that sink in. "Never, not ever. None of my family, no matter who they are or what they do."

A tendon shifted in the president's jaw.

"Maybe I should go explain that to the *men*." Kenna turned and walked the hall back to the main room, Jax beside her. "Do you have cell signal here?" she whispered.

"No." He slid the phone back in his pocket. "We need to get out of here, before they decide they need us for something else. I'm pretty sure Marine One is outside. What do you say we steal the president's helicopter?"

They passed two Secret Service agents standing near the door.

Jax said, "Kidding."

Kenna thought it was a great idea. "We don't need to get arrested. But I agree we should get out of here."

He held the door for her, and she strode in like she was the one in charge here. A little command presence so they remembered she wasn't someone they could push around.

"Where do I sign?" She glanced at the general, who stood on his side of the table with his hands braced on either side of a long paper. Petyr sat on the far end, his arms folded across his chest. Apparently, they weren't in agreement. "I'd like to get out of here. I have an appointment."

But right now, her biggest problem was that Ramon, Zeyla, and Bruce where nowhere to be found. Where had they been taken?

"Whatever you have so far, figure the rest out later. Send me an amendment, and I'll e-sign it." Kenna stopped about ten feet from the table, Jax beside her. "I'm done here."

The major general straightened, a look on his face that she didn't like at all. "I'll get the ceremonial dagger. We can all spill our blood and sign."

Kenna nearly walked out right then. "I just have one question. For Petyr. Why did you pretend Schnell was trying to kill you?"

She presumed the lawyers were pawns caught in the crossfire, but maybe it was someone's idea to target them as the perpetrators. The president, maybe? Would she cut down women she should consider sisters? More likely it was either Petyr himself or Schnell even.

"You malign my integrity?" the general said, a deadly severity in his tone. He picked up a dagger from the table and slid it from its sheath. "Sign." He pointed the knife at the Croatian president.

Petyr stared at him. "And swear an oath to terms that are favorable only to you? I don't think so."

Kenna rolled her eyes. "We've been going over this and over this for hours. You aren't going to get a better offer than what's written in that agreement. It's been in the works for months, if not longer." She'd been listening to them drone on and on for hours.

A boom sounded from somewhere not in this building, though it shook. A window shattered on the far end of the room.

Jax's arms surrounded her, and he turned her around. But neither of them could tell where the threat was coming from.

The general yelled to one of his soldiers.

Jax said, "What's going on?"

No one answered him.

Petyr stood up and said something loudly in Croatian.

Secret Service agents shoved open the door Kenna and Jax had entered from the side hall. The president in the center of the huddle, surrounded by her protectors.

"This way." The lead agent said, heading for the door.

But the president shoved out of the huddle. "What is the meaning of this?"

"Ask her." The general pointed at Kenna.

"I didn't do anything. It sounded like a bomb went off." Although, no one had located Amara, so maybe it did have to do with her team. Just not Kenna specifically. "Where are my friends?"

The general said, "I supposed we're all making sacrifices today." He grabbed Petyr's hand, and before the Croatian could get free, the general sliced his palm open and slammed it down on the paper. Then he let go, doing the same with his own hand. "It's signed."

Petyr's face reddened. "These are not our ways!"

The Secret Service agent closest to the president said, "Ma'am, we need to get you out of here."

"Let's go." Kenna squeezed Jax's sides. They headed for the door, right behind the huddle of Secret Service agents.

Out into the open where the air was laced with smoke.

A presidential helicopter had landed farther from the entrance than the chopper Kenna, Jax, and Zeyla had arrived in. Armed Marine guards stood on either side of the open door.

President Tetherton yelled, "Wait!"

The agents wouldn't agree to that, but she was their boss.

The president walked to the side, all of them still guarding her. She wasn't the target of a threat. But this situation wasn't without its dangers.

Jax held Kenna's hand, and they headed for the corner of the building. "Let's see what she's looking at."

Kenna nodded.

The guards were gone. Most of the soldiers were nowhere to be seen, until she looked all the way past this building to the far end of the base.

Smoke rose into the sky, thick and black. People poured out of the destroyed concrete structure. All of them dressed in white scrubs. At least a dozen interspersed with Kenna's team, who were assisting the "patients"—if that's what they were. Many were bandaged or missing a limb. More than half of them at least.

"What on earth?" Jax breathed out the question on an exhale. Kenna held on to him, seeking comfort from her husband.

The general shoved past them and looked around, as if unsure where to go.

Jax moved in front of Kenna, guarding her just in case. She looked at the president and saw the horror on the woman's face and the faces of her team. "She can't ignore this. None of them can."

"Agents, arrest Major General Schnell and all his men!" the president screamed. "And call the FBI!"

Chapter Thirty-Eight

President Tetherton stepped up to the microphone, Assistant Director Ranturno of the Secret Service on her other side. Kenna stood with Jax beside her. An ocean of reporters in front of the podium, in rows of chairs that covered the grass behind the White House. And behind it, the president cleared her throat. "Thank you all for coming today."

Zeyla, down the end of the row past Jax and the rest of their family, shifted nervously. Then again, she was wearing a dress and flat shoes. She'd especially made a face about the shoes.

Kenna had Converse on with her maternity black slacks and blousy white shirt. Jax had his FBI suit on, Ramon was standing beside him dressed similarly. Bruce and Amara stood next to each other like they'd face whatever came exactly like that—watching out for each other. Between Amara and Zeyla were Craig Stairns and Maizie Morrow.

Not Kenna's choice, but the president had them retrieved from Colorado before the base incident even took place. Which meant she'd been planning this. Or something far worse if it hadn't gone to plan at the general's base of operations.

"As president of these United States, it falls to me to protect the citizens of this great nation."

Cameras flashed, and Kenna blinked. The afternoon breeze on Pennsylvania Avenue drifted hair across her face she had to tuck back behind her ear.

Jax's fingers found hers, and she clasped them.

President Tetherton continued, "When I became president through tragic circumstances, I undertook to continue the work of my predecessor. One of those tasks was to oversee the continued success of a very specific taskforce." She waved one arm toward them. "The men and women of this team have successfully rooted out a deep corruption that was poisoning the bedrock of this nation and spreading its tendrils to other countries.

"Thanks to their actions, all information relating to this corruption is now public knowledge, and those responsible have been arrested. I am certain that their hard work will enable justice to be found in this case. Major General Schnell betrayed everything this country asked of him and used his position for his own gain and that of his followers.

"His people kidnapped innocents and experimented on them for his private military's gain. He disposed of anyone opposed to his ideals. Thanks to the tireless work of these independent investigators, lives have been saved and no more will fall victim to Schnell and his group."

Half the reporters were about to jump out of their chairs to ask questions.

Even the Secret Service agents seemed surprised, despite the fact it had been all over the news since Maizie remotely leaked the entire base network onto the internet for all the world to see. Including lab results, videos of experimental surgeries, and everything the general had been planning for decades.

All of it at the president's request.

"Accordingly, the major general and all his followers have been stripped of any military rank, authority, compensation, or benefits. They are currently in custody awaiting trial. As such, I consider this matter concluded, and it is with great honor that I present the Presidential Medal of Freedom to each of these investigators, who risked their lives to make this country a better place than it was yesterday."

President Tetherton stepped back, and the crowd around the reporters erupted into applause. They had to stand there while she laid medals on their necks, from Zeyla all the way down the line to Kenna.

Beside her, Jax said, "Thank you, Madam President."

The president stepped in front of Kenna.

"You were as surprised as I was finding those people on that base," Kenna told her.

Tetherton took the medal from Assistant Director Ranturno and lifted it over Kenna's head. "We're not doing this now, Kenna."

"We need to talk, Miriam."

She'd forced their hand by bringing Maizie here, exposing her to public scrutiny. The media wanted to know who each of them were, and their stories. They wanted to know their histories and what skills they had.

Maizie had been thrust into the limelight, and Miriam Tetherton knew it. Because that was her goal. To cripple Kenna and her team's ability to conduct an investigation. With the spotlight on them, she'd completely destroyed their privacy and put them in a position where they'd never be able to question her publically.

"All's well that ends well," President Tetherton said. "Isn't that the saying?"

"Not even close." They both knew she didn't mean the saying.

President Tetherton laughed like Kenna had said something hilarious, then turned and put her arm around Kenna. Forcing her to smile for the cameras. It lasted so long Kenna's cheeks started to hurt. Then the president leaned over and whispered in her ear, "You do what I say now." She pinched Kenna's shoulder and walked away.

Down the row, Zeyla and Ramon flanked Maizie the whole time, keeping the girl from being accosted by reporters. Bruce and Amara stood nearby. As soon as they could, they all retreated inside the White House, where the entrance had been set up for a reception.

Kenna wanted to hug them all for taking care of her girl. She and Jax stood side by side outside, fending off reporter questions so they would keep off the backs of their team.

When a journalist asked what she planned to do next, she smiled. "Maybe I'll will write a book like my father. I'll need something quiet to do after the baby comes." She laid a hand on her abdomen, playing the part of independent task-force boss about to have a baby.

Thanks to the president's actions, the entire law enforcement community was angry with Banbury Investigations. Miriam Tetherton had destroyed all the goodwill Kenna and Jax ever had by telling the world they'd been working behind everyone's backs for years, investigating the secret society *Dominatus*.

Half an hour later, she managed to get inside, dragging she was so exhausted. To say she was ready to get out of there was an understatement given they'd talked about it repeatedly a week ago before they were kidnapped.

Inside, she went over and sat on the carpeted stairs in the lobby. The whole place had been turned into some kind of elaborate reception with bar height round tables covered with tablecloths around the room, each with hors d'oeuvres and groups of champagne glasses.

Jax winked at her, then went to talk with Bruce and Amara.

Kenna sighed, glad this ridiculous farce would be over soon. But apparently, they were being forced to endure this reception event with high profile government officials, a glaring secretary of defense and the FBI and CIA directors.

Maizie came over. "I still can't believe we're in the White House."

Kenna held out her hand, and Maizie sat beside her. "She destroyed your privacy."

"Ramon and Zeyla have been working on that for me. We'd already come up with an airtight backstory. I just didn't think I'd have to use it. Turns out I'm a runaway from Canada and a tech genius. No one is going to discover the truth." She hesitated. "Hopefully."

Kenna bit her lip, because anyone who'd known Maizie when she was a captive child bride had seen her face all over the media. The teen would be under full-time protection for the foreseeable future.

Craig Stairns wandered over and stood in front of them. "Not the outcome I expected when we got kidnapped from the house."

Maizie leaned against the outside of Kenna's arm. "Me either." She shook her head. "I'm not used to being 'escorted' places by federal agents. Is that normally what it's like to be kidnapped by them?"

Kenna shook her head. "There's nothing normal about any of this."

"I know." Maizie nodded. "Because we're *in the White House.*"

Stairns snorted. He looked at Kenna. "It's good to see you."

She held out her hand as he helped her to her feet, then gave him a hug. "It's really good to see you, Craig."

He chuckled. "Elizabeth wants the president's autograph before she leaves." He shook his head. "I'm glad she came with us, even if it was technically a kidnapping."

"At some point, you should let it go." Kenna backed up and sat on the stairs by Maizie again. "But not for a while."

Any further conversation about that was going to happen in Colorado and not here in the vestibule just inside the North Portico. These walls definitely had ears, and not just when *Dominatus* sat in the president's chair.

No way was Kenna going to believe this farse was anything but Miriam Tetherton's attempt to seize control. She had no idea where Petyr had gone after the military base, but she planned to track him down before leaving the area.

Kenna glanced from Stairns to Maizie. "Does the lawn have room for one more vehicle?"

Maizie's eyes widened, and she gasped. "You're coming to stay?"

Kenna hugged the young woman she and Jax had adopted. Her daughter. "I need a safe place to have this baby, and I can't think of anywhere I'd rather do it than at Elizabeth and Craig's house."

"You need to see Cabot! She misses you." Maizie put her head on Kenna's shoulder. "We all do."

"Jax and I will be there." Kenna smiled.

They'd talked about it just this morning. After joking that they should park the RV in the Rose Garden because it would be a safe place to live. But the reality was, neither of them had any desire to be near Miriam Tetherton. They would only be dragged into it all again, party to some drama she concocted, and they'd find themselves working for her—for *Dominatus*.

Jax came over with a plate of meats and cheeses, surrounded by a fan of crackers. "It's not a cheeseburger, but I figure it will do."

"My hero." She took the plate and shoved a bite of cheese in her mouth.

"Can I ride back to Colorado with you guys?" Maizie asked. "I need to commune with Jolene."

Kenna's gaze found Jax's, and she widened her eyes.

He grinned. "I love that idea. We can go visit the world's biggest rubber band ball. Maybe we can all convoy, and you can ride for a while with Ramon and Zeyla and then with us for a while."

Maizie hopped up. "Yes!" She hugged Jax and rushed off.

Stairns shook his head and walked away smiling.

Kenna let the tears fall, because it was a beautiful moment.

Their cat had been on the step of the RV when she and Jax had returned. All the neighbors had wanted to know who they were and why they'd been kidnapped by the military. After the president broke her story as the truth things got even worse, and now no one would leave them alone. The RV park had been inundated with reporters just hours later and many were still camped out there. At the base, some of the captives the general had been holding did media interviews. Most were currently receiving medical care ahead of being freed, and more than a few had been reunited with their families—which the president also took credit for.

Jax shifted to stand in front of her. "You okay?"

"What on earth are we going to do about this?" She had no desire to go to war with the president of the US.

"How about we have a baby, enjoy this season of our lives, and worry over what we're going to do about it later?" He tipped his head to the side.

"Maizie is in danger." Kenna bit her lip. "Someone will come for her."

"You think any of us is going to let anything happen to her?"

Kenna shook her head, blinking back tears. "God protected us, and the baby. He'll protect her, too."

"I know He will." Jax held out his hands, and she stood, moving into his arms.

Kenna touched her lips to his and decided not to worry about anything.

Until it was time.

Chapter Thirty-Nine

The convoy of vehicles driving through the gate of the private airport consisted of two cars and an RV. Dawn was barely breaking, and the Learjet on the runway was about to begin startup procedures. The pilots walked around the plane, doing preflight checks, while the five passengers waited in the yellow glow of the open hangar door.

The man in the center wore a suit, and watched the RV pull up. Park. Two men got out of the cars—one dark-haired man who walked with the stride of a predator, and the other an older guy in a Hawaiian shirt. Neither was the kind a person would want to run into when they had ill intentions.

Kenna stepped out of the RV, Jax beside her, and they crossed to speak with Petyr. He studied them as they approached.

"Leaving?" The question was redundant, but Kenna needed an opener and "good morning" didn't seem right.

"There is nothing more to do."

"You have the treaty?"

He shook his head. "She likely burned it. Isn't that what presidents do with papers they don't like?"

"And there's nothing you can do?"

"I tried. That's why I stayed so long, I was hoping I'd be able to convince her to rework the agreement."

Kenna wondered if that was the first honest thing he'd ever said to her. "And all that business about who is my father?"

The skin around his eyes flexed.

Kenna tugged her big coat tighter around her. He needed to take off soon, before the snow started. They were supposed to get four inches here today.

"To be the grandfather of the first offspring of a new generation is a great honor."

Kenna scoffed. "You mean it gives you leverage against everyone else."

He said nothing.

"Is she the *Imperatoris* now?"

"That position is only decided by popular vote." He scratched at his jaw, and she noticed he had stubble there. Too stressed out to shave.

Kenna wasn't sure she wanted to have any sympathy for him. This man wasn't a positive part of her life. He'd shown up in it during her worst moment in recent years and hung around like a persistent sore she couldn't get rid of.

What happened to her, or her family, next wouldn't have anything to do with him. Their lives would part ways here, and she didn't know if she would ever see him again.

Jax shifted his stance. "I'm surprised she didn't implicate you in the operation Schnell was part of. She could have had you arrested as a co-conspirator and taken you both off the board."

"No one would have believed it. They'd have seen immediately that it was a ruse." Petyr shrugged one shoulder. "None of us work together in that way. It's just not done."

As it was, the news reports all failed to mention his presence. That had been the easiest way for the president to control the narrative.

"I'm surprised she didn't have you killed," Kenna said.

"What makes you think she didn't try?"

She met his gaze, refusing to be sympathetic about that. There was nothing about his presence in her life that should make her care about him. And yet, the love of Jesus in her wanted to offer him something. She held the words back, warring with the fact he deserved nothing from her. He'd been part of tormenting her and never once showed empathy unless he was going to get something out of it.

"Now you're going home?" Kenna asked, purely to move the conversation along.

He nodded. "My people need leadership, and my task here failed spectacularly. There are measures to be taken and plans to be made."

"Long as none of that involves me, we'll be good." She folded her arms, determined not to owe him anything. And yet, the still small voice nudging her toward forgiveness said otherwise. "Sorry you didn't get what you want, but my family has nothing to do with your war. I'm not getting dragged into it again." She swallowed, aware she needed to say it. "I forgive you for all the fear you put me through. And I hope I never see you again."

"There may be a day when you need my help."

"More likely, you'll need mine," she said, "and you'll leverage my help to get what you want. That's all *Dominatus* does. Using people as game pieces on a board like they mean nothing aside from what they gain you. Either you win or the pieces are lost."

"And you intend to stop the game?"

"I intend to give birth to a healthy baby and protect my family from whatever comes next. Because there's always something around the corner, heading our way." She would do all that surrounded by the family she had chosen, people who willingly put their lives on the line for each other. "And none of it will have one thing to do with *Dominatus*."

"She won't let you go that easily."

Of course, Kenna wasn't presuming that the president didn't have a plan. That she wouldn't interrupt their lives with her own agenda. That was how these people worked, and with her bid to take over, she needed all the leverage she could get.

Kenna said, "We'll deal with that when it happens." Much like pregnancy, birth, safety, solving cases, and anything else. "As a family." She indicated behind her.

"I wish you well, Kenna Banbury. And you, Oliver Jaxton. But I doubt that's what will happen. So best of luck to you both." Petyr didn't shake their hands. He just walked away, flanked by his security team.

She watched him board the plane, staring at the open door for longer than she probably needed to.

Jax slid his arm around her waist and stepped in close to her back, his protective embrace covering the baby. "She's just letting him go?"

"If she kills him, her life will be fair game in recompense." Kenna leaned her head against his chin. "But for a second there, I thought the plane was going to explode."

"How about we get out of here, just in case?"

"You think it's going to blow during taxi, or takeoff?"

"I'd rather not be here to see it," Jax said. "We'll be late if we're detained by the police."

Kenna let out a long sigh. "Let's go."

They held hands back to the convoy of parked vehicles. Her RV wasn't exactly inconspicuous with the car hooked up to the back, the front wheels off the ground.

"Lot of miles between here and Colorado," she said.

Jax glanced over at her. "We'll get there soon enough."

"Maybe I can solve a cold case on the drive." She lifted her brows, as if challenging him to wager with her. "We can use the walkie-talkies between the cars to bounce ideas around. Try to figure out who the killer was."

He grinned. "Whatever passes the time, I guess. Most people just play road games."

"This is my road game."

He chuckled, holding the RV door for her.

Ramon and Bruce watched them climb in and returned to their cars. One more stop, then they would be on the road to Colorado, where she could have this baby on familiar ground. After they spent time with Maizie, Stairns, and Elizabeth, they'd go to Wyoming and take whatever maternity leave they wanted. Work when they felt like it, spend time together, and ignore whatever the president had planned.

Kenna had zero intention of losing sleep over Miriam Tetherton. The woman had made her choice, and the bid for power was going to be a fight she might not win. *Dominatus* operatives were far too set in their ways to allow a woman to be in charge. Which begged the question of whether her plan was to destroy them instead of lead them.

Kenna shook her head.

"What is it?" Jax slid into the driver's seat.

"Nothing." She buckled up and recited the end of

Psalm 91 in her head, where the passage switches from the human to the divine perspective. She had called on God, and He had answered her.

Kenna fully intended to live out the promise of being satisfied with a long life.

Starting now.

Chapter Forty

Kenna slipped the apron over her head and tried to tie it around her waist. "I'm not sure this is gonna work." She grinned at the man who wheeled himself into the room.

"As if we're going to make you do any of the heavy lifting." Jesse Lee Peterson grinned at her, then wheeled his chair back and turned it. "Come on."

She pulled the hair tie off her wrist and secured her hair in a bun so it didn't get in her face. "Thanks for reminding me I'm just eye candy for this operation."

Jesse Lee barked a laugh. "I'm nothing but a mission to you."

She grinned, following him from the food storage room to the kitchen behind the counter. "This is the deadliest operation I've been on in a long time."

He stopped by Jax and glanced between them.

Kenna's husband had an apron on also and held a ladle for Thanksgiving gravy in his hand.

Jesse Lee said, "I really appreciate you guys coming. It's going to mean a lot to the people who are here for Thanksgiving dinner, but I know we'll wind up with a good amount of donations because you're raising awareness of what we're doing here."

"If I'm gonna be famous I might as well use my powers for good." Kenna squeezed his shoulder and passed him. "You brought your gun, right? Just in case?"

Jesse Lee pushed through the swinging door, laughing. She heard him call out to everyone in the room, and they all quieted while he said a blessing over the meal. After a resounding, "Amen!" that thundered through the open hatch into the kitchen where her family stood armed and ready—with serving spoons and spatulas—they got started serving food.

Maizie wiggled into a spot on Kenna's right, between her and Ramon.

Jax looked over at Kenna, between scoops. "This was a good idea."

She grinned at him. "If we're gonna get snowed in, we might as well be useful." She scooped mashed potato onto a plate and said, "You're welcome," to the man holding it. Dirty coat, army patches, and in need of a shower. "Enjoy." She smiled at him.

The plan was to get on the road right after dinner and put some miles between them and the president before dawn on Friday. Usually, she'd have been driven by fear to rush out of town. Something deep in her had given her enough peace to hang around long enough to serve here.

Jesse Lee had made a difference in her life. When she'd been spiraling out, he'd counseled her and she'd taken the step back to right relationship with the Lord. He'd talked with her the way a pastor would, if she had a home church, and it had turned her spiritual life around.

She was thinking of asking if he wanted to be the baby's godfather but still had to ask Jax about that.

Maizie nudged her. "Do you still want to do that DNA test thing? Did you get a sample from…" She cleared her throat. "You-know-who."

Kenna pinned Maizie with a look.

"What?"

"Nothing." Kenna smiled. "I had a father, and he passed away. It's not just because of any of *them* that I don't want to know who it really is. I just… I had everything I needed. God provided me protection and safety, and now He's done it again."

"Because of Ramon, and Bruce. And Stairns?"

Kenna nodded. "Pretty sure I have all the father figures I need right here."

"She's right, kiddo." Bruce slung an arm around Maizie's shoulders and hugged her to his side. Elizabeth and Craig had taken a flight back to Colorado already so they could get things ready for extra guests in the backyard. The rest of them were here, though.

Including Zeyla and Amara.

"I have an entire family," Kenna said to Maizie. "More than I ever imagined I would have. I'm very blessed."

Maizie nodded in agreement. "I know you're worried since the president exposed who I am to the world, but I'm not worried." She looked around. "Because I have you guys. I'm not scared."

Kenna touched her cheek. "You're very loved. Don't forget that."

Jax put his arm around Kenna and kissed her forehead.

Maizie swiped a tear from the corner of her eye. "We should get back to work, or we'll still be here when the baby comes."

The next person through her line said, "Happy Thanksgiving."

Kenna smiled back at them, scooping extra mashed potatoes onto the plate. "Yes, it is."

And she had plenty to be thankful for. More than she'd imagined she would have—just as she'd told Maizie.

Thank You.

Keep Reading For...

- Where to find more great Lisa Phillips books.

- How to sign up for Lisa's newsletter and get a FREE book.

- Where to find Lisa on social media.

About the Author

Find out more about Lisa Phillips at her website, where you'll discover more romantic suspense fan-favorite series and heart-pounding thriller novels.
https://authorlisaphillips.com/

If you loved this book, please consider sharing about it on social media. Or leave a review at your book retailer website, on Goodreads, or on Bookbub. Your review will help others find great books to entertain and encourage them!

Signup for Lisa's newsletter by scanning the QR code below to stay updated on sales, new releases, and recommendations for your TBR pile. New Subscribers even get a FREE book!

Find Lisa on Social Media!

facebook.com/authorlisaphillips

instagram.com/lisaphillipsbks

bookbub.com/authors/lisa-phillips

Also by Lisa Phillips

Find out more about Brand of Justice at my website:
https://authorlisaphillips.com/product-tag/brand-of-justice/

Book 1: Cold Dead Night

Book 2: Burn the Dawn

Book 3: Quick and Dead

Book 4: Over the Limit

Book 5: Skin and Bone

Book 6: Dust and Ashes

Book 7: Long Road Home

Book 8: Dead to Rights

Book 9: Fear No Evil

Book 10: Out of Time

Book 11: Every Which Way

Book 12: One More Chance

Book 13: Storm and Tempest

Book 14: Now or Never

Book 15: Every Last Step

Book 16: Now Until Forever

———

Other series by Lisa:

Benson First Responders

Last Chance Downrange

Chevalier Protection Specialists

Last Chance County

Northwest Counter-Terrorism Taskforce

Double Down

WITSEC Town (Sanctuary)

———

Numerous other titles including several with

Love Inspired Suspense,

find the complete list here:

https://authorlisaphillips.com/all-books/

9 789888 552292